A RED WOMAN
WAS
CRYING

A Red Woman Was Crying

Nagovisi Stories

Don Mitchell

Saddle Road Press

A Red Woman Was Crying
© 2013, 2019 by Don Mitchell

Saddle Road Press
Hilo, Hawai'i
saddleroadpress.com

This is a work of fiction. No events, persons, depicted here are real, and no inference should be made to actual events.

Cover photograph and design by Don Mitchell
Author photo by Becky Cooper

ISBN 978-0-9833072-4-2
Library of Congress Control Number: 2013941337

"Fireflies Killed Her" is derived from "John Brown's Body," (*Humanistic Anthropology*, v. 23, no. 2, 1997).

"Dog Fights" is derived from "Dog Food" (*Green Mountains Review*, v. 12, no. 2, 1999/2000)

Portions of "My White Man" are derived from "Have You Seen Wanawo?" (*Humanistic Anthropology*, v. 34, no. 1, 2008)

Cover image: Osiropa of the Bero Tolesina at Wakoia, 1970

Books by Don Mitchell

Land and Agriculture in Nagovisi
Shibai: Remembering Jane Britton's Murder

v2.4

For Ruth, Ethan
and
all the Nagovisi

CONTENTS

PREFACE

This is a work of fiction set among a people called Nagovisi, who live on the west-central plain of Bougainville Island, in 2019 still a province of Papua New Guinea.

I worked among the Nagovisi as an anthropologist in 1969-70, 1971-1974, and briefly in 2001.

Although these stories are set in the time and place of my fieldwork and are informed by it, they rarely and only obliquely touch on actual events and specific Nagovisi women, men, and places.

The 2013 edition of this book included a number of Nagovisi myths and folktales; these have a new home online (a-red-woman-was-crying.com) although the eponymous Red Woman myth remains.

A Red Woman Was Crying

Literal translation of a foundational Nagovisi myth

A RED WOMAN WAS CRYING.

Her name was Koso and she was hungry.

On the ground she thought she saw flying fox bones, but they were leaf spines.

The people with Koso also saw the spines and were crying because they too had nothing to eat.

Some men came and said to Koso, "You had better go to Sekentu's house. If a pig's been killed there, you can eat it."

Koso did not know who Sekentu was. Her father took her to Sekentu's, and left her there.

Makunai, the demon ancestress of the Eagles, was Sekentu's mother. Makunai sat Koso down on a bed made of black-palm planks and told her she was now married to Sekentu.

Makunai said, "Stay on the bed until your husband returns from hunting pigs. When you see the bushes shaking, you'll know he's coming."

Sure enough, Koso looked up and saw the bushes shaking. When she saw her husband, he was a snake, not a man.

Koso said, "What kind of husband is this?"

She began to cry.

The snake Sekentu coiled up on a basketry platter under the bed and went to sleep without noticing Koso.

Koso's tears fell on Sekentu, waking him up.

He said, "What's up there? Why am I getting wet?"

Makunai said, "That's your wife."

Sekentu coiled around Koso. He put his tail in her vagina and ejaculated in her.

Sekentu saw that Koso was very thin. Her bones were showing and he felt sorry for her. He went out to hunt pigs for her. He caught pigs, he killed them, he brought them back, and the two of them smoked them over a fire.

Later, Makunai said, "You two had better go and see Koso's people."

When they arrived at Koso's village, Koso went to the cookhouse and Sekentu slithered to the feasting house.

The people at the cookhouse asked Koso, "Did you come alone?"

"No," she said, "I came with my husband, who is in the feasting house."

Her brothers went to the feasting house to see what their brother-in-law looked like.

They didn't see anybody, so they came back and said, "There's nobody there."

Koso said, "Ah, you think he's a man, do you? Did you look inside the slit gongs?"

So they went back, looked inside one of the slit gongs, and saw a snake.

They said to each other, "What kind of thing has married our sister?"

Sekentu, nestled in the slit gong, said nothing.

They went back to the cookhouse and said to Koso, "When are you two going back to your mother-in-law's?"

"Tomorrow," Koso said.

Koso set a date for coming back to her brother's place.

When Koso and Sekentu were ready to return to Sekentu's house, Koso's brothers hid in the bush along the trail to watch them.

They measured the snake as he slithered by.

When Koso and Sekentu returned to Makunai's house, Sekentu resumed hunting.

Makunai said, "When you are in the forest, gather lengths of the *kabe* vine and bring them to me."

Sekentu did, and Makunai took them and joined them and rolled them up.

Sekentu brought back pigs and they smoked them. Every day he went out and brought back more kabe and more pigs.

The day for returning to Koso's place neared, and finally came.

Sekentu and Koso left.

Koso's brothers were waiting. They had put tree trunks across the trail.

When Sekentu's snake body was draped over all the logs, the brothers jumped from the forest and each chopped Sekentu, cutting him into pieces.

In this way he was killed.

Makunai had tied a kabe vine to Sekentu's tail, and when she pulled back the last piece of his tail she knew he was dead.

She put his tail in the thatching above the food in her cookhouse.

When she cooked food, she said, "Come to life! Spill!" and salt water came down.

When she had enough, she would say "Stay!"

When she gave the food to her grandchildren, they asked, "What have you seasoned this with?"

Makunai answered, "Salt from your father."

Each day, the children played around the cookhouse, and each day they ate the seasoned food.

Each day they asked the same question and each day she gave them the same answer.

One day, a child hid in the cookhouse. When Makunai said, "Come to life! Spill!" he ran and told his brothers and sisters, "Our grandmother has something that she talks to, and it makes salt."

Another day Makunai went to her garden, and the children stayed at the cookhouse.

They built up the fire and cooked their own food, and when it was ready, they cried out, "Come to life! Spill!"

Sekentu's tail did as they commanded, and the pot was soon filled up. The children didn't know how to stop it.

They went and got coconut shells, and filled them up too.

Sekentu's tail kept spilling out salt water, and flooded the forest and everything all around.

Everything in the bush and even the villages were floating in Sekentu's salt water.

At her garden, Makunai saw what was happening and said, "My grandchildren have done this."

She ran and tried to warn people, "Look out! Run away!" but it was too late.

Sekentu's salt water killed Koso's brothers, but some of the people who ran away didn't die.

All their languages became different, and this island Bougainville was the only place left in the middle of the sea, the sea that Sekentu's tail made.

Namesakes

My patients call me Doctor.

Everybody else calls me by the name my mother gave me, Lalaga. I have a name from the Catholics over at Sovele Mission, but I use it so seldom it's hard to remember what it is.

When I have no patients and my wife has no garden work that day, she stays home and I leave my Aid Post and walk up the trail to Pomalate Village and talk to the American anthropologist Elliot Lyman. If anybody needs doctoring she sends word to me. It's not far, although there are two rivers to cross.

Most of the forest between the Aid Post and Pomalate is old forest. It hasn't been cut for gardens since before the Japan War. Even so, the trail is wide and because the sunlight falls on it, it's grassy. And muddy, of course. Nagovisi—that's what we call ourselves, and where we live—is a rainy place.

After you cross the Wetu river, you climb up and begin to see the falling-down houses of Old Pomalate, where the people lived until a few years ago. Sickness came, and so they moved the village.

Yes, sickness. Some days that's all I think about, because I'm treating sick Nagovisi. But other days, as I've said, I'm free to cross the Tavera, walk along that wide trail, cross the Wetu, and go talk to Elliot. To me, that makes for a good day.

I may be called Doctor but I'm only a Native Medical Orderly, in charge of a government Aid Post out in the bush, in the last place, the end of the road. If I'd been born after the Japan War I could have gone to medical school and I'd be a real doctor. It would be a strange world if we could control when we were born, and because we cannot, all I could do was take Medical Orderly training, and here I am.

I know what a scientist is, and I could have been one. There are many things to understand about the world and they all interest me. It's easy for me to see the connections between things, and it's easy for me to understand how to find things out. But when I was young, nobody went to University.

Before Elliot, I knew about biologists and geologists and botanists, and the people who study fish, although I can't remember what they call themselves—and insects—but I didn't know there were scientists who studied cultures. Kinship, beliefs, rituals, exchanges, even disputes and sorcery, fighting—I didn't know that anybody was interested in these things except us.

True, when I was a boy there was an anthropologist down in Siwai, but I didn't know what he was doing and

I hadn't thought about him for—let's see—I suppose thirty years, until Elliot told me that man was his teacher.

It amused me to imagine that Elliot might study us the way a biologist studies animals. We were having fun once and I told him I'd wondered whether, like a biologist, he'd kill us and dissect us or preserve us for a museum.

He laughed and laughed. "If I was a biologist I'd study"—and he pretended to be thinking—"flying foxes? Yes. Flying foxes. They're black and live in groups. Just like Nagovisi."

We were walking back to Pomalate at the time. "Yes," I said, "indeed. Go on."

He bent over and tried to go upside down, but he couldn't. "I want to live with flying foxes," he said when he stood back up, "and learn their language and hang upside down in trees," and we were both laughing, and I said, "And have us shooting you with arrows!" and he said, "Or shotguns, worse," and we went on and on like that until we were weak with laughter.

When we got to Pomalate, Elliot's neighbor Siro said, "Here are giggling schoolchildren."

With one voice, Elliot and I said, "Flying foxes!"

Siro's wife Siuwako came from her cookhouse and saw us being silly, and said the same thing. Giggling schoolchildren, I mean, not flying foxes.

Elliot does like to talk about flying foxes. He told me about an American moving picture he saw when he was a boy. A girl was carried off to another land by a whirlwind, and there were flying creatures who looked like little men and could snatch you up. "Then," he said, "when I was down in Buin Town on my way up here I went outside at night and these huge black flying things came flapping overhead and I said, 'They'll get me!' I was frightened. I admit it."

I said, "Frightened, and now you eat them," and he said, "I do, Lalaga, I do, but I cut their heads off so I don't have to look at their little faces when I fish them up out of the pot. As you know."

I've wandered, but I won't apologize. Elliot and I usually do wander away from what we start talking about. Far, far away sometimes, and that's good because that's how he learns. If we always stayed on the trail we started down, he'd never learn anything interesting.

When I was young, my white teachers understood that I was quick and wanted to learn, so they allowed me in their houses. They showed me *jigsaw puzzles*. I still remember the name.

Those puzzles made a big impression on me. Fitting the pieces together was easy. At first I fitted them together by shape. I didn't understand that they were giving me a test. I was happily making little clusters of pieces that fitted together. That's all I was looking for, the shape and fit. I paid no attention to the colors. They didn't show me the picture on the box right away, but when they did, I understood that getting that picture was the goal and that I'd missed what was drawn on the pieces.

Once I understood, I began to see that many things in the world were like that: even though pieces can fit any old way, if you don't fit together the *correct* pieces you don't get the picture. And even if two or three or ten pieces fit together, you cannot fit *all* the pieces together unless you pay attention to the picture that's forming.

Those were my jigsaw puzzle lessons and I have not forgotten them. I am not saying that after I learned about jigsaw puzzles everything in the world suddenly seemed different to me. I was too young for that. I'm saying that learning about jigsaw puzzles was good training for being an adult and even better training for somebody who wants to understand his own people.

I never wanted to be a leader but I am the one people go to for advice, and that includes Elliot.

Our leader Mesiamo and I *talk* to Elliot. I'm saying *we*, but it's not as though the two of us always sit with him together, and it's not as though we're the only Nagovisi he talks to, or learns from. Not at all. But we teach him the important things.

Of course all of us know our language and everybody knows how to behave, what ought to be done and ought not to be done, how we're related, and all the rest. But it's true that most Nagovisi don't bother thinking about what it all means, how it hangs together, how it changes, what the bones, the skeleton of our culture are, and all the rest of the things an anthropologist wants to understand.

Elliot says that it's the same in every culture, including his own. Most people don't think about their own culture. They do what they're used to doing, or what they're told, or they do things because everybody else is doing them. It's obvious that those aren't the kind of people he should sit and talk with. Nevertheless a great many Nagovisi who don't know much about anything come to visit Elliot just for the pleasure of talking with a white man who speaks their language and doesn't look down on them. And for tobacco and sometimes medicine, of course.

Elliot says there's something to be learned from everybody, but often enough I've gone to his house and found him stuck with some old fool who's going on and on about something that never happened the way he's describing it, or trying to explain something Elliot already knows all about. He sneaks me a glance and makes the face that means, "Help!" and I always find a way to send that fool off.

Mesiamo and I don't just say "here's how we do this, here's what we say about that." We *explain*. We never just *name things*. If Mesiamo and I only gave Elliot the pieces and not the picture on the box, and said "Here, friend, here are the pieces of Nagovisi. Do your best to assemble them," he would have gone home long ago. So neither of us ever did that except a few times, as little tests. Otherwise we talk about some pieces and then we talk about how they fit together, and then we talk about the picture, which is Nagovisi.

And then it can get complicated, and more interesting, because we like to talk about the Nagovisi-picture not only as it is now, but as it was in the past, and as it might be in the future. That last thing, Elliot likes to talk to me about that. He doesn't talk to Mesiamo about it.

Mesiamo isn't like me. Mesiamo thinks of himself as the teacher, and Elliot as the student. He tells Elliot what he thinks he needs to know. If Elliot doesn't want to know about something, Mesiamo doesn't care. He tells him anyway. If Elliot wants to know something that Mesiamo doesn't want to talk about, he doesn't tell him.

What *I* want is for Elliot's book about us to be based on a deep understanding of our ways, and I'm the one who can help him with that, more than anyone else. I know he has his own ideas—he tells me what they are, never mind that he shouldn't, because that can contaminate not only what I say, but what other people say. I remind him that I'm a doctor and understand contamination and I know how to keep my mouth shut.

When I walked through Siro's coffee plantings and into Pomalate, I saw a gang of boys from Bakoram Village coming up from the Wetu River.

I heard them calling, "White man! White man! Want a cockatoo?"

What they were really shouting was "White! White! Want a white?" because the name for the bird and the name for the color white and the name we often use to refer to white people are all the same: *kakata*, white. True, we usually refer to white people as *mono kakata*, white body, but by now if it's about Elliot most of us drop the "body" and call him Kakata. I refer to him that way but when I'm addressing him I always use his name. And why not? It's the name his mother gave him.

I didn't think he saw me coming, so I stood behind his house and listened. That's not something I like to do. I don't spy on Elliot. Even so, if I learned he was doing something wrong, something that might harm Nagovisi, I'd tell Mesiamo, doctor's confidence or not. I wouldn't like doing it, and I'd be very sad, but I'd do it.

Elliot taught me the American expression *when pigs fly*. We Nagovisi have many pigs and I expect they'll all be flying like kakatas, among the trees calling *oink oink* to each other before Elliot does something against us. But Mesiamo remains wary.

I was standing out of sight so as not to interfere with what was going to happen. I understand Elliot's non-interference rules, the ones he tries to live by. I knew whatever was happening would unfold differently if I went around to the front. Anybody who's not a fool knows that things go one way or another depending on who's involved and who's not, not to mention who's watching. What I mean is that I understood how important it was in Elliot's work.

I heard him ask, "Can it fly?" and the boys answered, "No, we cut the feathers on its wings."

Elliot obviously understood they were trying to sell it, because he asked "How much?" and one of the boys said, "Five sticks of tobacco."

I heard him walk up his steps and go to the room where he keeps his strongbox with the twist tobacco in it. I heard it open, I heard him walk back out, and I heard the boys calling excitedly, "He bought it! He bought it!"

Elliot called after them, "What does it eat?" and they yelled back, "Sweet potatoes and greens."

And then I heard what I knew I'd hear, because I knew about this particular kakata, who was insane—its crazy call, *eeeewwww, eeeewwww, eeeewwww.* I couldn't see it nodding its head while making that noise, but I'd seen that often enough at Bakoram village.

I walked around to the front of the house. Elliot was holding a stick with the kakata on it, looking pleased with himself.

I said, "Kakata's kakata," and he said, "It's true."

I told him that I'd heard what he'd said to the boys, because I didn't want to pretend I knew nothing about what had just happened.

He said, "Now I can do name-sharing with this bird," and I said, "It's named Elliot?"

He gave me a look.

"You know what I mean," he said, and I said, "I do. But where are the bird's kin to welcome you as one of them, and help you? Where's your new kakata mother, your kakata sisters—"

"In the forest," he said, laughing and gesturing toward the other side of the Wetu, and I said, "I'll watch you fly over there and roost with them."

I sat down on his steps. He handed me the kakata, which tried to bite me, as I knew it would. I held it while he found a stick and made a perch between his porch poles. Then he tied the bird to it with a bit of vine he pulled from his thatching. Kakata bit him while he was tying it.

"It bites," I said, and he said, "As I've just learned," and then he gave me a surprised look and said, "How did you know?"

I didn't have to answer because just then Siro walked around the corner of the house and said, "Man! What's that?" and Elliot said, "As you see, it's my namesake," and the kakata began its *eeeewwww, eeeewwww* and Siro shouted, "That's the crazy Bakoram kakata! You're going to be sorry about this," and when Elliot said, "Why?" he said, "Because of the noise. Hear that noise? You're going to hear that noise all the time, all the time that it's not sleeping. Why is it here?"

Elliot looked at me and then at Siro. "Because...I bought it," and Siro said, "How much?" and when Elliot said five sticks of tobacco he shook his head.

"Five sticks for a crazy bird. It's not worth even one stick," he said, "Better we kill it now and eat it. I'll kill it if you don't want to," and Elliot said, "Me? A cannibal? This is my namesake, another white," and Siro just laughed and said, "I'm going to tell Siuwako about this. She's going to have to send over sweet potatoes and greens," and Elliot said, "How did you know that's what it eats?"

Siro threw his hands in the air. "Kakata! How did I know? Everybody except you knows about this crazy bird. This kakata's going to shit all over your steps. No one will visit you because no one wants to sit on kakata shit."

Siuwako came from her house to see what the shouting was about. Her little daughter Nuai was on her hip. Elliot looked unhappy—anybody could see that—and I suppose Siuwako did because she handed Nuai to him. He loves to hold her. She reached out to the kakata and Elliot pulled her back.

"Bite baby, bite baby," he said.

Among the things I never expected to see in this world was a white man talking Nagovisi baby talk. But there it was, and crazy kakata or no crazy kakata, it pleased me.

I said, "You can wash your benches. I'll sit on them if you throw water on them. I don't care about a little bird shit." I wanted to laugh but I didn't.

Elliot said weakly, "I thought it would be nice to have a bird, and better to have a white one I could call my namesake."

Nuai cooed and played with his hair.

The kakata, which had stopped its *eeeewwww, eeeewwww,* started up again.

I hadn't been up to Pomalate for a week and when I went there on a Sunday afternoon to visit I saw that he'd built something new. It seemed to be a cookhouse but it wasn't separate and dirt floored, the way ours are. It looked as though he'd broken down a wall and made a new room, but not at floor level and not at ground level either. In between.

I slapped on the siding and he came out. I said, "Why didn't you build a little cookhouse on the ground, instead of this thing?"

He said, "I wanted to be like everybody else and have a place to sit around a fire, but I also wanted something different. Siro helped me." He seemed defensive.

I said, "This is different, all right. Nobody has anything like this."

Secretly, I was pleased. The new room was an odd thing, but it suited Elliot and in truth it suited the way he lived among us. He's both one of us and not one of us. Of course he knew that, but I didn't think he built that room to symbolize anything. He built it like that because if he'd simply extended his floor, he'd have to rebuild his thatching, and that's something you need an expert to help you with. So he and Siro cut the wall and built a new floor low enough so you could step down past the eaves.

He said, "Everything about me is different isn't it?" and I laughed.

"Yes," I said, "but some things about you are more different than others," and then I went up his steps and down into the new room. I sat.

"No kakata shit here," I said, and he said, "Indeed."

He started a fire and did a good job, except that he used matches. It was pleasant in the room.

I said, "Let's call this your *false-cookhouse.*"

He said, "Can't it just be my cookhouse?" and I said, "No. If you cooked in it, but I don't think you ever will."

He grunted and kicked at the fire. I said, "Speaking of different things, did I ever tell you that when I was a boy I went down to Siwai and I saw your teacher's wife and she was the first white woman I ever saw?"

He said, "No, you didn't, and I can't imagine why sitting in my new cookhouse made you think of that—" and I interrupted him, "False-cookhouse," and he said "Oh never mind, but I don't know how you got from here to there," and I said, "because I was thinking about things I'd never seen before, this room"—I waved my arm around—"and also about white people, that's you, and it came to mind. I don't know why I never told you about it."

He poked the fire in an irritated way and said, "Well, you didn't."

I said, "I asked a Siwai, 'What's that?' And he said, 'A missus.' I said, 'It looks like a woman to me, a white one,' and he said, 'Bush boy, that's the word for white woman.'"

Elliot said, "You never told me that," I said, "I know, you already said so," and he said, "Well, I thought perhaps you weren't listening because you were making fun of my cookhouse," and when he said that I realized he was in a bad mood.

I should have noticed it earlier but I was so pleased by his false cookhouse that I didn't pay attention. He didn't see that I was pleased, and I suppose that was my fault. I didn't want to change the subject, though, because that would have been the same as dismissing him.

"I didn't talk to her," I said, looking at him, "she didn't even look at me. So it was nothing."

He grumbled something that sounded like "It wasn't nothing," so I said, "I didn't tell you when I saw the District Commissioner, either, or the Bishop."

He said that wasn't the same thing, and I should know it.

I stood up and stretched. I said, "If you say so," which I thought might finish it off. I didn't want to talk about it anymore.

"Let me see if I can find us some betel to chew," I said, "but I might have to go to Biroi and get it from Mesiamo."

I thought a few moments alone would improve him. I suppose I shouldn't have said "If you say so," but I had and there was nothing to be done about it.

Elliot said, "I'll go with you," but I didn't want him to. If we both went to Biroi then the three of us would have to sit and chew and talk, and I was in a mood to have Elliot to myself. But I didn't want to admit that to Elliot.

I said, "No, you stay. If you go with me, anybody I ask will think I'm using you to get betel. Somebody will say, 'Ah, Lalaga's afraid I won't give him betel if he doesn't bring our White Man along.'"

Elliot sat down. He looked irritated. "Our White Man?" he asked, "Is that like our radio? Our tape player? Our medicine? Or maybe I'm *your* white man?"

I threw my hands in the air and turned away.

"Go," he said. "Maybe chewing will make me feel better."

I'd started down the steps, but turned back to look at him. "What?" I said, "You're sick?" I didn't want to admit I knew he was in a bad mood. I sat down at the top of the stairs, my back to him. Sometimes it's better not to have to look at somebody at all, because you might look away when that person thinks you shouldn't, and whatever's wrong is made worse. I didn't have any idea what was wrong.

He said, "Not sick. Just not happy. Sad, I suppose."

No, he was *irritated* about something and didn't want to admit it. I said, "Missing America?"

He said, "No. Yes, a little bit. All right. The betel. I mean, what you said about going to get betel, it made me sad."

He paused, but I said nothing.

I could hear him stirring the fire. After a moment he continued. "We understand each other. I know I'm a white American and you're a black Nagovisi, but when we talk I think you're talking to me, the one sitting here."

Well, of course. I didn't see where he was headed, beyond that it had something to do with being white. I said, "Instead of?"

He said, "Instead of something like—the statues in Padre's church. Like a Saint."

I laughed and turned around to face him. "You, a saint?"

He grimaced and spread his arms. He said, "No, let me finish. It's—the statue isn't the saint, everybody knows that. What I mean is, sometimes I think Nagovisi look at me like the statue of all white men, not a real person."

He stopped. I said nothing, and then he said, "I know I'm not being clear."

I stood up and went over to him. I sat on one of the new black-palm benches. "These are nicely-made," I said, "did you split the trunks?"

"No," he said, "Siro did, but I did the smoothing with my machete."

I said, "This is a good bench." I exhaled. "It's true, what you say. But it's only true for Nagovisi who don't know you. To those people, yes, you're the White Man statue. But to us, the people around here," I waved my arms expansively, "not to us. We know your ways. Not everybody likes you, some are suspicious, but those people, those people too, they think of you as a person. We don't know everything about you but we know what you're like."

Again he looked irritated, and poked up the fire. "Ah. So everybody understands everything about me, is that it?"

I stood up again. I thought maybe I should leave, and then I thought I shouldn't. "That's not what I said. Are you trying to fight? It looks like it. If you are, that's all right. Do you think we Nagovisi don't get cranky?"

"I'm sorry," Elliot said, slumping down against the wall, "It's true. I *am* cranky today." He looked up at me. "I'm like the plant *nado*, if you touch me, I'll sting you."

I don't know what was wrong with me. I shouldn't have said anything. How many people can make analogies in another language? Even so I said, "No, not like nado. You're like the little fern that folds its leaves when we touch it."

Elliot turned away from me, and hit the bench with his hand. "Shit!" he said, "Ah! Fuck! I don't even know what I'm like, is that it? Nado! Nado! You had better not touch me because I'm nado."

I wasn't sure what the best thing to do was, but because Elliot and I are always direct with each other, I said, "You're not making sense," and he slumped over and kicked the fire and said, "I suppose not," and I said, "I think I'll go look for that betel, and you stay here. If I don't find any, maybe I'll go back to the Aid Post. If you're sitting here I'll stop on my way and see if you're still cranky. You can be cranky if you want to, is what I'm telling you. Everybody gets cranky."

He said, "You, I don't know. Yes. People hide it from me. Maybe they're cranky but when they come here, they hide it. I don't know what anybody really thinks, Lalaga."

I shook my head. "Elliot, who does? True, we Nagovisi here, we know each other very well, much better than you do. But when you came here, you didn't know any of us, and now you do. We didn't know you, and now we do."

I stopped, in case he wanted to say something, but he didn't.

So I asked, "Isn't it true, what I'm saying?" and he mumbled, "It is," and so I went on, "You know more about us than any white man ever has, because you live with us, you talk our language, all the rest. For us, it's the same. We see you every day, we look at you, how you walk, what your face looks like. We know you get happy and cranky and silly. Don't think we don't, because we do."

He said, "Good." And he looked ashamed, but he shouldn't have been. Certainly it was true that having our own white man had been a new thing, like his false cookhouse, but by now whenever we talked about it, most of us felt as though he'd been with us a very long time. Even so, he was a white man and therefore something else, to most of us. Not to me.

I said, "You don't understand that most people don't know what to do with you. If you're in a bad mood, what should they do? They don't know how to cheer you up, except Siuwako, by giving you Nuai to hold."

"That's true," he said, hugging himself, and I continued, "You never act angry, but there's nobody who doesn't get angry. So they know you're hiding it. You don't hide it from me, but I don't live near you. And even if they know you're angry, what should they do? When the other whites get angry, we get out of the way. So what *should* people do when we think you're angry? People talk about it."

He said, "People talk about it?"

I gave him a little punch on the arm. "In their real cookhouses, yes. They talk about you." I raised my voice, "I'm speaking the truth. If you think about it, how could it be any other way? You're not the Kiap at his Patrol Post, not like Padre at Sovele Mission. You're here with us in our place and we *want* to treat you like anybody else but we're not sure how to."

He made a noise but didn't say anything.

I wondered, could it be that he doesn't understand how close to him I feel? I said, "As for me, I can imagine being so angry with you, and you with me, that we would stand up and yell at each other. I can, and that's because I think I know you well. Mesiamo, yes, maybe Siro, and I'm not sure about the women, Siuwako yes, maybe Big Nuai. Some of us trust you enough to imagine getting angry at you. I'm saying a true thing when I say that I don't think anybody else around here feels that way."

Elliot sighed a great sigh and slumped over.

The kakata started making the *eeeewwww, eeeewwww* noise.

"Shut up," he said, "Oh please shut up, fucking kakata."

The young men also mix English curses with our language. He muttered "fuck" again and then he said "True, yes, true. It must be hard for the Pomalate people. I know it's hard. It's hard for me, too. But you know that."

I said, "I know it," and after a moment he said, "Sometimes it feels like I'm a kakata in a cage, for everybody to look at."

It seemed a good time to slow things down again, so I took out my paper and tobacco and started rolling a smoke. After a moment I said, "Let me have that burning stick, will you?" and after he passed it to me and I lit my smoke I said, "Like your kakata up there on his perch? He's not in a cage, he's tied up."

Elliot said in an irritated way, "All right, he's tied up, all right, it's not a cage."

I tossed the stick back into the fire. It seemed I'd pushed him just as he got his balance back. That was unfriendly.

I cleared my throat and spit through the planks of his new floor. "Is this the first spit on your floor?" I asked, and he said, "Only if it didn't go through without touching," and I laughed and continued.

"So when you said 'Kakata in a cage,' you didn't mean the bird, you meant the man we describe by his skin color, never mind that it's no longer white, our own not-a-bird kakata, even though he's not a bird, and isn't in a cage. Is that it?"

Elliot looked as though he wanted to laugh and was trying not to. He said, "You're giving me a headache. That's what I meant, and you know it. You're trying to trick me into being happy by talking about what thing stands for what thing and what's really something and what's not."

I cleared my throat. "Well?"

He smiled and laughed. "Well." He paused a moment. "Tell me you knew what I meant about the kakata and the cage."

I said, "I think so."

He said, "Lalaga, what you've said makes me happy, yes. You didn't say, 'I knew!' but instead you said 'I think,' and that makes me happy because I know you never say 'I know' when you mean 'I think' and that's why I like talking with you."

My cigarette had gone out. I picked up the stick from the fire, and relit it. Elliot started to say something, but I gestured at him to wait. I drew on my cigarette. "Some of us believe we know you very well. I'm one of those people and if that's news to you I'll be very disappointed."

Elliot said, "As for me, the same."

I grabbed his upper arm and shook it gently.

"Try hard not to worry so much," I said, "You are a human being so you worry. Try not to do it so much."

The kakata said, *eeeewwww, eeeewwww.*

Elliot said, "I'm glad you came to see me."

I went up to Pomalate on a week night, instead of Sunday. I needed to talk to Mesiamo, but I stopped in to see Elliot. I lifted my lantern to see Kakata on his perch. He greeted me with his annoying noise. Many of his feathers were gone, but otherwise he seemed his crazy self. Elliot didn't answer when I slapped his wall, but then I heard his voice from next door, so I went over there.

He was sitting with Siro and Siuwako and playing with Nuai and their son Nema. When I came into the cookhouse Elliot talking about how many of his penicillin syringes he'd used on sick Nagovisi. He was saying he only had thirty left, and so by way of greeting I said, "I'll give you as many as you need," and Siro said, "Stealing from the government!" and Elliot said, "Mine are American, better than your Australian ones," and that's when I realized they'd all been chewing strong betel.

I sat down. There was no need to hurry to Mesiamo's.

Siro asked Elliot if he'd ever been sick enough to use one of them, and he said no.

Siuwako said, "I don't know how you'd shoot yourself in the butt," and Elliot said, "I'd ask Siro to do it."

"No!" Siro said, and switched to Australian-accented pidgin, "A *kanaka* is not allowed to put a needle in a white man."

"Lalaga, the Native Medical Orderly, is allowed to inject white men," Elliot said in English, and I said, "Government give me power!" and Siro said "No English! No English! I no understand English." He said that in English. We all started laughing and Nema and Nuai joined in.

Nuai had been crawling around on the dirt floor. Elliot picked her up and put her on his hip. She tried to put her arms around him, as she always did.

I liked seeing Elliot with Siro and Siuwako, because although he and I are completely at ease with each other, I rarely see him sitting and talking easily with anybody else. Of course if I lived next to him, I would. But I don't.

I said, "Speaking of being sick, what's wrong with Kakata? He looks like a plucked chicken. Take care you don't eat him," and Elliot said, "It's true. He's sick."

Siro waved his hands in the air and said "He's pulling out his feathers because he's crazy. The kids made him crazy, and now he's worse because there are no kakatas around, showing him how to behave. If he was with the other kakatas, he wouldn't do that."

Elliot said, "About other kakatas, there's me."

Siuwako laughed and so did Nuai. She was bouncing up and down in Elliot's lap and he was letting her flop backwards onto his thighs.

Siro reached over and tickled Nuai's belly. She squealed.

"Maybe you're crazy too," he said to Elliot. "That kakata is a bird, you're a human. We're talking as if there's no difference, because of the white color and the name..."

Elliot interrupted. "We humans and birds walk on two legs, don't forget that."

I wanted to get in on this, so I said, "Don't you forget that our clans are related to birds."

Elliot said, "I know, but that bird at my house isn't a hornbill and it isn't an eagle and I never heard that any clan is related to Kakata except the white clan and that's my clan and I don't see why I can't teach it to behave."

Siuwako laughed, "White clan!" and Siro said, "Human kakata, you're crazy yourself. If you can teach it, why haven't you? Then it wouldn't make its ugly noise and shit on your steps."

Elliot said, "No one can teach a bird not to shit. However if we're going to talk about bird shit as well as bird totems, I know all birdshit is called *kutu*. But if the Hornbill totem black possum's shit is called *maa*, the same as human shit, then why doesn't hornbill shit or eagle shit have the same name as human shit?"

Siro made a noise. Siuwako said, "That question's too hard for young people."

I said, "I can't answer that either." Actually, it was a interesting question. It's odd that only one kind of totem shit has the same name as human shit. I never thought about that before. Later I'd talk about it with Mesiamo.

Siuwako said, "Why are you men always talking about shit? When the baby shits Siro runs away as if he thinks that his clan is forbidden to touch baby shit."

We all laughed. It's true. Men will clean up their babies but not if they can make their wives or the young girls do it. How many times have I seen a man hand the baby he's holding to a woman, even if it's only pissing?

I'm different but that's because every day I deal with sick people. Elliot seems to be the same way, Siuwako says. She told me that he'll clean Nuai's bottom if she needs cleaning, and that she's seen him wipe her nose with his fingers and then wipe his fingers on his shorts. She said to me, "When I saw that, I thought 'he's one of us, now.'"

Siro snorted. "Never mind insulting my clan," he said. "What matters is that the kakata pulling out his feathers on your porch is a bird and being around a human kakata doesn't make any difference to him. We've taught you, but you haven't taught him."

Siuwako said, "Elliot tried to teach Kakata to talk, but Kakata would only say his name."

Elliot said. "My name's not *eeeewwww eeeewwww*."

"No, *ka-ka-ta*," Siuwako said, imitating the kakata's cry. I was surprised at Siuwako, who usually doesn't get silly. Maybe the betel was unusually strong.

"Ah, you're both foolish," Siro said, "Am I the only one who understands that a bird can be the same as a human without being human? Lalaga?"

I made a noise, "Yes, of course."

Elliot gestured towards Siuwako. "We do, I do. We are not idiots. But I still say Kakata is sick and needs medicine."

Siuwako said, "Your needles are too big for a bird."

Elliot grunted. "I have some pills that will work."

"Give him pills, then," she said, and Siro grunted. "Give him a little pill like you gave Lopana when he had diarrhea, and he didn't shit for three days. Give one to Kakata and you won't have to clean your steps."

I said, "I'm going to Mesiamo's. I'd stay here longer if we were talking about anything useful."

All three of them shouted, "Go!"

I was walking up to Pomalate to see Elliot on Sunday. I never go to church and neither does he, but most people do and that means on a Sunday morning villages are mostly empty except for the lazy or the pagans. And Mesiamo's the only pagan except perhaps for Elliot, who doesn't seem interested in God and Jesus except to know what other people believe.

I was thinking that maybe Elliot and I would go to Biroi and visit with Mesiamo.

After I'd crossed the Tavera but before I got to Gerum, I saw Elliot walking towards me. It was the wide trail, where it's straight, which means you can see anybody coming even when they're too far away to be sure who it is. It was obviously Elliot, and I knew this not so much from his skin as from his height. No one is as tall as he is.

When we met he seemed uneasy, as if he hadn't been expecting to see me. This surprised me. Why would he have been on the trail at Gerum except to come see me? Even more surprising was that he had his kakata on a stick. I couldn't think what he was doing on the trail with that bird. It was so strange I asked him straightaway, instead of greeting him.

"Why are you walking with your kakata, Kakata?" I said, even though I almost never call him Kakata. I said, "Kakata's not very kakata, with all those feathers gone. It's worse, isn't it?"

He laughed, but it was a nervous laugh. He said, "It's worse, but as for walking, everybody knows white people take their animals for walks," and I said "Indeed, but those animals are usually dogs, and what you have there is a bird."

He said, "But it's my namesake," which was true but couldn't have anything to do with why he was walking around with it.

When Elliot stumbled on, talking about how he was showing Kakata his ancestral home so that when his feathers grew back he'd know where to fly, I knew he was making up a story to cover up what he was doing, whatever it was.

He knew I knew that the boys who caught the kakata had caught it in the big bush beyond Bakoram, not here near the Tavera. I thought that inventing a story I'd recognize as a lie meant that although he was doing something he didn't want to talk about, he was willing to have me work it out.

I said, "Stop with me, wherever you're really going. Kakata won't care. We'll chew some betel, if you have lime."

Most people who stop to talk along the trail stand and talk. But luckily for us, there was a good sitting place at the trail's edge—two coconuts planted close together, so I sat down and motioned Elliot to do the same. He went off balance trying to get down while keeping the stick level. Kakata screamed and Elliot called him a brainless man-bird and then laughed.

It was pleasant there on the trail, leaning against a coconut, my legs out on front of me in the grass, and somebody interesting to talk to, especially now that I knew there was a mystery to solve.

Then Kakata started with his noise, the one that's so annoying that the Bakoram people sent the children to trick Elliot into buying that bird. I don't think anyone's told Elliot that it wasn't the children's idea, and I'm not going to either. They did get to keep the tobacco for their trouble, though.

We chewed and didn't talk about anything while we did.

Elliot spit carefully near the kakata, and I said, "Why don't you blow out a cloud of red spit and turn that white bird red?" and he laughed and shook his head. "Because where it's pulled out its feathers it's reddish already," he said, "and that would make it redder, so it would be red bird, white man and we couldn't be namesakes."

I said, "You still get sunburned sometimes," and he said, "Only if I walk around with no pants, Lalaga. The rest of me is all brown, and here we are back again where we were with kakata-in-a-cage."

"It's true," I said, and spit.

After a while I said, "Before you came, I never thought about white people when kakatas flew overhead calling their *ka-ka-ta*. It was just their noise, they were just birds, and they never made me think of anything except what they were."

He said, "Different now?"

I said, "Certainly. Now *ka-ka-ta* makes me think of you, not the birds, and often about white people generally."

Elliot said, "I admit I can't say the same when *kavokavo* the crow caws," and we both laughed.

I knew Elliot was tangled up in the white man, white bird idea, and I thought he was probably sorry about it. He'd been covering it up by joking, but I thought it was bothering him more and more.

I also knew that he wasn't afraid to kill animals if there was a reason—he chopped the heads off his chickens when he wanted to eat them, the same with the flying foxes—and I couldn't see why he didn't kill Kakata and be done with it.

I put all these things together and decided that he was probably meaning to toss Kakata into the big bush and walk away, and that's why he was down near the Tavera. If Kakata lived, good. If something ate him, well, that wouldn't be Elliot's fault. It wouldn't be the same as twisting its neck.

I was sure that was what was going on, but I didn't want to say it plainly. I thought I could make him start talking about it, and then I could suggest what he do with the bird. It's never hard to get Elliot talking about anything and I think this is because he's always working at getting us to talk to him.

"You were talking about white people and their animals," I said, and spit.

He grunted, "Yes, I was."

I said, "When I was in Rabaul I saw white people with kakatas in cages. I think white people like our birds more than our other animals, because I don't think people keep possums or crocodiles or snakes, isn't that right?"

"And not spiders, either," he said, "lucky for that."

I said, "Yes, a spider *pet*—isn't that the English word?—would be foolish. You couldn't know where it would spin its web, so even if you liked looking at it you'd have to search for it each day."

Elliot gave me a shove. "That's a good one," he said, "it must be fun to tease somebody who doesn't like spiders," and I went on to what I'd seen that interested me. "I think whites treat their animals like people, more than we do," and he said, "I suppose. Even so, Nagovisi give their dogs names," and I said, "You have to call your dog, and if everybody called his dog *Dog*, then imagine how confused everybody would be," and Elliot said, "Especially the dogs, yes, but how many women treat their pigs like their children?" and I had to agree, because it was true.

I said, "Let's go back to dogs and cats, and birds. We don't eat dogs and cats but we do eat birds, but I'm trying to think whether anybody here who keeps a bird in the house gives it a name, and I can't. I don't think anybody does. People say 'my hornbill,' or 'my mynah,' or like you, 'my kakata.'"

Elliot shook Kakata's stick. "I'm a Nagovisi then, because my kakata has no name unless we talk about how my name is kakata and therefore it has my name, and it looks as though I named my bird after myself, a very foolish thing."

I laughed and spit, and said, "You've eaten kakata, haven't you?" and he said that once in the bush Tagilali shot a kakata and they built a little fire and cooked and ate it. "There wasn't much to eat," he said, "and I had better say that if I told people in America that I'd eaten kakata they would be disgusted and think I'd done something wrong, because parrots are pets, not food."

I said, "White, white, they would call you a cannibal," and he shook his head and laughed. "No, that's too complicated for them. They would only think about a pet, and not about its color."

I said, "I'm wondering something about whites," and Elliot laughed and said, "That's hard to believe, what a thing," and I said, "True, but this is indeed something I've wondered about."

He said, "Ask."

I knew where I was headed and I hoped Elliot would quickly see it. I said, "Suppose you're a white man and you have a dog or cat. Say a dog. Now, the dog's old and sick and needs looking-after, but you don't want to care for it any longer. What happens?"

Elliot said, "Here in the Territory, or in America?" and I said, "Here," and he laughed and said, "You make your houseboy care for it."

"No, really," I said, "what do you think?" and he said, "In truth in America when the dog's too hard to look after, or too sick to treat, its owner takes it to an animal doctor who gives it an injection and it dies and everybody's sad and they bury it."

I hadn't known that. I'd never bothered thinking about it, either. Here, somebody will kill that dog with an axe and that's the end. But going to a doctor to have the doctor kill your dog seemed a strange thing and worth asking more about, so I did.

I said, "This is the same doctor who looks after the animals when they're sick, and heals them?"

Elliot made a noise. "Yes, it's true, and I can tell you think that's not right, because what human doctor does that?"

I said, "I'm not thinking *not right.* I'm thinking about confusion. Don't you think it would be hard for that doctor?" and before he could answer, I said, "I do. You heal the animals but sometimes you kill them."

Elliot said that he'd never thought about it that way. "I just think, well, that's part of what animal doctors do, and I never stopped to think about it." He paused. "Looks as though you're being the anthropologist here, making me see things about my own people."

I was pleased. I slapped him on the thigh, startling Kakata who started his noise again. "Oh, sorry," I said, and then I asked Elliot what kind of drug he thought the animal doctors used. He said he supposed it was some kind of sedative.

I was even more pleased by that. I said, "You have sedatives, don't you?" He knew I knew he did but I was willing to say an obvious thing to move him towards killing that troublesome bird.

I said, "How do you think the animal doctors use them?"

"An overdose," he said, "I'm sure of that. They would give a big overdose," and then we talked for a while about how much it would take to kill a cow or a horse, or a pig, compared to a dog.

After we stopped I put my hand on his shoulder and squeezed it. I felt as though I'd gotten us to where I wanted. I didn't want to push him about the sedatives unless I had to. Instead I said, "Elliot, go down that little trail over there and put Kakata in a tree and let's go see Mesiamo," and he made a *don't want to* noise and I said, "The idea of the white man and white bird namesakes was funny but it's not worth keeping an annoying insane bird only for the fun of it," and he looked at me—a sad look, really—and didn't say anything.

After a moment I said, "Let's go sit with Mesiamo, then," and Elliot said, "Let's go."

It would have been perfect if a pair of kakatas had flown over, calling White! White! but there was only the sigino bird calling, and the sound of the Tavera. Kakata screamed, which was better than his annoying noise, and we headed to Mesiamo's.

I was going to Sovele to borrow malaria pills from Sister Mary Agnes, so I stopped off in Pomalate. It was early in the morning, but smoke was coming from Elliot's false cookhouse, so I knew he was awake even though his shutters were down.

I slapped on the wall. Elliot asked who it was, the polite way.

I said, "It's me, Lalaga. I'm going to Sovele and I don't see Kakata. Did he run away?"

Elliot said, "Lalaga. Come in."

His voice didn't sound right.

I opened his door and stood in the doorway, getting my eyes used to the darkness.

I closed it behind me and then I saw him in his false cookhouse, sitting near the fire, with Kakata in his lap.

I said, "Ah, there he is. Kakata must be worse, because he's letting you hold him."

I stepped down and sat beside Elliot, who was stroking Kakata's throat. Clearly Kakata was sedated, because he wasn't biting. Elliot opened one of Kakata's wings and ran his finger along the stiff clipped feathers, making a little thrumming noise.

I reached over and opened Kakata's crest and let it fall back closed. Kakata's eyes were open but unresponsive, and his breathing was shallow.

Elliot said, "I gave him some medicine, and it put him to sleep."

Medicine. I wondered what he'd used. "What was it?"

"Ah. Well…phenobarbital."

"How did you give it?" I asked, and he said that he'd crushed up half a tablet in the night and put it in his food.

I said, "Ah. I see. It's good for centipede bites. You haven't been bitten yet, have you?"

He said, "Ah, not yet."

I made a noise. "Did you think a centipede bit Kakata?"

I paused but Elliot said nothing, so I continued. "Most likely one bit him. Making him sleep through it is good idea."

I was going to go ahead and invent a story for him, but he said "Lalaga, I…."

I put up my hand. "I've used phenobarbital more than you have. He needs more."

Elliot said, "Lalaga, in truth I'm…" but I interrupted him. I said, "No, no, don't worry. I'll do this. Get your medicine dropper."

He took Kakata with him while he went looking for the dropper. I got up and went to the counter, opened the phenobarbital bottle, crushed two tablets into a spoon, mixed in water, and drew the slurry into the dropper that Elliot handed me.

I said, "This should be enough. Shall I give it to him?"

Elliot said, "No, I will. He's still my namesake."

We both sat on the bench and I handed Elliot the dropper.

He opened Kakata's black beak and dribbled the liquid into his throat, past his thick black tongue. Kakata swallowed. We sat without talking and before long Kakata stopped breathing.

I said, "We tried, but it didn't help. Soon I'll have to go to Sovele, but I'll sit with you in your cookhouse for a time."

"You go on," Elliot said, not meeting my eyes. "Go," he said, "Go," but as if he'd said nothing, I said, "We'll sit."

And so we sat. The children were leaving for school. Women were coming up from the Wetu with their wet laundry and putting it on the lines. Chickens, dogs, piglets. Noise. It had seemed quiet while we were doing what we'd done, but I knew it hadn't been. I said nothing. I thought that the next time Elliot asked me to go, I would. But until then I'd sit with him.

Elliot got up from the bench and put Kakata down on the floor by the front door, his head inside and his feet pointing out. The door was still closed. He went to his office and came back with his camera case. He picked up one of his camera bodies, chose a lens, and clicked it into place. I recognized that lens because I'd looked through it many times. It showed a very wide area. He opened the door.

He knelt and photographed Kakata lying on his side, on the black-palm planks in the doorway. His lens was close to Kakata's head. I knew that Kakata's head would be large and the village small in the background. The planks would be wide, and then narrow away. He snapped once only.

He picked up Kakata and came to sit with me. He put Kakata in his lap and his camera on the bench and said, "I didn't use color film. This is black and white. You've seen it, black, grey, white."

I said that indeed he had showed me negatives.

He said, "Kakata will be black, the floor white."

I said, "It will be," and he said, "You can train your eye to look at the film and make the black white in your mind, and the other way around," and I said, "You taught me," and he looked at me and nodded. There might have been tears in his eyes.

Later, Elliot told me that when he developed the film and held the negatives to the sun and examined the single Kakata frame he thought he could see his crouching figure reflected in black Kakata's white eye.

I'm Going to Sovele

Everybody calls me Lunta, which means *deaf.* The young people don't know my other names, but I don't care. It's just a name, and it's a good name because indeed I am deaf, although not as deaf as I pretend to be. They don't know I hear them imitating me, but I do. Everybody thinks it's funny when I say "I'm going to Sovele. I'm sick," because I say it so often and, it's true, I do shout it. Sovele's where the hospital is, so why shouldn't I go there when I'm sick? It's closer than Lalaga's hospital.

Not long ago a mountain man I knew died. We don't speak the names of people who have recently died, so I'll call him The Dead One. He was a man I'd fought, long before the Japan War, when we were both young—little more than boys. In that battle we killed five of them, and four of our people died, but it was all even because someone among the mountain men had already killed our leader Mesiamo's father by sorcery, and that made it five each.

I tried to kill The Dead One and he tried to kill me. We both failed but in the end here I was, alive, and there he was, up in the mountains, dead. I didn't go up there to cry for

The Dead One and dance around his funeral pyre with the other mourners, even though I wanted to. I was afraid, and that's the truth.

Among the mountain men you can still find skilled sorcerers, as skilled as the one who killed Mesiamo's father. And cremations are dangerous. All sorts of spirits come to cremations, you don't know what might emerge from the dead person's body, the smoke can carry poisons, people are moving and close together so there's a chance somebody could put something on you, or blow something at you, or even stick you with something and you wouldn't know until it was too late.

The other Pomalate and Biroi people didn't go up either. Our leader Mesiamo is a fierce man but he never seeks out trouble. Even though the deaths were settled long ago, we think the mountain men are holding what we Nagovisi call *mudemude*, an anger that stays hidden for years. You never know about mudemude until someone reveals it, maybe by doing something on account of it.

Another reason was that they didn't invite us, and although it's not wrong to go uninvited to a cremation, it's never a good idea if you think there might be trouble.

If there's mudemude it's because the mountain men think that Mesiamo has no right to their clan brother Leau's head, which we cut off in that battle. I haven't seen that head since the Japan War, and I don't know where Mesiamo hides it or even if he still has it. But I suppose that doesn't matter to the mountain men.

I was one of the men who killed Leau, and watched his head being cut off. If it weren't for that business about the head, I wouldn't fear going among the mountain men. Indeed because The Dead One and I had become friends, sometimes went up there to visit. I always returned safely.

True, I was careful.

I thought that if I didn't go up there for at least part of the funeral, The Dead One's relatives would be angry. They'd say, "You didn't come to cry for your old enemy, you didn't care about him, it seems he was nothing to you. Shame!" Then they'd probably try to kill me because The Dead One couldn't.

So I knew I had to go, but I knew I'd need to be careful up there. I thought that the safest event would be the little ceremony when The Dead One's close relatives would resume having fires, eating hot food, and could return to their gardens.

This is a simple ceremony and it wouldn't matter if I missed the actual fire-lighting. I'd cry a little, rest, and go home. They wouldn't have many chances to poison me, even if they wanted to.

With sorcery, there are two things to worry about. One is leaving behind some part of you, like a hair, or mucus you might have coughed up, or earwax, even piss. When I'm going to a dangerous place, I ask someone to brush my hair vigorously, so hair won't fall out. The sorcerer can use anything that's been in your mouth, like a betel nut husk, so you shouldn't leave those things behind.

The other thing is to watch what you put in your mouth. Everybody's food is cooked together and you see who's serving you, so that's not a worry. But there are other things you put in your mouth that other people have handled out of your sight, such as unhusked betel nuts, and betel peppers, and sometimes tobacco.

The most difficult thing is taking care while acting as though you're not. If your hosts think you're protecting yourself against them, they feel insulted. They might decide to harm you even if they meant you no harm before.

I put on the warm shirt our white man gave me, because it's cold up there, and I get cold easily. Then I went over to his house to borrow a flashlight because I knew I wouldn't get back before night. I didn't think I'd get up there until late in the day, and nothing could make me stay there overnight.

"Are these new batteries?" I asked him, and he said he couldn't remember, and went back to his metal box and got two new ones for me. I put them in my bag. "Do you know how to change them?" he asked, and I said, "I'm old, but I know that," and he said, "Go, then."

I told him where I was going but not why, because he would want to come along. I didn't want to be responsible for anything that happened to him up there.

It's a long walk, and while walking I thought it would be a good joke on the mountain people if they poisoned me and nobody down here realized what happened because I'm sick so often.

When I got there the sun was almost down, and the fire lighting ceremony was over. I wanted to stop where the funeral pyre had been—the blackened area stays for a long time—and cry a little, to be polite. But I was tired and went on to the feasting house to rest. There were a few people there but while I was sitting on a bench, warming myself at the fire, more came in and sat down—some on the benches, some on mats on the ground.

When I realized that they were all gathering around me I was a little frightened, but nobody seemed threatening. I didn't say anything. Then I thought perhaps they wanted to ask me about the old days, when I fought The Dead

One, but I hoped not, because that might make them angry, even though it wasn't I who killed him.

So I just looked around, nodding and saying useless things about the fire and the weather and the trails, and showed them our white man's flashlight, because it wasn't the sort of flashlight an old man would have.

In this way I learned they wanted to ask me about our white man. They knew about him, a few people had shaken his hand, but he hadn't ever walked this far into the mountains and they were curious about him.

I was happy to talk about him because that wasn't likely to make anybody angry at me. Probably it would please them, help pass the time, and then I could go home.

I told them I didn't sit with him regularly, the way Lalaga and *Our Leader* did. I wasn't going to use Mesiamo's name up there among the mountain men, because of that business about the head. I said I talked to our white man from time to time, usually when we met along the trail to Sovele.

I said, "I'll tell you what happened one day when I met him on the trail, and you'll see what kind of man he is. You can ask me questions, and I'll answer them if I can hear you."

This was going to be a new thing for me, but I didn't see anything worrisome in it. If I kept them interested and amused, what was hidden might stay hidden.

I settled myself on the bench, getting as close to the fire as I could. That way I could keep warm and also spit into the fire, where nobody could get my spit.

I said, "Here's what he's like. I was on my way to Sovele ..." and I heard a voice like my own saying "I'm going to

Sovele, I'm sick," and I had to laugh. The man who imitated me—Meteko—did it very well.

"It's true," I said, "It's true," and when people calmed down I continued. "I saw our white man walking toward me. He had a small parcel of mail. I suppose they were letters from his mother, or maybe from that woman Anna who writes to him. When the children are running along the trail carrying our white man's letters they are usually singing 'Anna, Anna, Anna,' but he wasn't singing."

The people laughed. Of course the mountain people knew that *anna* is another word for *woman,* and they knew it was also a white name. I told them about the letters because I knew that letters from a woman whose name was *woman* would amuse them.

The mountain people are a more serious people than we lowlanders are. Sometimes they can be a surly bunch, so I thought that amusing them would be good, as I've said.

Usually surly or not, it seemed that everyone was being pleasant. You would never have thought they were mountain people in mourning. This mourning business is never easy, so I was thinking they might be happy because the first part of it was finished. But then I thought maybe it was because they were looking forward to poisoning me, and so I thought I had better try to keep them laughing and in a good mood.

Someone I couldn't see said, "Speaking of women, tell us about his people. His mother, if you know anything." We Nagovisi trace our lineages through our mothers, so that was a good question to ask. I told them I knew he had a mother—more quiet laughing—but that even though I'd seen her picture, I didn't know her name. I said that when he showed it to me he said "My mother," and instead of asking her name I said, "No father?" and he showed a picture of his father, and again I didn't ask for a name.

Somebody I didn't know asked why I hadn't, and I said, "Deaf as I am, I'd hear it wrong and say it wrong, and he'd think I was insulting him." Meteko shouted "What? What?" and the people sitting next to him pushed him around and said, "Quiet! Quiet!" There was a lot of laughter, so I smiled and nodded my head. I thought it might be genuine.

I thought I had better laugh too, but that made me cough. I spit safely into the fire. A woman I didn't know asked if I wanted water, and I said no. My plan was to wait until I was so thirsty I couldn't talk, and then say I had to piss. I could hardly piss in the feasting house, so no one would think it strange if I went outside, and no one would go with me. I could sneak a drink from someone's rain barrel with my hand, pretending to be splashing it on my face. That way I wouldn't have to drink from anybody's cup.

I admit I was pleased to have an audience. I'm not an important man, so most of the time people are wanting *me* to listen to *them*. But this was the other way around and it was very pleasant although as I've said, worrisome.

I said, "I'll continue. On the day I'm talking about, our white man greeted me and then asked if I had any betel. He said he had lime and one old pepper."

I told the mountain people I had a betel nut in my bag, and that I knew he was expecting me to lick it all over before handing it to him, so I did.

"He knows what that means," I said, "Lalaga told him," and a woman interrupted me, asking "He's learned about sorcery and poison?" and I said that was true, and then I quickly said I didn't think he would ever use what he learned.

I could have said "He knows what that means" and stopped there, but I thought that talking about poison as if I knew everything about it and didn't worry at all what a white man who learned about sorcery might do would remind them I was no easy mark. In truth there's no telling how lethal a white man who knew our poisons might be, because he could put that together with *his* people's sorcery and that could be very dangerous, yes. Very.

I said, "I licked it because I wanted to show him respect. I wanted to do what I knew he was expecting me to do," and there was a murmuring that seemed approving to me, and then I said, "True, I was sick," and before I could continue someone said, "And on your way to Sovele," and again there was laughter.

I hadn't meant to be telling the licking story as a funny story, but that's what was happening. I don't see what's funny about proving you haven't put poison on a betel nut.

I said, "What happened was that he took the betel and said, 'My jaw's sore. I'll open it with my knife,' and that's what he did. He popped the nut out and cut it in half with his small knife, just as we taught him!"

Someone said, "I wonder what else you're teaching him," but I had no idea what she meant, so I went on. True, sometimes people say things like that to trick someone into talking about something they'd like to keep hidden, but I didn't have anything hidden apart from how they were worrying me.

I said, "He handed half to me. He opened up his tin of lime, broke the pepper in half, and we shared it. It was a big pepper but old and limp," and some of the women laughed and one said, "What does *his* pepper look like, I wonder," and then it was all laughing and carrying on.

Mountain women are easier to be around than mountain men are.

When the laughter died down, Meteko said, "Have you taught him to spit, then?" and I said, "Certainly. He does all the spits properly, although he painted his face red when he was learning," and I passed my hands all over my mouth and chin. I continued, "If you heard his *kuioto* spit"—that's the explosive one you spit to summon spirits but mostly so that everybody in hearing knows you're chewing—"but you didn't see who was spitting, you'd think it was one of us."

I wasn't surprised when someone interrupted me— "He does kuioto? What a thing! White men hardly spit at all"—so I waited while people said one thing or another about not-spitting whites, and then I continued. "Even so I'm not telling a story about spitting. I'm talking about what happened when I met our white man along the trail to Sovele," and again someone started "Because…" but another person shushed him up.

I said, "I'll continue. We sat chewing and spitting. Our white man didn't know it, but we were sitting where our she-demon Topegina lives, and I decided to tell him about her, because although he doesn't believe in our spirits, he wants to know about them. I said, 'Over there is the she-demon Topegina's place,' and he asked me what kind of demon she was, as I knew he would."

Someone said, "Did you tell him what she does?"

I said, "I didn't want to tell him all at once. I was in no hurry. I wanted to have some fun with him, even though it was dangerous to talk about Topegina in her own place. So when he asked me what kind of demon Topegina was, all I said was 'She takes the form of a beautiful woman,' and he seemed surprised. He said, 'No one's told me about a beautiful demon,' and I said, 'White Man! Here we're on the trail to Sovele, a trail you walk all the time. Are you telling me that the Pomalate people let you walk through this dangerous place without warning you?' and he said, 'Warning me? About what? A beautiful woman?'" and some people started to chuckle. These were the people who knew about Topegina, I suppose.

I made a motion with my hands—calm down—and I said, "I told our white man that yes, Topegina is a beautiful woman, and he asked 'Why is she dangerous?' as I hoped he would, and I said, 'She takes you into the bush and screws you,' and he opened his eyes wide and said, 'What's bad about that?' and I shouted, 'Afterwards your penis swells up and falls off, White Man!'"

Everybody was laughing. Somebody called out, "What did he say, Lunta?" and others were shouting, "Tell us! Tell us!"

I waited until it was quiet and then shouted, "He asked … 'Does that hurt?'"

Now everyone was laughing, and loudly. I told the people I answered, "Does it hurt! White Man! Who cares! You die!" and that he started laughing, so I knew he was teasing me. I said I thought he knew about Topegina already, but was keeping it secret.

A woman I didn't know said, "Probably Lalaga told him," and Meteko said, "Lalaga, the man who knows everything but believes nothing." Indeed that's what I think myself. No one is smarter than Lalaga, except perhaps Mesiamo and our white man, but if you ask him about the spirit world he always says it needs to show itself to him before he'll believe it. Mesiamo says that also, but there's not a person in Nagovisi who doesn't think he knows the spirit world very well.

But I didn't want to talk about Lalaga, in case somebody started thinking, "Doesn't believe? I'll show him!" because Lalaga was far away and there was only me to be shown, so I continued. "Our white man said, 'Are you saying that if a beautiful woman finds me on the trail, I shouldn't go into the bushes with her?' and I answered, 'Don't do it. Being a white man won't will help you. Your white penis will fall off.'"

I waited for a moment and then said, "Too bad I'd chewed my pepper or I'd have made it white with lime and wiggled it at him," which got the women going again.

"White pepper" they screamed, and pushed each other. "Limp white pepper!"

I began to think that making them laugh might be the thing to do. People having a good time laughing won't start thinking about poisoning the one who's amusing them.

I'm not very strong anymore, and I don't mind a break from talking. I always have to talk loudly so I can hear what I'm saying, and that's tiring. I decided to smoke. I reached in my bag and pulled out my pipe. Smoking a pipe is safer than rolling cigars or making cigarettes from newspaper, because you know where the mouthpiece has been.

Someone I didn't recognize called, "Do you have tobacco, Lunta? I have plenty," but I pulled out a leaf of bush tobacco and waved it at him. "You can have some of mine," I said, and that man started to laugh and said, "Have you licked it?" and again they were all laughing but this time it was at me, and I didn't like it. Of course I hadn't licked it. It's hard to light tobacco after you've licked it all over. They should have known that.

After I lit my pipe, I went back to my story. I said that, as usual, our whiteman began to ask me questions even before he and I calmed down from laughing. "Does it hurt? Does it hurt?" someone said in a loud voice, and I said, "Yes, and I'll continue. He asked me when the last time Topegina took a man into the bush was. He always asks questions like that—when, how long, where. I told him that it was in my lifetime."

Agata said, "That's all, Lunta? That's all that happened?" and I said, "No, no. How fast do you think I can tell this story?" and people laughed. I thought I'd make them wait. I stopped and looked around. They were all looking at me. I suppose that did make me an important man and I liked that, but because envy can be a reason for sorcery, it would be best not to seem pleased about sitting and talking easily with our white man. He would have sat and talked easily with any of them, too, but they didn't know that.

I smoked a little and then I said, "It was like this. Remember we were chewing. Our white man chewed and spit, and I did the same. Then, just when I thought he probably had no more to say, he asked me if Topegina could turn into a white woman, which was an interesting question, don't you think?"

The feasting house people made noises of agreement. Someone said, "Indeed his spirits must be white," and although I didn't see what that had to do with anything, I nodded my head.

I nodded my head again. "Yes," I said, "That question surprised me and I had no answer. I thought he might be teasing me, but when I looked at him he seemed serious. I said, 'If she can turn into any woman, I suppose she could turn into a white woman,' but he wasn't satisfied and said, 'But if she never saw a white woman, what then?' and I said, 'She could have seen one of the nuns,' and he said, 'There's no nun who could tempt me into the forest,' and I said,

'How would you know, they're always covered up,' and we started laughing again.

"Even before we stopped, our white man said, 'Clothes, what about clothes, what do spirit clothes look like, or would she be a naked white woman?' and I said, 'Another good question, White Man, because I never saw Topegina and I can't say whether she would be naked or clothed. I think naked.'

I could see people elbowing each other. A woman called out, "Only naked in the days we didn't wear clothes," and another woman shouted, "Today she'd wear a skirt and blouse!" and again everybody started laughing.

One woman pretended to take off her clothes, and a younger woman said, "You're not beautiful," and she gave that woman a shove, and although it's true everyone was laughing I was thinking that laughing or not, they might be in a violent mood.

After the laughing died down, Meteko cleared his throat. He's a serious man and I was glad he was talking. He's never been accused of anything. He said, "Indeed, Lunta. Good question. I wonder if your white man knew anything about our mountain spirits who do the same thing"—I shook my head—"because in case you don't know, ours never change their shape and never look like anybody except themselves"—he motioned at me—"and before you ask, yes, always beautiful. And the rest is the same, about the penis."

The women again screamed with laughter. "Yes! Imagine our demon Kado-orem looking like one of us," a woman shouted, "How would a man know the difference?"

"That's the kind of question our white man always asks," I said, "because he hides what he knows," and a man said,

"What do you mean, secrets?" He looked troubled and more than one person shifted on their seats or moved around a little. I didn't mean for that to happen. If they thought our white man had dangerous secrets, then they might think I knew them, and fear me, or envy me, or both.

So I made sure they didn't have the wrong idea. I said, "I suppose he has secrets, but that's not what I mean. What I mean is that if he already knew about Topegina, he would never say so. We know this because sometimes a woman will say to another woman, 'I told our white man about that,' and the other will say, 'As I already did,' and the first will say, 'He never said he knew.' When I asked Lalaga about it, he said our white man wants to know everybody's story, and if he says 'I already know that' then he'll learn nothing new. So he always says he doesn't know, and that may be true or not true."

By then I suppose I had twenty people listening to me. I was still tired, so I thought I'd stretch out my story, and that way I could recover completely before I went back down.

I saw that a man whose name I knew—Kebotai—had come in and was sitting next to Meteko. I didn't know him to be a sorcerer, but he was a talker, so that was probably good.

Kebotai and Meteko whispered to each other and then Kebotai called to me, "A man who keeps what he knows secret sounds like a priest to me." That didn't sound like a priest to *me*, but I wasn't going to argue. I know many people think that priests are keeping secrets from us, but that's not what I meant. I said nothing, and Kebotai continued, "I'm wondering if your white man could be a priest of a religion we never heard of. We heard there's some new religion down in Buin Town and he was in Buin Town before he came to you, wasn't he?"

I hadn't heard about that new religion, and I said so. "Where did you hear about it?" I asked and Kebotai said, "At the copper mine they were talking about it," and I said, "I don't know, but I doubt it. For example, our white man never tells us what to do, except simple things like 'don't get water on that bandage,' or 'if you see my mail at Bereteba, bring it to me.' Things like that, and I never knew a priest or one of those Methodist missionaries who wasn't always saying 'You must do this, do that, do the other thing otherwise God will be angry, or Jesus, or Mary,'" and after I said that there was a lot of head nodding and people were saying, "True, it's true," and things like that.

Even so I didn't want them thinking our white man was carrying any kind of religion to us, because they might think I was part of some secret religion and be suspicious, or angry. I said, "I can say that our white man asked me if I thought that the old days were more interesting than now. I said, 'Well, we don't fight any more,'" and as soon as I said that I wished I hadn't reminded them that I had helped kill Leau. So I quickly explained what I meant about the old days.

I told the people in the feasting house that I told our white man it was easier in the old days because we didn't have to worry about the white man's spirit world or the white man's laws or the white man's money and that we had our own spirits and demons, and we understood them well. Then I paused because again I was sorry about what I'd said. Why was I always talking about dangerous things? Was there no way to talk about pigs or exchanges or cocoa or whether there would ever be a tractor road up here?

Kebotai said, "I can tell you what I would have told him about the white spirit world. I would have said, 'God, Jesus, Mary, and those Saints are your spirits and we don't understand them.' That's what I'd have said, and then I would have said, 'If God and Jesus are everywhere, like Padre says, then they must have been here too, so why didn't they show themselves…'"

I interrupted him without thinking. I said, "Maybe the beautiful women along the trail were really Mary pretending to be us," and after I said that there was a lot of shouting, especially by the men, the ones who were religious. Even among the mountain men there are strong Catholics, which has always surprised me because of how far they have to walk to get to Sovele.

Even now I'm not sure why I said what I said, considering I was thinking about tractor roads. I shouldn't have started people thinking about how Mary might take a man into the bush. But in the church at Sovele, there's a statue of Mary and in truth she's beautiful. I haven't seen many white women, but I like the way Mary looks.

Someone I couldn't see said, "Mary's a virgin even yet, so she can't have taken men into the forest," and someone else shouted, "Makes no difference, virgin or not," and Mekala the catechist—I hadn't seen him come in—stood up and shouted, "Stop this sinful talk that foul-mouthed Lunta has brought here," which was something I didn't like hearing. It wasn't me who talked about Mary's virginity. Was Mekala the only one angry at me?

I thought I ought to get away from Mary and be done with religion, because catechists can be dangerous. Yes, angering a catechist is dangerous. If we make him angry, then that makes Padre angry, and if Padre's angry that makes Jesus angry, and if Jesus is angry, he might kill our children, unless his mother Mary stops him. That's how I understand it.

It's true that I never heard Padre say that thing about Jesus. I overheard a man named Karesa tell someone he heard one of the catechists say it, who said that one of the teachers at Sovele told him he heard Padre say it. It must be true, because a mother can usually stop her son from doing something he shouldn't. Otherwise there would be more dead children than there are.

I wanted to calm Mekala, so I said, "If I said anything sinful, I'm sorry about it. I'll confess to Padre and be done with it, and why don't you let me finish with our white man along the trail at Topegina's place?" and people said, "Go ahead, Lunta, go ahead and tell us." Perhaps no one was angry, after all. Even so, Mekala continued to look crossly at me. I thought that if I got to Padre before Mekala did, I'd be safe.

I was going to continue, but I was thirsty. Lucky for me it was dark by then. I excused myself to go piss, and I took my bag along. I took my time pissing over the cliff. There were probably pigs down there but I never heard of a pig-sorcerer. Then I went to a rain barrel, splashed water on my face and secretly drank some.

When I got back, I reminded them that when we got off track about the secrets, our white man and I were talking about whether Topegina could take the shape of a white woman. I said that our white man was pressing me about the naked white woman, and indeed we both thought it very funny, but I wanted to make sure he knew that Topegina could take the shape of living people.

When I said that, both men and women began laughing and making noise. I hurried so that no one could spoil my story. I said, "I told our white man that after the Japan

War Topegina was taking the shape of his grandmother Warabai."

Women laughed but the men didn't. I said "Our white man only knows Warabai as an old woman, but I told him she was very beautiful when she was young," and some of the old men said, "Yes! Yes, she was!" The women fell silent.

I told them our white man said that he'd heard the same thing, but he wasn't smiling anymore and he didn't seem ready to laugh, so I said to him "You heard that Topegina was taking her shape?" and he said "No, that she was very beautiful," and looked away from me and I couldn't see his expression.

Before anybody could steal my story, I quickly told it—I told our white man that when Topegina took Warabai's form, many men went into the bushes with her. And nobody's penis swelled up and fell off and nobody died.

Some people made noises, but nobody laughed. I was surprised because to me, that's very funny. Nobody said anything for a moment, and then Meteko's wife said, "Lunta. I don't think you should have told him that. It was a long time ago and although it's true that we heard about it up here, not everybody believed it," and I said, "Believed what thing?" and she said, "About the penises, that they didn't fall off," and I said, "Why wouldn't you believe that?" and she started to laugh so hard she could hardly talk, but managed to say, "Because you Biroi talk so much about penises we think you must have lost yours and are angry about it," and nobody could say anything for some time because of all the laughter.

It's not true, about the penises. We do curse much more than they do, but it's hard to curse without naming penises, and she should have known that. I suppose people who don't curse wouldn't know that, now that I'm thinking about it.

But why had they all been silent before they started laughing? I couldn't understand. Certainly they knew the story, but they didn't laugh until Meteko's wife scolded me. So they were laughing at *me*, not at something I said. They were laughing at me because that woman scolded me, and yet what had I done? I was only telling them about our white man, as they asked. It made me nervous. But what could I do?

I said, "I'm sorry our white man didn't come up here with me, because he would have liked that joke, very much. As I did. But now I'll continue, because I have more to tell you."

I told them that when I said the thing about all the penises staying where they were attached, all he said was, "Ah." I was going to go on, but Kebotai said, "It must be that he started asking questions," and I said, "That's it. He said, 'What you've told me is interesting. Do you think Warabai knew Topegina was taking her shape?' and I said, 'I suppose people talked about it,' and he said, 'And did anybody ask her about it?' and that's when I realized he was asking me questions I couldn't answer, to slow everything down while he worked out what to do."

I could see people nodding their heads. One of the old women—I recognized her but couldn't remember her name—said "I never asked that woman but certainly we talked about it, even up here!" and the other old women started laughing.

Meteko's wife looked as though she wanted to talk again, and that was all right with me. I thought I knew what she'd say, and it was better for her to say it than me. I gestured to her and said, "You talked about it up here?" and she said, "Oh yes. As Nuapaga has said. In truth I remember very well that all the men, even our men up here, wanted to believe it was indeed Topegina, and so did their wives, even more," and some woman said, "I remember! Yes!" and Meteko's wife continued, "Having your husband tricked by a dangerous spirit and surviving was one thing. Having your husband go with the real Warabai was another," and I said "I wonder if you were in the forest listening, because that's what I was thinking, sitting there on the trail with our white man."

Meteko's wife nodded her head. "Yes," she said, "I remember that, and feeling we were lucky, because Kado-orem never did that."

I said, "I didn't know," and then I cleared my throat and said, "I'll finish about our white man. I thought he and I might as well be done with this, so I said, 'You know Warabai. Can you imagine asking her? Perhaps you're not understanding me?' and he said, 'Oh, I've been understanding you,' and then he spit a long, slow spit"—I bent over and imitated him, being careful to spit into the fire—"'but I admit no one's taught me what to do when somebody's joking about my grandmother. If it's all right to laugh, or not, I don't know,' and it was good, that he finally admitted he didn't know what to do."

People said, "Yes, good," and "He admitted it," and things like that. But nobody asked any direct question so I went on. "I was glad to hear that. I was glad to know he was thinking about what he should and shouldn't hear about his grandmother. 'You can laugh,' I said to him, and he laughed and laughed until he started coughing.

"I hit him on his back. He hit me on my thigh and spit a perfect kuioto and then he said, 'I'll never tell. Was she really like that?' and I smiled at him and said, 'People say,' because it was one thing to tell him that about his grandmother, but another to name names."

What I didn't tell the mountain people I said was, "We're not talking about your sister," because they are so careful up there that even a hint as to what a man must not hear about his sister would offend them. For dangerous sorcerers, they're prudes.

People were shifting around in their seats. They didn't look angry, but in the darkness it's hard to tell. I said, "Our white man and I sat for a while, and then he got up. 'Go on to Pomalate and read your letters,' I said, 'but if a woman steps out of the bush around here, don't stop. Never mind whether she's black or white, wearing clothes or not,' and he shook my hand and went along the trail."

"I turned in the other direction because I was going to Sovele," I lifted my hand and said, "No need to—" but it was too late. They all began imitating me, even the women, and very loudly too, and two young men stood up and started walking the way I do, bent over, coughing and shouting, and more men did the same.

It was insulting, and I wanted to say so. I'd done what they asked, and here they were making fun of me. But what could I do? If I'd shouted back at them they would have thought I wanted to fight, and who knows what would have happened?

I had no weapon except our white man's flashlight. I may be an old man but I would have broken some heads with it, I can tell you that, just the way I broke Leau's head with my axe, broke that head before we cut it off and took it home. Yes, we did and would do it again, too.

I thought, *May mudemude heat these rude prudes so much they try something against Mesiamo,* and I came very near saying it. Instead, I got up from my seat, put on an angry face and turned from side to side. I shouted, "Enough is enough! No need to insult an old man who's come to help you mourn," but they wouldn't stop. Everywhere, people were imitating me. It was intolerable but in a moment I realized this offense was giving me my chance.

I pushed my way through the crowd, refusing to shake hands with the women offering theirs, giving strong looks to Meteko and Kebotai and the other fools—Mekala the catechist also—and not taking the hands they offered me. Who knew what they had on them?

I was shaking, but not with cold and not with anger. With relief. Yes. It was clear I'd been in grave danger but I'd seen my chance to escape, unharmed, by using my old wits.

The Dead One also failed to kill me, I said to myself as I walked from the feasting house. I turned on our white man's flashlight and I walked slowly, to show them I was unafraid.

I paused for a moment at the pyre because I know what proper behavior is. I also didn't want He Who Died angry at me. After I said some things to him I started walking and I didn't look back.

I could hear them shouting and laughing farther down the trail than I expected. When I could no longer hear their insults I cursed them with their dogs and pigs and their sisters and their brothers.

Then I walked a little faster because there was no way to know who might have heard.

Fireflies Killed Her

My name is Polanara.

When my daughter gave birth to a boy, our white man Elliot exchanged names with him. Now my grandson has an American name, and Elliot has a Nagovisi name, Kanai. Elliot killed a pig for his namesake, making them one person. I am their grandfather.

I'm not like the younger men. It's hard for me to be at ease with whites, because before our white man came to us, no white man had ever done anything except give me orders. Make me work for him. Obey. Not talk to him beyond saying, "Yes, master."

Even though Elliot did none of these things, it wasn't until he became my grandson that I felt at ease with him. I understood that he wanted to learn things from us. Yes, even from me, an old man.

When he lived with us he studied our gardens. He loved gardens more than anything and was always asking questions about them, especially the taro gardens from before. When the Japan War came to us, the taro died and never grew again. The war, all the killing, the death of taro, these are bound together in ways none of us, not even Lalaga, can understand. It's possible that my grandson is here to study these connections. Maybe some day he'll tell us, unless it's a secret.

Since the Japan War, I've had a question I wanted to ask an American. I've seen one or two Americans since the fighting, but I never thought I could ask them anything. It wasn't only because they couldn't speak our language. I thought they wouldn't want to tell their secrets to someone they didn't know. When I became Elliot's grandfather I thought if I asked him to reveal American secrets, he would. I was waiting for the right time.

One day he asked me to show him my old taro garden, so he could study it. I thought that would be the right time and place, the garden where we were on this day I'm telling you about.

Even so I almost didn't ask, because it was so direct. But then I reasoned that because he asked me to help him, and I did, that he would want to make us even by answering my question. Even exchange is very important to us and he understood that.

We were at the garden's edge, but now it was forest and undergrowth, but there was a log and I sat on it. My grandson stood, although there was room for both of us in the shade.

I said, "Grandson. Here we are. I've told you everything about this garden, the garden we made before you were born. I remembered where I felled the trees, and I showed you the stumps. I showed you where we planted taro and sweet potatoes, greens, where I made the fences, everything. I showed you, I helped you cut lanes so you could measure, and I held the end of your tape, and you made your map. Are you finished?"

He said that he was.

I said to him, "Now that we're standing here, I have something to ask you."

He looked at me, and although I was used to that open look of his, the look that always says, "Ask me anything you like," it was hard for me to ask my question. It wasn't a question such as "What's the name of your village?" or "What's your mother's name?" Many people ask him simple questions like that, and he always answers them.

Mine was more difficult. True, men like Siro and Lalaga are always asking him about America, and the young men and women, they talk about modern things. I know because I hear them talking and it's clear they are talking easily about things that are not secret or forbidden to talk about.

I know that the world beyond Nagovisi is a different world. But I'm an old man now, so knowing that it's different is all I want. I don't need to know *how* it's different, or *why*. The new things like radios and tape recorders, I just listen to them. It's not necessary for me to understand anything about them, or learn how to operate them, and I don't want to.

The same with cacao. I grow some cacao, and my daughter and son-in-law dry it and take to the Co-Op and they bring back money, and we buy tinned meat or rice with it. Without cacao I wouldn't have any money, but that would be all right. I help my daughter in her garden and she feeds me, and when I'm too old to go to the garden, she'll still feed me, and then I'll die and the Lolo women will come for my body and probably cremate me, because I'm not strong for the Catholic Church.

I was thinking all these things while my grandson was standing there not saying anything. Now that I'd finished helping a white man do his work, my thoughts returned to what happened there long ago. Being in my old garden brought back memories of fear, of death, of dead bodies, of mourning, of cremation, and most of all, of trying to understand new things.

I got up and walked a little distance from him as if I had to do something with my knife, which was easy because in the bush there's always something to do with a knife. I was deciding how to phrase it. He waited, standing.

When I was ready I turned and walked back to him. I said, "My question is, do you know who killed my wife Katenai, your grandmother, here in this place?"

He widened his eyes. He seemed only a little surprised, and I thought that might mean that he knew that he might be asked about it. He said, "It was an airplane, that's what everybody told me. An American war plane. No? Are you saying that it wasn't an airplane?"

I said, "No, no, it was airplane guns, I know that. I asked *who*, not *what*, because an American man flew the airplane and shot the guns and because you are an American I am wondering if you know whether that man was black or white."

That last thing was my true question.

Many old people believe that the American pilots, the ones who bombed us, the ones who sprayed poison on our gardens, that these were black men, not white men. I believe this might be true.

My grandson said he knew that an airplane killed Katenai, but he never heard the whole story. He asked me to tell it to him. I thought he might be trying to slow things down, so as to have time to think. Whether he learned that from us or it was already his way when he came to us, I don't know.

I began telling him. I remembered everything about it, even the little things.

In my mind I could see the garden the way it was. I asked him if he could see it too, and he said that he could. He's been learning about gardens from Siuwako, and he can clear away trees and brush and vines in his mind and see what any place looked like a long time ago. She taught him that.

I pointed to where my wife had been restarting the fires from the day before, and I told my grandson, "It happened over there."

He nodded his head and said "Tell me, Grandfather."

I said, "I was swinging my machete around, deciding what to do first, maybe repair the fence, maybe weed, maybe cut some new bush. It was still chilly. I was turning around, moving, and then I heard the airplane."

I paused. When I was silent, my grandson asked if I knew what airplanes were then, before the fighting.

"Yes," I said. I told him I knew what they were, and I knew they carried cargo because Lovio's plantation master at Rabaul sent him to the airstrip to unload cargo from one. That was the first time he saw one up close, and when his contract was over and he came home, he told us about it. But I didn't know they could be used for fighting. I thought they were like cargo ships, except they traveled into the air. They were just another machine that white people used to carry things from place to place.

I told my grandson that before the Americans came, airplanes were rare. Sometimes we heard them but rarely saw them, and when we did, they were high in the air. Big Nali walked to Buin and saw some on the ground there, and told Mesiamo about them. They were Japanese.

Then after one killed Katenai they were always overhead, not droning in straight lines but diving, tossing like bats, flitting. Usually we saw them in pairs, like hornbills, but sometimes they were all together, like crows mobbing an eagle.

I stood up and asked my grandson to come to the cliff with me. I cut some bush and when it was open enough so he could see out over the Tavera River, I pointed to the bend and I told him that I heard a sound that wasn't the airplane sound I knew coming from downstream. It wasn't steady. It was changing pitch, and although I thought it was an airplane I couldn't see one in the sky, which confused me.

The feel of that day was returning to me. I put my hand on my grandson's shoulder and spun him around, and I said "Look, you see? This was all clear, from *there* to *there* to *there*"—I was pointing—"you know what a garden on a ridge looks like, so I could see the sky but there was no airplane in it. And I turned around and around, looking, like this," and *I* spun around, looking up, and I said, "Katenai was busy with the fires, kneeling, making noise with the branches, concentrating. I'm sure she heard it too, because she turned around. The sound got louder and louder and then suddenly it flew around the bend, so fast, fast, right at us. I hadn't seen one except high up, from underneath, the wings, but here we were, suddenly the airplane coming at us."

I slashed at the air with my machete. I knew my voice was changing. I said, "I was so surprised. It shot lightning, winking, but slower than lightning, and I remember thinking *fireflies, fireflies in the morning*? I couldn't understand it. I turned towards Katenai and I saw the earth around her spurting up, I'd never seen such a thing before, and blood spurted from her, too, from her back, because she had jumped up from her fire and then she was driven backwards, spinning around."

It was so fast. I clapped my hands three times to show my grandson how fast it happened. One, two, three claps, finished.

And the roaring! And a crackling sound like fire, only louder.

I said, faster than I meant to, "And it seemed like a wind flung her over there, Grandson, when the blood shot out, it was right over there, there, it shot out," I pointed with my machete, "over there." And I said again, "Over there. Over there."

My grandson looked at me without saying anything. His mouth was open.

I said, "Now I know it was *bullets* hitting her that flung her back onto the heap, like when wind, wind rushing before a storm, takes a rain cape. That's what it looked like. You know how wind sweeps down from Wakupa, you hear the noise, look up, see brown clouds, then it's on you, the wind, you run to the garden house to be safe, the thatching jumps and slaps. This was more sudden. No wind from Wakupa ever came so fast, wind never made that noise. No storm ever swept in with fireflies for lightning. No. No. And the blood spreading."

I sat down, then I stood up again. It was hard for me because this was something I never talked about. Telling my grandson about it made it real again, and that made me angry and frightened. We Nagovisi say fear is sometimes anger's mother and sometimes anger's child but on this day I'm talking about they were sisters.

My grandson said nothing. He was looking at me and his eyes told me he understood. I could see that I'd taken him there with me, back to that day. He was seeing it as I saw it, feeling it as I felt it, and that calmed me, as if I had transferred my feelings to him.

I said, "Grandson, after she was down I couldn't do anything. I stood here, stunned as if lightning had struck near me, and I remember thinking *fireflies killed her*, even though I knew the airplane had done it. I knew she was dead but I couldn't understand how."

I took my grandson's arm and pulled him to where Katenai died.

I said, "I ran to her, here. Around her was red, blood on the dirt, blood splattered on the leaves she was burning, and the fire was heating the leaves and they were brown and curling up around the sizzling blood. Even though I was confused and terrified all I could think of was how much it looked like betel spit into a fire, the way it hisses and boils on hot wood."

He said, "Oh, Grandfather."

I told him I looked at the blood and I looked at Katenai and I didn't know what to do. I was frightened. I pulled some branches over us, and I hid there with her until I couldn't hear the airplane any more.

I could hear her body making noises, but I knew she was dead.

My grandson put his hand on my arm. I slashed a little at the leaves. I said, "Katenai did nothing to the airplane and neither did I. An American pilot came and killed her for no reason and although I could not see his face, some people say that the pilots were black men from America."

My grandson said, "Black men? Is that what people say?" and before I could answer he said, "This is a hard story to hear, especially in this place. I wonder if you can tell me what happened next?"

I wanted to be sure he understood, so I said, "Black men is what people say, but I don't know whether that's true. American black men."

He didn't say anything. He nodded his head as if to say, "Tell your story," so I did. After this long, I could wait a little for an answer.

I said, "I had to carry her back. It was very hard. I crept out from under the brush. I was still afraid of the airplane. I pulled Katenai out and I slung her across my shoulder and started carrying her back to the village. I had never carried a dead person by myself. All the way there were noises louder than anything I ever heard, and more airplanes too."

He asked me if I'd stayed on the trail.

I said, "Yes. On the open parts of the trail I tried to run, because I was exposed. It was hard to run because when I did she bounced up and down on my shoulder. It was terrible to feel that. Can you understand?"

He nodded his head *Yes* and then he shook it, *No*.

I went on. "When she bounced on my shoulder, her body made noises. So I held her tight, but that felt wrong. I knew she was dead but I was thinking *Maybe I'm hurting her.* That's how crazy I was. I held her tight and ran a little faster than walking, and when the bush hid the trail I slowed, but I never stopped."

My grandson said, "It's very far from here to the village."

I said, "Very far, yes. It was terrible. My back and chest were covered with blood, and it mixed with my sweat, matting my body hair. When I looked down at my chest it seemed *I* was the one bleeding. Blood ran down to my elbows and dripped off, and her arms were slap slapping against my back, her feet bobbing in front so she seemed alive."

I put my hand on my grandson's bare back and struck him rhythmically, so he could feel what I felt.

"Slapping," I said, "bobbing, bouncing, and I could smell her. Smoke, sweat, her wrap, woman-smell. It was terrible. Finally I came into the village but no one was there. I stood at the center. I was so tired and frightened that I didn't know what to do. And sad."

"I slid her down through my arms, Grandson, that was awful because her head hit my shoulder and I had to look at her dead face. I couldn't put her down. I turned her and I cradled her like a child, and then I called out, without clearing my throat or catching my breath, and what came out of me was a huge voice screaming 'Katenai is dead! Dead! An airplane killed her!'"

My grandson took my hand.

I said, "And all the people who were in their gardens, but no airplane attacked them, all those people who ran from their gardens when the noise began, all those people who ran carrying food and infants, all those people hiding in the bush around the village, all those people ran towards me to see if it was true. When they saw me holding bloody dead Katenai they knew it was true."

My grandson said, "Grandfather, I'm crying for you," and I could see that his eyes were wet and I believed him.

"Cry," I said, "Weep. And I will tell you what happened. The people came to me. When they saw Katenai with big bloody holes in her they made noises but they couldn't speak. People couldn't control themselves. Some people belched. Some groaned. Some farted. Some covered their faces and sobbed. Two or three ran back into the bush. The rest made a ring around me, and I kneeled on the dirt and put Katenai down on her back. No one helped me. I arranged her arms properly and put her legs together."

I took my hand from my grandson's and wiped my own eyes. "When I stood up my body felt as though it would rise into the sky. On that day I thought I would rise like smoke and airplanes would kill me. Then the women began circling her body and singing the mourning dirge immediately in full sun, and the men joined them. They didn't wait to wash the body and lay it out in a house. Nobody went to get a mat to cover her. That was not our way but no one was thinking clearly."

My grandson touched my arm. He said, "Did you stay with her?"

I said, "I stood next to Katenai. I should have joined the circle, but to me it was like a dream. I thought I might be dead, too, with the mourners singing and dancing around me. The center is for the dead and the circle outside, the singing and dancing, is for the living, but I was so confused it seemed I was dead and alive at the same time. I joined in the singing, *My wife, o my wife, o my wife,* which told me I was alive. But the other singers were surrounding *me,* which told me I was dead."

My grandson asked me if I'd stood there for a long time, and I said that I didn't think it was very long, but it seemed a long time, and he made a noise but said nothing.

I said, "Mesiamo came and took me away from the mourners. 'Let them sing,' he said, 'come away now.' He took me to my cookhouse and made me sit down and drink water. Then he gave me betel. I didn't want to chew because of the red, but he made me. He prepared it for me and put it in my hand and put my hand to my mouth, so I took it in and chewed. I didn't want to spit red, because I was remembering the red blood that came from Katenai's mouth, so I swallowed my spit."

"And then?" my grandson asked, "What then?"

I said, "Mesiamo asked me, 'Was it a Japanese airplane?' I said, 'I don't know how to tell,' and he said, 'Did it have red circles on it?' and I said, 'I didn't see any red circles,' and then he said, 'Did you see anything?' and I said, 'No, it was so fast, but no red circles,' and he said, 'It was not the Japanese,' and then he said, 'This is bad because we don't know who is killing us.'"

My grandson said, "Grandfather, what happened then? Did you cremate her?"

"Yes," I said, "Mesiamo sent men for wood to build the pyre. The men couldn't make the proper ritual meal but even so they went for the wood and cut and split it and chopped down Katenai's betel palms for the supports. The women washed her and covered her with a mat. All this was done in a rush when the sun was still high. We laid her in the body-crib and I put fire to it."

"And that night?" my grandson asked.

I said, "Everybody came to me that night and made me tell my story over and over, because Katenai was the only one killed. Everyone wanted to hear it. I told them, 'Why must you hear the story so many times,' and Big Kenema from Osilaada said, 'Because if we can understand what she did to anger the airplane perhaps we won't be killed,' and Lunta asked me, 'Why did it kill her and not you?' and that was my question too. I couldn't answer it."

My grandson said, "It must have been very hard. In the morning she was alive and working in her garden and by nightfall she was burned to ashes. So sudden, so fast."

I said, "It was terrible. All in one day. And that night, questions, questions, and the people surrounded me in the feasting house. 'Why? Why?' they kept asking and I had no answer, and then I became angry and I answered 'I don't know, I don't know, why are you asking me, I don't know' to every question, and finally Mesiamo said 'Stop!' and he made everybody leave."

My grandson asked, "You were alone that night?"

I said, "Yes. I left all the people in the feasting house and went to our house. I lay down on a bench in the cookhouse and covered myself with a mat. I couldn't have a fire because of the death, but I didn't want one, because of the airplane. I was afraid that it would see the fire or see me, the one who escaped, and come winking like a firefly in the night and kill me."

Again my grandson made a noise and touched my arm.

I shook my head and made a noise myself. I said, "I fell asleep and dreamed that in the garden Katenai flung *herself* at the piled up brush, that when she staggered to the heap she was escaping under branches and logs.

"And in the dream I ran to her and she called to me from the heap, 'Husband, I'm not dead, under the logs I'm alive,' and I pulled the tree branches and vines from the burning heap but I could not find her. I pulled and pulled and she called 'I'm alive, I'm alive,' but she wasn't there."

My grandson said, "Grandfather, I'm very sad about all this," and I said, "I know you are, and I'll continue. When I woke from the dream I knew she was dead. I could smell the pyre, I could smell her flesh burning, I could smell the blood that was still in my chest hairs because I never went to wash. And Mesiamo was sitting with me, not talking, just sitting. I was not an important man, that he should sit with me while I slept."

I paused, remembering all this, how strange it was.

I said, "And I remember thinking, *We are in a different time now.*"

In the garden I sat on a log facing the little area I'd cleared while telling my story. I pushed my machete in and out of the dirt and said softly, "I couldn't ask you about the pilot before today. I thought maybe you wouldn't tell, if you knew, because it might be an American secret we are not allowed to know. Then you asked to study my old garden and I thought, 'I'll ask him there, I'll show him the spot and when he looks at it and hears about my first wife, his grandmother, killed there, shot for no reason, maybe he'll tell me what he knows.'"

"So that's what I think," I said, "that maybe you know, and if you do, that you'll tell me. Now I've said everything I have to say."

My grandson said nothing for a little while. Then he said, "Grandfather, please ask your question again. You told me this sad story and it made me weep, but I'm not sure what your question was."

I wondered if that was true, that he had forgotten, but it wasn't important. We all say things like that.

I said to him, "I want to know if the pilot was a black man or a white man."

My grandson was silent for a moment. Then he breathed out heavily and made circles in the dirt with his bare feet. I said nothing.

He cleared his throat and said, "In the books I have read about the Japanese War, there is nothing about black pilots. The black pilots were in the place called Europe, where the other part of the big war was. So I can tell you that the pilot who killed Katenai was a white man, not a black man."

I thought that was probably true. If my grandson didn't know which pilots were black and which were white, then no one I could ever talk to would know.

He said, "Grandfather, I'm wondering why you are worried about this."

I said, "I have seen many things in my life, but one thing never changed until you came to us—that white people boss black people and if it's ever black fighting white, the whites kill the blacks. So it's easy to understand what to do about white people, which is to obey them always. Otherwise they might kill you."

We sat there for a while without speaking, and I decided to explain why I wanted to know. I felt sure he'd understand.

"Grandson," I said, "Grandson, it's like this. I think that everybody, black or white, that everybody is unhappy if the world seems upside down, not the way you think it should be. Don't you agree?" and he said that he did, but that was all he said.

For a moment I said nothing. I'd asked him a difficult question but this was almost as difficult.

"Grandfather, tell me," my grandson said, and so I said, "It's like this. If the pilot was black then everything I understand about the world is wrong. But if the pilot was white then the world is as I have always thought it was."

I looked at him and said, "Do you see? Do you see?" and he said, "I see," and I said, "Then you understand it comforts me, that the pilot was white."

My grandson looked at me and I could see he was sad. I could see that he wanted to say something, but he didn't. After a while he said we should start back to the village before the rain came down from the mountains.

Dog Fights

When our white man Kakata came into our cookhouse, my dog Koria growled at him.

"Why does Koria hate me, Siro?" he asked as he sat down across from me. He made a face at Koria, who growled again. "I'm tired of it."

"Koria will stop hating you when you stop being white," I said, and Kakata stuck an arm out towards where Koria was growling under the bench I was sitting on and said, "If he used his eyes he'd see I'm brown, not white."

I said, "You can't fool him. He saw you were white when you came to us, and he hasn't changed his mind. Besides, he uses his nose and you smell like you did when you came."

"Like I did? Then why do people tell me my sweat stopped smelling like a white man's sweat when I started eating sweet potatoes instead of meat? If a person can tell, why can't a dog?"

"Because he's a dog and dogs can't talk," I said, knowing that was a useless response. But I wanted to say something, and I didn't really want to talk about Koria with Kakata. There's no help for what's going on, so why talk about it? Yet Kakata keeps bringing it up.

"I can talk and I say that's a bad dog," Kakata said, and reached into the pot for a sweet potato and started eating it.

A person who only saw him taking a sweet potato and eating it, a person who didn't notice his hair and skin, would think he was one of us. We talk about people as if we recognized them according to what they look like, and this is certainly true, but it's also true that we recognize them by their movements, the way they hold things, whether they're at ease with those movements or not.

Before Kakata came to live with us I never thought about things like that. I've watched Kakata change—we all have—as he learns our ways. It's as though he's growing up, the way a child does, but he's no child, our white man. Even so I think it's not very different. Children grow up not only by getting bigger, but by learning things. Kakata's no bigger than he was when he came here, but he's learned a lot.

Kakata's always telling me that the outsider person sees things that the insider person doesn't. The first time he said that I could easily see it was true, although it wasn't something I'd ever thought about.

And now, after all these months, it's interesting to think about how much Kakata is an insider and not an outsider. It's not an easy question to answer, because certainly he's a mixture. When he does something like take a sweet potato and start eating it as if he's been sitting in a Nagovisi cookhouse all his life, I shake my head.

If you take away his brown-white skin and long straight hair, will he ever be just like us? No, because there's not enough time for him to learn everything. But already he's so much like us that some people are beginning to say they don't think of him as a white man anymore. I don't either, except when he and I take ourselves among the whites.

I looked at him sitting there eating. He seemed happy, except about Koria. I didn't want to talk about the sweet potato thoughts because I didn't think it needed talking-about. But since we were going to see some white people, I thought I'd say something about that.

"Kakata!" I said loudly, startling him. "Kakata! Today we're going to see your namesake kakatas in their nest." I must have startled my daughter Nuai too, because she woke up. She'd been sleeping on one of the benches. When she finished rubbing her eyes she crawled over to Kakata and climbed into his lap.

He started raising her arms and talking English, while she babbled and laughed. The first time he did that, I understood only 'baby' and 'big,' but he taught me white people baby-play talk and now both Siuwako and I sometimes play with Nuai saying, "How big is baby? Sooo big." She likes it.

I wonder if that doesn't make us black people playing at being whites, and I wonder if an American hearing us saying the baby-play saying would think we were Americans playing with an American baby. I think not, because I can't imitate Kakata's English well enough.

What does it matter? An American says baby-sayings to our baby in his language and the baby doesn't care what language it is and neither do any of us.

I cannot think of one thing in this world that would change according to whether Kakata talked to my daughter in English or Nagovisi or any other language, or that her mother and I did. Lalaga likes to talk about what things mean and that's good but sometimes it's not necessary. At least not for a man like me who tries to decide what's worth thinking hard about, and what's not, and on a day when we were going down to Buin Town it was only worth thinking about because our white man was going in among other whites, and not alone. With us, and therefore it would be as complicated for him as it always was.

We shared some betel, spitting red onto the hard dirt. I tossed Kakata half of my husk and he gave it to Nuai, who started chewing it. Kakata took a cup of water from the water pot and rinsed his mouth.

"Ah, let's go," Kakata said, "we don't want Genenai to leave without us."

On the other side of the village Tagilali and Nalokasi were waiting. Tagilali's only half Nagovisi. His mother was a Rotokas, the people up towards Buka that we always joke were cannibals. I don't think they were, but that's what people say. He's black like us, so you wouldn't know he wasn't one of us unless you started talking with him and he told you. He never tries to hide that it's only his father who's Nagovisi, and he doesn't hide that the Biroi women decided to treat him as a Biroi, fitted him into the kinship system, even though his mother wasn't a Biroi. Tagilali's a little younger than Kakata. He's worked at the copper mine, Rabaul, New Ireland and other places in the Territory. He understands many things about whites, and about machinery. He and Kakata are easy with each other. They sit around talking on his porch, at least when he's not off at my garden, or making maps, and he sometimes helps Kakata when he needs to go look at something far away and wants company. Or isn't sure he knows the way.

Nalokasi had finished Standard Six but he hadn't been to Buin before. I thought this would be a good trip for him. I told his mother that somebody had to teach the boys about towns before they try getting jobs up at the mine, and better it should be me and Kakata, so that he gets used to being around whites.

We walked through Biroi. Mesiamo came out with his list, which he gave to Kakata. Mesiamo can't write, but he knows what he needs and he tells his son, who writes it down.

"I'll pay you when you get back, White Man," he said, and Kakata said, "Good."

Mesiamo always asks Kakata to buy cargo for him at Missus Loo's store in Buin. I always ask Kakata whether Mesiamo's given him the money, and he usually says the same thing, "In the end, he pays."

I know what he means, because it's the same for us. In the end, the Big Man evens things up but he's never in a hurry to do it, and if he owes you money, the way he makes it equal might not be with money, no matter whether you wish it was, or not. He might make it equal by helping you with a dispute, or protecting you in some way, or seeing to it that your wife's not left out of a land distribution.

Or protecting you, the way he did when our football team went over Moratona side to play a match with another village. We heard that they had put magic things along the trail, to make us weak. Mesiamo said, "I'll go with you, and I'll be first in line. Anything they put will fail, because of me."

We all understand that's how it is with him. Our idea about what's equal doesn't say that it must be exactly the same thing passing back and forth. Even so, with money—

that's difficult. Sometimes you need money for things that you can only do with money, and if the Big Man uses your money but returns something else, it can be troublesome.

I'm helping Mesiamo by keeping watch on Kakata, and that's not going to be repaid with money. It's never been talked about, but I know that after Kakata goes home, Mesiamo will pass control of some land to my wife. Not to me, because among the Nagovisi only women own land, except for Mesiamo. But I won't talk about that now.

Kakata didn't understand about Mesiamo and money in the beginning. Kakata asked me why I thought Mesiamo wasn't paying him for the cargo he bought, and because I saw he didn't understand, I said, "He's letting you live here, he's teaching you, he's looking after you and he would never say 'pay me for this,' but in truth, Kakata, money's the only thing you have that's useful to him."

That wasn't true, but I couldn't tell Kakata that Mesiamo was hoping to learn from him what plans the copper miners and the government had for Nagovisi, if any.

Kakata looked disappointed. He said, "I'm feeling stupid because I should have understood that," and I said, "But you didn't know that when you came here. You had to learn it," and he said, "Really, I did know it because Mesiamo isn't the only leader of this kind. Remember that my teacher studied Big Men in Siwai and so I knew," and I said, "I see," and he said, "I only feel a little bit stupid, because I thought that money, the new thing, that money was money and money exchanges would have new rules, but I see that I'm wrong."

On the trail from Biroi to Bereteba we walked sometimes single-file, sometimes side by side, talking about the trip.

Where it was especially muddy, with water ponding, we split up and walked on opposite sides. But we never stopped talking. Nalokasi asked if we were going to drink and in one voice we shouted Yes! I said I might let Nalokasi drink or I might not. It would depend on how well he behaved.

"What do you mean?" Nalokasi said.

"He means if you can screw a Buin girl while we're waiting at the store, you can drink. Everybody knows Buin girls screw for anybody, even a school boy whose penis has only been getting hard since Christmas," Tagilali said.

Kakata and I laughed. We were the senior men. I said, "Don't talk about screwing in front of this white man," and Nalokasi said, "Why are you making fun of me?" and Kakata said, "Because you're my uncle," which meant nothing except that when Kakata shared names with little Kanai, Nalokasi became his uncle.

When we walked past Lolo Village, their dogs came out and barked. Kakata shouted, "Fucking dogs!" and we all laughed.

It's always the same. They bark, he yells, they run away when he stoops and pretends to pick up a stone.

I said, "It's because of you. They wouldn't bark if it were just us."

He said, "You mean if you three walked down the road without me, the dogs wouldn't bark?" and I said, "Yes."

"Liars," he said, raising his voice, "Liars. Every place we go, the dogs bark."

Tagilali said, "It *is* because of you. Nagovisi dogs only bark at whites."

He said, "What bullshit you're talking. Koria barks at the mountain people when they walk through Pomalate." He gave Tagilali a push in the back.

I said, "That's because you're watching. If you weren't watching, he wouldn't."

Kakata muttered something in English.

"Please speak clear English, master," Tagilali said, "We kanaka boys cannot understand."

That made Kakata laugh. He stood up straight and said in a deep voice, "I will speak simple English for you schoolboys. I said, 'If a tree falls in the woods,'" and then he threw up his arms and said in Nagovisi, "meaning, 'You're all liars.'"

Nalokasi said, "What did you really say, nephew?" and Elliot gave him a push and said, "It's too hard to explain."

We let it go because we knew, even Nalokasi, that one day he'd say it again and would explain.

Kakata barked like a dog and gave me an elbow in the ribs. He changes his manner when we get away from our village. I think it's because he's not near Mesiamo and he doesn't have to be serious. He can be foolish. He can act like what he is, a young man my age thinking about going to town. And about getting drunk on the way back, too.

As we approached Bereteba, where the tractor would be, I said to Kakata, "Are you ready to speak English? Have you forgotten how to speak it?" I said this because in the village he only speaks English with some of the young people who have gone to high school and want to talk English. I also said it because I knew that in Buin there would be some language fights.

The whites always speak English to Kakata, no matter whether we're with him or not, and this is true even of whites who can speak good pidgin. It's as if they don't want us to know what's being said, even though they aren't talking about anything secret. I know this because Kakata tells me what they were talking about.

It's worse when the white man decides to speak pidgin, because then he speaks pidgin even when he knows that the native can speak good English, like a schoolteacher. Most of the whites are like that. Not all.

I don't care about English between English-speakers, but it's wrong to start speaking pidgin to one of us who speaks English. The worst thing of all is when the white man begins in pidgin, the native answers in good English, and the white man continues in pidgin. That's insulting. I think that means the white man doesn't want to let the schoolteacher into his "English Club," the same way he won't let natives into the Buin Club. It's wrong.

I talk about this with Kakata. He doesn't like it either but he says nothing to the white man when it happens, except that if the native speaks English, Kakata switches to English no matter what the white man does.

But if the white man's only talking English to Kakata, and Kakata has to talk to us, he switches to Nagovisi, which puts the white man on the other side of the river, a river he can't cross because no other white man speaks our language.

Kakata says that someday if this happens and the white man complains, he'll say to him, "Oh, you didn't speak pidgin to my friends, so I too didn't speak it," and see what the white man says. I don't think he'll do it, though. He always finds ways to avoid an argument.

We all know that Kakata wants to show us that he's on our side, even when there's no problem and it doesn't matter. It's his way. As for me, I like it. Many of us do. What other white man does this? Padre, of course, but I think that Padre defends us against the Adminstration because we are his Catholic children and he's in charge of us. It's as though we belong to him, so he protects us.

That's different from what Kakata does. Kakata's saying "I belong to the Nagovisi and therefore I owe the whites nothing." It's true, but one of us should tell him that he doesn't need to show it time and time again.

When I was working in Rabaul I went to the movie theater and saw moving pictures. I couldn't understand what people were saying, but in those cowboy movies it seemed clear to me that white people admire men who say, "I'll fight your battles! I'll save you!" Some day I'll start talking about moving pictures and I'll ask Kakata about this.

One Eye Genenai was waiting for us. He must have washed his tractor, because it was clean and blue. It would be dirty soon enough, because there's no part of the road that's sealed, and only some that's gravel. The rest is dirt. Mud, mostly, if it's been raining for a few days. I know how to talk about the trip in miles—seventy each way—but none of us measure it like that. We know that if a tractor starts for Buin in the morning, it'll be long after dark by the time it's back. And that's if nothing goes wrong.

The bags of cocoa beans had already been loaded on the trailer. Kakata and I climbed up and sat on bags next to each other. The ride down is always easier than the ride back, because the bags of cocoa are comfortable to lie on. Maybe that's why we get drunk on the way back, although if somebody buys enough rice there are bags for everybody. If not, there's nothing soft to sit on, but if you're drunk— never mind. Tagilali and Nalokasi sprawled a few feet away, and we settled in for the ride.

Genenai said, "Let's go!" and we all echoed him, "Let's go! Let's go!" He waved a hand in the air, then reached down and grabbed the throttle lever and shoved it forward and the trailer jumped and we were on our way.

Tagilali lay back and closed his eyes but Nalokasi seemed excited. He opened and closed his mother's black cloth umbrella, playing with it in the wind. I knew she'd be angry if he lost it or the wind turned it inside out, but I said nothing. Let him learn for himself.

I lay on my bag in the sun and my thoughts went back to Koria and the other dogs. I wanted to ask Kakata about something I'd seen. It seemed clear to me at the time. Even so, maybe I'd misunderstood and it would be easy to check it with Kakata.

He seemed to be dozing, but I reached over and shook his arm. "Kakata," I said, "Kakata. About white dogs," and he said, "Ah, white, brown, black, spotted, what about white dogs," and I said, "I mean white peoples' dogs," and he said, "What about them?"

I said, "I've seen white people feed their dogs meat from tins, and I'm wondering if that's meat the white man would eat if he wanted it, or some kind of special dog meat."

Kakata made a noise, but he didn't laugh. He said indeed it was meat for dogs, not people, although there was such a thing as dry dog food that looked like…and then he stopped and said, "I can't think of what it looks like that you know about, except maybe Cheetos, but it's harder than Cheetos and not yellow." Then he laughed and said he wondered whether that was the first white food he'd had trouble describing because Nagovisi had never seen it. "It's little brown pieces, and you put some water on it and the dog eats it."

I said, "What I saw was meat. What came from the tin looked like meat to me, like corned beef, and so if it's not meat people eat, then what kind of meat is it?"

Kakata was laughing. He said, "I don't know. It's strange, I admit it. It should be that meat is meat but among the whites that's not so. Some of them eat only meat that comes from some kind of animal, and the other kinds, they won't. Or they eat only meat from some parts of the animal and not from others."

I groaned and laughed, and he said, "You can laugh, but Nagovisi won't eat a pig nose or a pig tongue or anything to do with the pig's head,"—I interrupted, "You don't know where that pig nose has been!"—and he laughed and went on to say that in case I didn't know it, some people ate pig heads, pig cheeks, pig everything, including pig feet— Nalokasi shouted "No!"—and there was an American saying about eating *everything but the squeal,* which made us laugh.

Of course I know that the whites have animals and they kill and butcher them and that's where the packages of frozen meat in Missus Loo's freezer come from. But usually we don't think about that and therefore we don't think about what happens to all the animal parts that don't come to Missus Loo's freezer.

Kakata said that he thought dog meat was usually horse meat. He said, "Did you ever see a horse?" I had seen horses in all those cowboy moving pictures. Tagilali said he'd seen horses in Buka, but never in Nagovisi. But, like me, he'd never seen anybody kill and butcher and cook and eat one.

"I haven't either, but people in France eat horse," Kakata said, "it's true. In America, no," and we all made gagging noises. But Kakata kept at it.

"I wonder why Nagovisi don't eat dogs, the way people do in Tahiti?"

I made a vomiting noise. Everybody thinks that other people eat disgusting things, it's true. But eating a dog *is* disgusting. Even the thought of killing a dog and gutting it and skinning it and cutting it up disgusts me. I think this is because we never do those things with our dogs—except kill them, when we have to—and so every part of what you'd have to do if you wanted to eat dog is strange to me and seems wrong.

When I see men butchering a pig I'm happy but if I saw men doing the same thing with a dog, I'd say "What's wrong with you?" In truth, what's the difference? They're both meat. Another time I would have enjoyed talking about that with Kakata, because it's the kind of thing he loves to talk about.

Kakata asked me why I'd been thinking about dog food. "Really," he said, "We've been having fun but I think you're worried about something."

I said, "You know what it is. Koria's killing chickens and I have to pay compensation, and that's bad, but it's worse that he's made me a white man, buying food for him."

Kakata said, "Ah, true. Your dog's sins have made you an Australian, buying chickens for his food." Kakata knew I was unhappy about that. It was costing me money, and more money because of him. Some people said, "White Man would give me a dollar for the chicken Koria ate," and if I said, "You know it's worth two or three shillings to us," that person would say, "White Man pays more," and insist on it. I reminded him of that and he shrugged his shoulders and said, "What can I do?"

"Nothing, I suppose," I said.

He sat up and turned towards me. I think he didn't want the others to hear. "Remember how long it took for my namesake to, ah, get sick and die?"

Certainly I knew, because Lalaga told me. He asked me not to question Kakata too closely about his bird because there was no reason for it. Lalaga told me that Kakata was having trouble being a white man, and that this was because he thought he had to behave the way *we* thought white men did—not killing their pets—instead of being his own kind of white man.

I knew Kakata understood my problem, although it wasn't the same one. I didn't want to kill my dog because I liked him, and so did my children. But he was causing us trouble. Kakata didn't have to say anything about his bird. But he did, and I liked that.

We rode for a while without speaking. Nalokasi dragged a stick over the side until it caught on a stone and was gone. He hadn't lost the umbrella, though. Tagilali had his eyes closed again, but seemed to be listening. One Eye Genenai was singing Slim Dusty cowboy songs to himself.

I thought we might stay in this easy way until Buin, but Kakata said—this time, to everybody—"Why did you ask me about dog food, really," and what could I do? I had to answer, not only because he asked, but because everybody in the trailer and even Genenai in the tractor seat knew my Koria problem.

"Because," I said, "because I was thinking that before I kill Koria I'll give him something good to eat for once. He's been a good dog."

Kakata said, "He's not good to me," but I didn't want to joke, so I answered "You know what I mean. Everybody will laugh if I give the chicken-eating dog human food, like Ox & Palm corned beef, but if I give him dog food they won't, and maybe Missus Loo's store has dog food." I was hoping that could be the end of it, because what I said was the truth. But no.

Tagilali sat up and said in a loud voice, "Koria's Last Supper," and I said, "Shut your mouth," but he just laughed and said, "We'll get eleven Chicken Apostles."

Then everyone started laughing except me. "Why not twelve?" Kakata asked, "There were twelve Apostles."

Tagilali was laughing so hard he screamed, "Because Judas Siro would make twelve."

That was too much. It was funny to them, but not to me. I shouted, "Hard-on! Why don't you go fuck a dog instead of making fun of me?"

The three of them made hooting noises. Kakata said, "Oh, oh, oh," and I said to him, "You, Kakata, do you think I'm happy about this? It's your fault!"

That last thing, I didn't believe it. I said it to see what might happen. And I was angry, a little. I've had Koria a long time and although he's troublesome and I know he has to be killed, I feel sorry for him.

Kakata slid off his bag and went on his knees. "My fault? It's my fault, O Padre I have sinned so hear my confession now," and I said, "Oh just be quiet, Elliot," using his name even though I almost never do. But I couldn't shut him up.

He said. "As long as we're talking about religion, do you know that in English God is dog spelled backwards?"

"'G-o-d, d-o-g,'" Nalokasi spelled, "Is it a sin to say this?"

Tagilali rolled over and began drumming on the trailer's side. "I never thought of that. God-dog, dog-God, English is a good language! What about 'Jesus Christ, Our Lord?' Does 's-u-s-e-j,' *susej*, spell anything? No? D-r-o-l, *drol*? What about 'N-a-t-a-s,' *natas*?

Kakata clapped his hands. He seemed pleased with what he'd started. He said, "No *natas*, but *drol* sounds like an English word that means 'funny.'"

"How about '*drof*,'" One Eye Genenai called back.

"You're just pretending you can spell," Nalokasi said, "You're looking at the tractor," and Genenai shouted, "Can't spell? Did you fill out the shipping papers, schoolboy? All you did in school was try to look up the teachers' skirts."

"Never mind dogs," Tagilali said, "Let's do more words."

As the tractor bumped along we spelled Nagovisi, English, and pidgin words backwards, yelling at each other. We were laughing, writing in the air. I became less and less troubled. *Words are good*, I thought. *God, dog, satan.* The big bush and the road slipped by, the water in the fords was low, and the mud wasn't bad, all the way to Buin Town.

Missus Loo's cocoa shed and warehouse were behind the store. One Eye Genenai drove around back and the warehouse dog ran out and started barking at us. That dog never bites any of us, but it always barks. Missus Loo's white son-in-law Frank Williams came out from the shed, grabbed the dog by its collar and tied it to a post. He made a motion to One Eye Genenai to come into the shed with him, and the dog stopped barking.

Kakata said to me, "What do you think? If I get down, will Frank's dog start barking again?" He made a face.

I shook my head and bulged my eyes out. "Is mynah's son mynah?" I said, and Kakata said, "Perhaps mynah's son is kakata," which made me laugh, even though it didn't mean anything.

The saying about mynah's son means, "Did you expect something different?" Kakata was just playing with the bird names. All the same, when he climbed out of the trailer the dog didn't bark and I don't think any of us except perhaps Nalokasi, who had never been near that dog, thought he would.

When Frank and One Eye Genenai came out of the shed, Frank waited until One Eye Genenai got back onto the tractor seat before untying the dog. It started barking again, that mynah bird dog.

Frank said in pidgin. "Take the cocoa to the other warehouse and my boys will unload it."

Kakata was on the ground near the trailer. I knew what was coming, because Kakata does the same thing always. He hesitated as if he didn't want to leave us. Then he started to walk to where Frank was, but slowed and started talking to us over his shoulder. When he does this, it's as if he's saying, *I won't forget you! I'll come back to you! And I'll show whose side I'm on by talking your language!*

What he really called to us was, "I'm going to talk to Fart Breath. Genenai, you should run over his barking dog."

One Eye Genenai smiled and replied, "It just barks."

"Well, I think it's a bad thing," Kakata said while waving his hand at us.

One Eye Genenai grinned, but Kakata couldn't see it because his back was turned. Finally he was headed for Frank, and while he was shaking hands with him One Eye Genenai called, "It's nothing. It's how it is. Dogs bark. Please yourself talking English," and started driving towards the warehouse.

Tagilali and I yelled at him that we wanted to climb down and stay at the store, so he stopped. The dog barked at us until we turned around the corner where the store's entrance was. When we went into the store Nalokasi's eyes widened and he started making little noises.

There are three Chinese stores in Buin Town, and Missus Loo's is the biggest. All the stores sell the things we natives like, but Missus Loo's has what the whites want.

She has a freezer filled with meat, and more white shorts and white socks than the other stores do. You can also buy airline tickets at her store, and she's the one who has things like chain saws. All the stores have beer and strong drink, but only she has wine. None of us like to drink wine, so again it's something for the whites.

The thing about Missus Loo's store is that for Buin Town, it's big. I suppose at least twenty or thirty people could be in it at once, and she has five or six clerks. She has a big open space at the front, and it's covered. There are always people sitting and standing there, drinking Fanta and eating whatever they've just bought in the store. There's usually a tractor or a Toyota pulled up in front, loading cargo to take out into the bush.

Everybody says that if a store clerk belongs to your people, you'll get special low prices. I think that's probably true, but there are no Nagovisi clerks in that store, so I don't know.

I remembered the first time I went to a big store, how astonished I was, how there were so many things I'd never seen before that I looked quickly from case to case, shelf to shelf and really saw nothing until I slowed down.

Nalokasi said, "I thought a Chinese store was like the Mission store," and I said, "Someday you'll see the store at the Panguna mine, and then you'll say the same thing about Missus Loo's store." He didn't answer because he was picking things up and putting them down, and holding shirts up to his chest.

Tagilali and I stayed near him while he walked around the store. We had been teasing him, yes, but at the same time we wanted him to enjoy himself. We also kept watch because we didn't want him to do anything ignorant or foolish, so that the Buin people would cough or clear their throats or laugh, saying "Looks like we have some of those bush Nagovisi in here."

Everybody knows Nagovisi is the Big Bush, the Last Place, the end of the road, and they think of us as *bush kanakas*. It used to bother me, but it doesn't any more. I look at those Buin people, so proud of their little town, and I think of my days in Rabaul, which is probably a hundred times bigger than Buin Town, and in truth I feel superior.

And Nagovisi is closer to the copper mine than Buin is, much closer. When there's a road from Nagovisi to Panguna, the mine, we'll be the people closest to the modern things and the proud Buin people will be the last place.

Yes. It's going to happen, but I don't know when. As for right now, we Nagovisi are careful about looking like ignorant bush kanakas, and that's why we were watching Nalokasi. In the end he did nothing wrong, except that it was clear to everybody that he'd never been in a big store before.

As for me, I tried not to act like an ignorant bush kanaka when I asked about tinned dog food. The clerk said loudly, "Dog food?" in pidgin, and people turned to look. I gave him a strong look and said, "Yes, that's what I asked for. That's what I want for my dog, if you have any," and he went into the back room. I stood waiting, people looking at me.

When the clerk came back he was holding a round tin, which surprised me. I thought it would look like tinned beef. It had a picture of a dog on it. The clerk said, "We keep these in the back because some people think it's tinned dog meat and get angry at us for selling it," and

I laughed. Everybody laughed. I only wanted one tin but I also didn't want to seem like a poor wretched thing from the bush, so I asked him to go back and get me two more.

"That will be enough for now," I said, and paid more money than I wanted to. When we left the store I felt people looking at me, probably shaking their heads and wondering why a native was buying dog food just like a white man. I didn't like that feeling. I didn't like thinking that after I left, they'd all be talking about me and surely somebody would say, "What a thing, a Nagovisi imitating his white man, another day the fool will be buying wine."

I imagined going back in and saying, "In case you town people are wondering, it's for my dog that I'm going to kill. Nothing to do with that white man I'm with," but that thought made me feel even more a fool so I stopped thinking about it.

When Kakata walked around to the front of the store, I was sitting on the steps waiting for him. I had the dog food in my bag. Usually when he comes back to us he looks relieved, like a schoolboy who's just gotten out of school. But this day he looked angry.

I said, "Kakata, what?" and he clapped his hands and said, "Never mind. Nothing. Did you load Mesiamo's cargo? I paid for it in the back."

I nodded and took the dog food from my bag.

"Good," he said, "now Koria's a white dog."

"Or I'm a white man," I said, meaning to be funny. But he didn't answer. I put the tin back in my bag. I didn't intend to show it to the others.

Nalokasi and Tagilali were up on the loaded trailer, and One Eye Genenai was in the driver's seat, idling, waiting to go.

Kakata looked at them and turned to me and exhaled strongly. He muttered something under his breath, and then he said, "Let's get some extra beer and Cheetos and get out of here. I want to drink."

There was no way to know what was wrong, except that it had to do with Kakata and Frank. He climbed up on the trailer, found himself a bag of rice, and said nothing until we cleared the edge of town. I could see from his motions that he wasn't himself, although I knew that already.

Siuwako tells me that sometimes when Elliot's working in the garden or playing with Nuai, or looking after her, that instead of moving naturally as we all do—sometimes smoothly, sometimes not, sometimes hesitating—he moves slowly, but always correctly, and everything he does is carefully-done, so much that it calls attention to itself.

When this happens, she thinks he's disturbed about something or is uncertain and wants anybody watching him to see him behaving correctly. She thinks it's because he's afraid he's done something wrong or offended somebody. She says it's as if he's saying "See how good I'm being," the way a child might.

She never says anything to him because she thinks that if he's trying to send a message without any words, that she shouldn't respond with words. So all she does, when this happens, is to go about her business but in a lighter way, if she can.

I know Siuwako and Elliot are very close to each other and have a connection I don't understand. I know that they're constantly talking about gardens and food, because that's what she's teaching him to do—be a gardener.

In truth it's odd, and sometimes I worry about it, because it's a kind of closeness that husbands and wives have, and they usually don't have it with anybody else unless it's with somebody they're meeting in the bush.

What I'm wondering about is whether this all means anything bad about Siuwako and Kakata. I think not, but it's possible. Siuwako and Kakata are never alone. My son Nema is always with them and he's old enough to pay attention to what's going on, and to talk about it if I ask.

I could ask. Everybody knows I could, just as everybody knows that the only reason Siuwako and Kakata can garden together without any trouble is because of Nema. This is no secret. Lalaga and Mesiamo explained it to Kakata and told him to make certain that he was never alone with Siuwako. Even so I don't care to think too much about how Kakata and my wife communicate without words.

It's not as though we were riding along in silence, apart from the tractor noise. No, Tagilali and Nalokasi were talking and talking about Chinese stores and Buin town. Nalokasi kept naming all the new things he'd seen in the store, for example a necktie, which he thought was for tying around the head. Tagilali said "It's a *neck tie* and if you knew English you'd know that's where it goes," and Nalokasi said, "But why?" and Tagilali said, "Because that's what white men do," which was a useless answer but for Nalokasi it was enough, because he was excited, and having fun and jumping around between things he knew about and things he didn't.

Tagilali told him how small and pathetic Buin was, compared to Rabaul. I wouldn't have done that, but I didn't tell Tagilali to stop because I thought if they kept on talking it would let Kakata settle down.

Finally Kakata said, "Time to drink," pulled open the case of South Pacific Lager Green, and started handing them out. I said, "Not the Browns?" and he said, "The Greens are colder," and I said, "They'll stay colder longer, then, so we should start with the Browns" and he said, "Oh never mind. I like the Greens better," and I said, "Why didn't you say so? It's your beer," and he widened his eyes and shot me an irritated look as if I'd said a thing that didn't need saying, which I had.

Tagilali must have decided to make Kakata talk. We hadn't talked among ourselves about Kakata's anger, but we didn't need to.

"Hey, Elliot," he said, "did you enjoy talking English with Frank?" Everybody understands that it's a great relief to talk your own language when you've been with people who don't speak it. For once, talking's easy and it doesn't matter what you talk about.

"I had a good time talking English," Kakata said, "But Frank talks cranky. All Australians do. Never mind, it was English."

Nalokasi said, "What did you ask him? You ask us about everything." I was surprised at that. Nalokasi was just a boy and I didn't think that the children paid much attention to what Kakata did.

He said, "Nothing. I didn't ask him anything because I didn't come here to study Australians."

After a moment, Tagilali said "Maybe we need Nagovisi anthropologists. We have to figure white people out for ourselves, watching and listening. They don't like it when we ask questions. Did he ask you questions? He probably wants to know everything about you, because you're not like the other whites."

Kakata grunted and belched. "It's not the first time we've talked. And what would he ask? He isn't interested in me. To him I'm the crazy white man who lives in Nagovisi," and he held up his hand as if one of us was going to push him, "I mean, he doesn't understand why a white man wouldn't live in a town, speak English or pidgin only, and try to live the way white people live in Australia except doing it here in the bush towns."

Nalokasi said, "We know you're not like those whites, Elliot," and Tagilali gave him a shove and said, "You've met one white man who wasn't Padre or the Kiap and you know all about them, is that right?"

Nalokasi pushed Tagilali back and said, "One? Two. Our white man and the one with the dog," and Kakata said, "But you didn't meet dog-man. You only saw him, Uncle. You had better not talk about white people until you know ten or twenty, like Tagilali and Siro," and Nalokasi said, "I talked to Brother Michael once."

Tagilali made a noise and said, "It takes more than that, schoolboy," and I snorted and said, "And when you talked to Sister Mary Agnes about the sore on your ass, did you think you were talking to a white woman instead of a nun? You know all about white women now? White men? Chinese men? Chinese women? Nalokasi goes to Buin once and now he knows everything."

Nalokasi wrapped his arms around himself. "Why are you insulting me?" he said, "I never said those things," and Kakata said, "But you were thinking them, we know you were, we all know what you're thinking on your first trip to Buin." It would have been a good time for one of us to say, "We were all like you when we first went to town," but nobody did.

Nalokasi said, "Give me another beer, then, Master!" Kakata tossed him one. He opened it with his teeth and we cheered.

"At least he's learned something," Kakata said.

We were still in Buin territory by the time it was completely dark. One Eye Genenai's headlights showed us the road but nothing else. To the sides it was dark, and behind us, the same. If I looked up I could see the dark sky over the tops of the trees. Going through the forest at night, even when you know the road, is confusing. You think that such-and-such a village is a long way ahead and then suddenly there it is. Or the other way around. The best way is to pay no attention to the surroundings, if you can. Or talk, but for a long time nobody had anything to say. I didn't mind, but I was still troubled by Kakata's anger, or whatever it was.

By Siwai a half moon had appeared, which meant we could see the forest. But nobody really cared by then, because we were getting drunk. The beers were warm, but that was all right.

Kakata broke the silence by saying, "Genenai! How come you don't mind that dog?"

He was turned away from me so I couldn't see his expression. His voice was a little angry. "Is he angry about that dog?" I said to myself.

One Eye Genenai turned his head back and said, "He only barks. He never bit me. As I said."

"It's not right," Kakata said, "He should teach the dog not to bark at you. You go there all the time. The dog should know who you are by now. Dogs know one person from another. He could teach it not to bark at you. Dogs can learn."

"It doesn't matter to me." Genenai waved his arm in the air. "It's just a dog. It would be different if Frank bit me," and we all laughed.

Kakata said, "Frank probably has a tail hidden under his shorts, a dog tail," and we laughed at that, too. A dog-man.

I suppose we were all remembering when Osipari told Kakata he wanted to tell a story to the tape recorder, and he told a long story none of us ever heard before, about a dog who pretended to be a girl's grandmother and the girl was saying, "You have long ears," and "You have big teeth," and after that part Kakata started to laugh and shout but he kept the tape recorder running.

We didn't know that Osipari was giving Kakata one of his own stories. But when they both explained it, which was hard because I don't know who was laughing more, we too started laughing. It was a good trick.

"That's a barking dog," I said after a while, even though it was an obvious thing to say, "It's European, too. It's not one of ours."

"I know what kind it is. It's a German Shepard," Tagilali said, "The police have them."

"White dogs don't have to be taught to bark at us," I said. "It's their nature, because they're European dogs. Our dogs bark at you, your dogs bark at us."

"It's not *my* dog," Kakata said. "If I had a dog it wouldn't bark at you."

"We smell different," said Tagilali. "White people stink. We don't stink so they bark because we don't smell like people to them."

I thought about saying that Koria never changed his mind when Kakata changed to smelling like us but I didn't want to remind Kakata about the dog who hated him, so I said, "No, it's because they're European dogs. Europeans treat us like dogs and so do their dogs, because they're *masta* dogs."

"Siro, you're talking bullshit," Kakata said, "Bullshit. If the whites treated you like dogs, they'd be good to you. Food. Like we were talking this morning. Right? Horsemeat. They don't treat you like *they* treat dogs. They treat you like *you* treat dogs."

Nalokasi said, "That's true," and Tagilali said, "What do you know about whites and their dogs? Today was the first time you've seen them," and Nalokasi said, "I know about our dogs, and that's what my nephew was talking about."

Kakata let out a belch. "Barking," he said, and then he said it again. "Barking."

Nalokasi and Tagilali started barking. Kakata tried to howl but he couldn't do it. It sounded more like somebody weeping than a dog howling.

When everybody quieted down, he said, "Never mind all of us acting like dogs. All this talk, all this talk about who knows what about Frank's dog. European dogs. Fucking dog Koria. I know why Frank's dog barks at you." He paused, then said, "I know because he told me."

I was quiet. Kakata was going to say whatever he wanted to say, I thought. After a moment, Nalokasi said, "Tell us."

Kakata took a drink of beer, and said, "This is what he told me, 'First you let your dog go into a cocoa sack. Then your boys close it up, beat on it with sticks, and yell in kanaka language. You make sure you're gone, then the boys open the sack. When the dog comes shooting out all he sees is boys and from then on he hates them and he'll bark at them, but he won't bark at white people.' That's what he told me. It made me angry. It's not right."

I thought, *So that's it*. Everybody shifted on their rice bags. Nobody spoke. In the moonlight I could see Kakata shaking his head. He stook up suddenly and threw his beer bottle into the bush. "Fuck it!" he said in English, "Fuck those white people and their fucking dogs," also in English.

Then he turned around and said in Nagovisi, "Nobody cares? It's nothing to you? That fucking Frank fucking Williams teaches his dog to hate you?"

I didn't know what to do. I would have been more worried if we hadn't all been drunk, but everybody knows that drunk people, black or white, say anything and get angry at anything. I didn't like hearing what Frank had told Kakata, but I didn't see any good in talking about it. Talk is only talk, and some kinds of talk are a waste of time. Nothing happens, except I suppose people feel happier in the end because they've insulted people who aren't there.

We Nagovisi have a ritual where we brandish ginger stalks at each other as if they were spears, something called *pidosi*. But there's always another side and they're doing the same thing to us. A pidosi with no opponents is senseless.

I can get angry when I'm drunk, although I wasn't angry there on the trailer when Kakata was. But I try to save my anger for times when it's useful, such as convincing somebody to do something, or not to do something. That's useful anger. I am not saying I never waste my anger, because I'm a man like everybody else, no saint, and I lose control sometimes, it's true. But I try not to because, as I've said, it's a waste.

I didn't know what to do. I never thought this day would turn into one where we were all drunkenly angry about a dog. True, some were angrier than others. I thought the dog business might disappear if nobody responded to Kakata. Then I thought that was rude. Also I wasn't sure it was only about the dog.

I edged close to Kakata and said softly to him, "Why are you angry, really?"

He said nothing for a moment. Then he turned at looked at the other two, who were talking to each other again, and he bent over towards me and breathed in and out and put his hands on his knees and said softly but with intensity, "Siro, because I said nothing to him, is why. I didn't say anything. I sat there and looked at him and said, 'Oh, really, is that right?' as if he was one of you and I was listening and writing."

I said in a low voice, "That's not wrong," and he shook his head and reached out and put his hand on my shoulder and said, "But it wasn't one of you, it was a fucking Australian I don't care about and even so I hid my anger and kept my white mouth shut. I'm angry at myself and I'm ashamed. I am no better than a small boy."

I couldn't think what the best thing to do was, so I said nothing. I thought that if he didn't know that I understood how he felt, he wasn't thinking carefully. Who hasn't had that feeling? No one. True, with us it's between ourselves and no two of us are as different as Frank is from Kakata, but even so it's still the same. Often enough when Mesiamo tells me something, I don't speak. I don't respond, and then afterward, exactly as Kakata did, ask myself why I didn't say what I thought, or disagree, or any of those things.

I belched politely. I put my hand on his shoulder. I couldn't be sure that anybody had heard what Kakata said. Not One Eye Genenai, that's for sure, and I don't think that drunk little Nalokasi was listening. Nevertheless had they looked in the dark they would have seen me and Kakata with our arms on each other's shoulder and wondered what we were doing.

I released Kakata and he released me. I said loudly, "Don't worry about that dog, Kakata. Be like Genenai and let it slide by you. It's just a dog."

Kakata made a noise and turned away.

There was some coughing and spitting, but no one said anything for a while except Nalokasi, who must not have heard because he went back to the dog-beating. He said "Siro never put Koria in a sack for you to beat, White Body, and he always barks at you."

That was the first clever thing Nalokasi had said all day, except that it pointed us all back not just at dogs and white people, but at dogs and Kakata. Also what Nalokasi said was true, so nobody could call him a liar and turn us away from it.

Even so I thought I'd try. Maybe I could turn it back to Frank and only Frank and his dog. I cleared my throat. I said, "What Frank said might be true."

Kakata pushed me. He looked sorry for himself. "What do you mean, 'might?' It is true, unless you're calling me a liar."

I said, "Kakata, calm down. Nobody's calling you a liar. I mean that what Frank says happens to the dog might be true."

Kakata said, "It sounded like you thought I was lying," and I said, "No. No. But I think what Frank did isn't the only way. Right? If all the whites put their dogs in bags and beat them even we bush Nagovisi would have heard about it by now, and we haven't. So I don't think it's something all the whites do. What Nalokasi says about Koria is also true. Dogs are like people. They don't like different kinds, and to a Nagovisi dog, you, Kakata, you're the different kind. We think you're one of us, but dogs are too stupid to understand that."

I laughed, because I wanted to make it sound like a joke. I didn't need to remind Kakata that he wasn't one of us, which was what telling him he *was* probably sounded like to him. In truth, what happened with Frank had reminded him of that.

Tagilali helped me out. "Frank didn't need to do all that work," he said, "What if his dog got hurt in the bag, or killed? And he would say, 'Shit! Now I have a dead dog that can't bark at any kanakas and I'll have to send to Europe for a new one.'"

That made us all laugh, even Kakata. Nalokasi began singing to himself, and Tagilali drummed against the side of the trailer. I didn't think the dog talk was finished but I wasn't going to start it up again myself.

I asked Kakata to open the Cheetos and he passed them around. Tagilali opened one of the cases of Ox & Palm and pointed to the tins inside. "Here," he said, "Let's eat some dog food, I mean tinned meat. We can put it on the Pilot crackers." I gave him a look—stop it!—but it was dark so it was a wasted look.

"That's Kobua's, for his store," Kakata said, "He'll be angry. We should eat some of mine."

Tagilali started taking tins out. He said, "Kobua won't mind if it's you, Elliot. You hired the trailer, so he owes you some meat. You can give some to us."

Kakata said, "Oh, now I'm a plantation master feeding his boys? If I were a real master you'd be bringing me cold beer. You'd be saying, 'Master Elliot, do you want another SP?'"

I said, "Well, Master Elliot, do you?"

Kakata stood up. "All you boys!" he said in bad Australian pidgin, "Tell houseboy he make dinner. Eat meat your master give you!"

One Eye Genenai turned around and said, "Yes, Masta!" I knew we were joking, but I wasn't sure about Genenai.

Kakata ate his tinned meat and drank more beer. I've noticed that when he's drunk, he speaks our language better than when he's sober. I am not saying he makes more sense. I'm only saying that it comes from his mouth more easily. This isn't a surprise to any of us, because it's well-known that a drunk Nagovisi who can speak any English at all will begin shouting things in English as he gets more and more drunk. And sometimes two drunks will have an argument in English.

"I'm still thinking about Frank's dog," he said, switching to pidgin, "I wonder why we don't go back, sneak up on that barking dog and kill it. We're not thieves or rascals, so if it barks only because we're black, why not kill it?"

Kakata speaks pidgin as well as anybody, and so I knew that if he said *we* he meant to say *we* and not *you*. I sat on my bag of rice wondering why he'd done that. The dog never barked at him. I ate the cracker with Ox & Palm on it that Tagilali gave me without saying anything.

I began thinking that all this was tiresome. I like happy drinking, not angry drinking. There was no good reason for Kakata to put himself with us, against Frank Williams, when we all said we didn't care about that dog. Something was bubbling inside him, finding a way out little by little. I wondered what it was. Maybe just drink.

Then I thought maybe he was really talking about Koria, the dog who barked at him only because he was white. It didn't make sense to me, but then I was also drunk so I wiped my hands on my pants and picked up my beer bottle from between my feet.

I said, "Koria barks at *you* because you're white. So maybe *you* should kill Koria first, and then another time we'll go to Buin and kill Frank's dog. We can all be dog-killers."

Kakata said, "I can't kill Koria. I'm forbidden to interfere."

I said, "And pushing us to go back and kill Frank's dog, what's that? That's Kakata getting in the middle between us and the dog, us and Frank Williams, and who would get the blame, who would go to jail if we were caught? Not you, except you would be the cause of it."

I found myself getting a little angry with Kakata. I wasn't bothered by anything until he started trying to get us to kill Frank's dog although it's true, I didn't think he meant it.

In my drunk thoughts I said to myself, *Nobody tells me to kill a dog*, and then in the way that happens when you're drunk, I remembered the time I did kill a dog, so I belched and said, "I killed a white man's dog once."

Kakata said, "What?"

Tagilali said, "Oh, the plantation dog."

I thought it would be a good story to tell, in case Kakata thought I wouldn't kill Frank's dog if I had reason to. Kakata needed a little lesson, and I wanted to be the one giving it. I said, "Don't wreck my story. Nalokasi, you shut up too. Kakata, give me another one of your beers."

He handed it to me and I said, "When are you going to learn to open it with your teeth? Even Nalokasi can," and he said, "Teeth too weak," and I said, "Bullshit. You don't want to because if you broke a tooth you'd have to go to Asatavi and have that nun fix your teeth and you'd have to admit how it broke," and he said, "Plus she would ask me about the betel stains, plus Missus Loo might have put poison on it," and when he said that I knew he wasn't too angry.

"All right," I said. "This is how it was. Rabaul." I belched. It was coming back to me. Not what I did, because I remembered that very well, but how I felt about it.

I said, "We were on a plantation full of bush kanaka Highlanders. We were line bosses but our master treated us just as badly as the Highlanders. The foreman had a dog named Skipper, who was a biter, but he was chained. Sometimes the bush kanakas forgot how long Skipper's chain was and got too close, and Skipper bit them. It was funny, because the Highlanders couldn't do anything about it."

Everybody laughed. Everybody knows that Highlanders are violent. If there's a problem, they like to solve it by fighting, so thinking about a Highlander being bitten by a white man's dog that he can't turn around and kill is very funny.

Some people think it's in their blood, but I don't know about that. I think they learn it from each other. It doesn't matter what the reason is because the violence is violence all the same.

Nalokasi had kept drinking and was drunker than anybody. He interrupted me, saying "Highlanders with their big beards are hairy like dogs anyway."

I reached over and gave him a shove. "Nalokasi! Stop interrupting."

I stood up and then dropped back onto my rice bag, this time on my knees. I said, "Look, this is how it was. I wanted to have some fun with the Highlanders, to make them fear me because they knew I wasn't a fighter. I got the idea of making them think I was a sorcerer."

"He did," said Tagilali, "I was there. It was clever."

"Nobody wants to let me tell my story!" I said, and drank more beer. "Here's how it was. There was a banana growing outside our house, and I told the Highlanders I could kill it with magic. They didn't believe me. Every night when they were asleep I boiled a kettle of water and I crept out to the banana and poured hot water around it."

I crept forward on my knees, which was the reason I'd changed position. I used my elbows and crept up to Nalokasi and pretended to pour something on him. We all laughed.

I said, "After a week it died and the bush kanakas believed I was a sorcerer."

Everyone laughed. Kakata said, "And the dog?" He seemed excited. I said, "The dog, yes. I was worried after I fooled the Highlanders because if they found out about my trick they'd be angry and attack me. So I decided to make them more afraid but also to believe I was helping them—kill that Skipper dog they feared."

"It worked," Tagilali said, "it really worked."

"Yes," I said, "it worked." I was remembering how pleased I was. I said, "the way I killed it was clever. I bought a lightbulb and a tin of Ox & Palm. I opened the Ox & Palm and smashed the bulb, and mixed the glass into it. I worked the whole thing into a ball about as big as my fist, and I crept out late at night and went down the road to Skipper's place and when he came running out I tossed the Ox & Palm at him and when he started eating it I ran away."

"Poison dog food!" shouted Nalokasi, and everyone started shouting things like "Poison! Sorcery! Evil Siro!"

Kakata said, "Siro saves bush kanakas from the devil dog!"

I raised my hand in the air, beer bottle in it. "Glass, truly. I saved them. In the morning I told the Highlanders, 'Two or three days from now, Skipper will die,' and he did."

Again the shouting.

Again I raised my arm. "Yes. The Highlanders owed me a debt *and* they were afraid of me. After that they did anything I asked. Truly, I was their Big Man."

I threw my beer bottle off into the bush. I was hoping it would hit a tree and we'd hear it smash to end my story, but it didn't.

When the laughter died down no one said anything. Kakata slid off his rice bag and lay on his back on the trailer floor, looking up at the moon and stars. I was wondering what he was thinking. I had told Kakata about many things I'd done, but they had all been the kinds of things young men do—drinking, girls, fighting, even stealing from the Chinese stores.

Some of those things were against the law, but killing Skipper was different. I knew it was different and I was sure that Kakata did also. What I did was something Mesiamo would have done, and I wanted him to be thinking about that. I'm not Mesiamo and certainly Kakata knows that, but I don't mind having him wonder what I'm capable of.

Kakata rolled over to the carton and got himself another beer, then shoved the carton in my direction. I gave another one to Tagilali and, even though I thought it might be a mistake, to Nalokasi.

Kakata said, "I'm tired of dog stories. Drink. Let's talk about bush demons or the pretty Buka nurse. I'm bored by Frank and his dog." I didn't believe him, but if he wanted to drop the dog-talk that was all right with me.

Soon we were all completely drunk, except for Genenai. We sang cowboy songs. Kakata sang one I heard on his tape, *I fell into a burning ring of fire*. Kakata told me that when we were cremating Laumo that song was running through his head but he asked me not to tell anybody.

We taught Nalokasi to piss over the side of the trailer. Kakata held his shoulders and said, "If you splash on me I'm pushing you over," and Tagilali said, "It's good you're holding him because he needs both hands to find his little penis," and we all laughed, except for Nalokasi, who said only "Fuck a chicken, Tagilali." Kakata started clucking like an excited hen.

When we came up on the Hupai, One Eye Genenai stopped the tractor in the water, and we stripped and started washing off the road dust and sweat. The water was cold. The Hupai is always cold because it's deep and fast-flowing, so the cold mountain water stays cold all the way down to the sea.

"A white man hides under your shorts," said Nalokasi, pointing at Kakata, "Ours don't hide anything."

Kakata splashed water at him. "If your trousers don't hide anything, why don't you go over to the school and pull them down for the teacher girls."

"Go fuck a dog!" Nalokasi yelled.

Kakata was laughing. He said, "That's your job. You should kill Koria by fucking him to death! Dog-fucker! That's you."

Everyone laughed and hooted. Tagilali climbed up on a boulder and waved his beer bottle. "Highlanders have red penises, yes they do! Highland women nurse pigs, too. A baby sucking on one, a piglet on the other!"

I groaned and made disgusted noises. "Highlanders are animals! They'll do anything!"

Tagilali began telling about a drunken Highlander who walked into a room at the mine where somebody was showing movies of people screwing. Everybody was drunk.

He said, "The Highlander can't believe what he's seeing! He's hardly seen white women *with* clothes, and here's a *naked* one with her legs spread. He gets excited and runs towards the screen. I yell, 'Look out, he's going to fuck the screen!' He trips over the projector, like this," Tagilali imitated a man tripping, losing his balance, "and the whole thing falls down. The whites yell and laugh. They don't care.

"But then there's a fight, Highlanders against the Papuans. People start throwing beer bottles. The whites grab the projector and run away. I'm trying to get out the door too. This other Highlander has a beer bottle and he comes crashing against me and I fall down like this . . ."

Nalokasi yelled, "Throwing bottles! Like this!" and threw his bottle at Tagilali. The bottle smashed on the boulder as Tagilali lost his balance and slid down onto it.

"Son of a bitch!" Tagilali screamed, in English, "You have cut me, you fucking bastard." He leaned against the boulder, standing on one leg, holding his cut foot out of the water, cursing in English. Some curse words of his, I didn't know.

Nalokasi flopped in the water and put his head in his hands. "This is a bad thing," he said, and threw up. One Eye Genenai went over to make sure he wasn't swept away.

Kakata and I waded over to Tagilali. The Hupai is a stony river, so we had to make our way around the boulders. He was making little *ah ah ah* noises like he was really hurt. We draped him over our shoulders, carried him to the trailer and laid him down on some rice bags. Kakata found his flashlight and we saw it was a bad gash, deep and wide and bleeding steadily but not spurting. "Not a big vein," Kakata said, and I said, "Yes, I think not." Even so I knew this was no small thing, Tagilali's wound.

I left Kakata with Tagilali and went with One Eye Genenai up on the tractor. I asked Genenai what he thought we should do, and he said we should go on because the only help was either in Siwai or at Boku, the Patrol Post. I went back to the trailer.

I said, "Genenai thinks we should get started now."

"Come in the trailer, Nalokasi," Kakata said, and gave him a hand up. Kakata's voice seemed calm and maybe he *was* calm, but I didn't think so. It wasn't good, what happened. We had finally become a bunch of happy drunks and now one of us was in danger and we weren't sure how much.

One Eye Genenai slammed the tractor into gear, and jerked up out of the river.

Kakata had his light on Tagilali's cut. "Drive faster," I yelled to Genenai, "Tagilali's really bleeding." I looked at Kakata, hoping he had an idea. "What should we do?"

He said, "The blood isn't spurting."

I said, "True, but it isn't stopping."

Kakata said, "Nobody knows about this kind of cut, from an axe or machete or a tin?" and I said, "Not this big."

"Here, I'll put my thumb on it," said Tagilali, "Stop it myself." He brought his foot up and grabbed it, but in a moment blood began dripping through his fingers.

One Eye Genenai called back. "Have you got the bleeding stopped? I can turn off into Siwai. There's an Aid

Station not too far in. It's theirs but I know the orderly. Or we could go to Boku. What shall I do, Masta Elliot? You tell me."

I heard Kakata say in a low voice, "Why do I have to be the masta in charge?" Then he said to me, "We're not in Buin where it matters who's white and who's not. We're in the big bush and Tagilali's bleeding and we can't stop it and we're drunk."

"It's true," I said.

Kakata said, "I'm not ashamed to admit that I'm frightened. I don't know what to do and you don't either."

We knelt around Tagilali, lying on three bags of rice.

Nalokasi said, "Nephew, You're getting Kobua's rice all bloody."

I said, "Shut up, stupid." I could hear nervousness in my voice. I said, "This is your fault. Never mind Kobua. Tagilali's mother will be angrier if he dies. She's your aunt and she won't court you but she will court me and probably Kakata too."

Kakata said, "Never mind about court, we don't care about courts here, put him on my rice. Fuck the blood. He won't die. I'm no doctor, but I say he won't die. I'm worried, but he won't die."

"I won't die," Tagilali said, "I promise."

Kakata said, "Put his leg up, his foot. Put a bag under. That's good. Put him on the floor and put the foot on two of my rice bags," and it did help. The flow decreased.

"Turn-off coming up," Genenai called back, "Shall I turn?"

"What are you going to do?" I asked Kakata, because it was clear that's what Genenai wanted, that Kakata should decide. Kakata said that last week Lalaga told him Dakta Bagarap was at Boku.

Bagarap was from Europe. Nobody knew his name. We called him Bagarap because when he looked at a wound he always said *emi bagarap,* which in pidgin means "it's broken." His pidgin was bad and the high school girls said his English was impossible to understand. The nuns said he was always drunk, but that even so he was a good doctor.

"Don't turn! Go on to Boku," Kakata shouted to One Eye Genenai, "Dakta Bagarap is there," and Genenai called "But what if he's gone patrolling?" and Kakata shouted "There's an Aid Post Orderly," and Genenai called, "What if he's patrolling too?"

"Never mind. Go to Boku, Genenai," Kakata said, and I thought, *Look at Kakata giving orders like every* masta *in the Territory.* And I said that to him, but I didn't mean it as an insult at all. It was the thing I was thinking about before, that he should do something rather than only slide out of the way.

He said, "Fuck a dog! Somebody has to decide and if you and Genenai won't, I will."

Good, I thought, *even though that doesn't fix the cut.* I told Kakata he'd have to wake Bagarap up and make him help.

Kakata said, "I can be our masta."

I smiled and I think he saw me smiling even though it was dark. It's true that I was worried but I didn't smell death around us, not that death smells like anything unless it's a corpse that's been dead a long time. I thought there was still some danger and if Bagarap wasn't at Boku, maybe serious danger. If he wasn't there, having our own masta wouldn't help.

One Eye Genenai said, "It's true, Masta Elliot. I'm glad you're with us."

"I'm still bleeding," Tagilali said.

Kakata said, "Never mind. Keep your leg up. Don't move. Boku isn't far."

Tagilali lay still with his eyes closed.

Kakata asked me if I knew how to make a tourniquet and I said I didn't. I didn't know the English word tourniquet but Elliot mimicked it so I knew what he meant. I had seen such things but didn't know where to put it or how to use it.

Kakata said he knew where to put it but not how often to slacken it, because you were supposed to loosen and tighten it so the part of the body beyond the cut could get blood. He said he would try it if he had no choice, but he didn't want to do it yet.

He asked me if I had any betel. He said he needed to clear his head and that his mouth was bad from beer and Ox & Palm.

"I have some left," I said. "I didn't bring it out because we were drinking. Here."

Kakata quickly chewed. I could see he was swallowing instead of spitting, so I knew he was worried about his thinking. Swallowing makes it stronger, but it also makes your stomach hurt. And I thought that maybe he didn't want to meet Bagarap with red lips like an Australian woman.

"Don't wake Dakta Bagarap up," Nalokasi said, when we reached Boku. "He'll be angry. Wait for morning."

I said, "Shut up, drunken boy. Why are we here?"

"Go to the hospital," Kakata said, "Genenai! Drive up to the hospital first."

The hospital was dark. Kakata and I climbed down. I pounded on the door, shook and rattled it, and shouted

"Hey! Anybody here? Hey! Wounded man," but nobody answered and no flashlight appeared.

One Eye Genenai said, "The Orderly must be patrolling. Dakta Bagarap sleeps at the Agricultural Officer's house. I know which one it is."

Kakata leaned his forehead against the trailer's side. He said, "The Orderly would be easy. Now I have to find a white man with bad English, and he's probably as drunk as we are. And I don't know what his real name is so I have to call him Bagarap and hope he doesn't get angry."

I said, "Don't worry. Everybody calls him Dakta Bagarap."

Kakata looked into the trailer. I shined the light on Tagilali's foot. It was still bleeding.

"Tagilali," Kakata said, "Wake up! How's it going?"

He said, "I'm all right. Are we at Boku? I haven't died yet. My foot really hurts. I feel faint. Are you getting Dakta Bagarap for me? If he won't, never mind. We can go home."

Kakata said, "You're babbling. I'm going to find him now."

Kakata grabbed his shirt from the trailer, put it on, and started walking up the hill to the house One Eye Genenai pointed out. Genenai drove the tractor behind him.

Kakata looked over his shoulder at us, but it wasn't Buin Town and I didn't think he wanted to say "Don't worry! I won't forget you!" When he got to the house he shook the screen door and shouted, "Dakta Bagarap! Hey! Dakta Bagarap!"

I walked up and stood beside him. I couldn't hear any noise inside.

"Hello! Bagarap!" Kakata put his ear to the screen door.

I heard a thump and the sound of a match striking. The yellow light of a kerosene lamp appeared in the darkness behind the screen, and a voice began to mutter in a language that didn't sound like English.

"Dakta Bagarap?"

"Yes, yes, yes" in English. And then in Pidgin, "I'm coming."

Kakata grabbed my arm and shook me. He turned and shouted in Nagovisi, "It's good! He's coming! Tell Tagilali!" and called inside in pidgin, "One of my boys is cut."

"Yes, yes. Wait," in pidgin, "Don't worry. I'm coming."

Kakata had been using two different languages and he didn't sound like a white man. I thought, *We will see what this white man does when he learns he's been talking to another white man.*

Bagarap held up the lamp and looked at Kakata through the screen door. He wiped his mouth with his hand, looked at Kakata again, and spoke English. "You have problem?"

Kakata spoke English. "My friend has a bad cut, Dakta."

Bagarap opened the door and stepped out past Kakata. He was swinging the lantern at his side. His breath smelled of gin.

He said in English, "You must be masta lives Nagovisi. Come. We go to hospital. I sew."

"Yes," Kakata said in English. "Yes, Dakta, yes. Thank you very much."

In pidgin I said, "Thank you, Dakta Bagarap."

Dakta Bagarap started walking to the hospital and Genenai backed the trailer around and drove down. Kakata walked with Bagarap, but I rode in the trailer with Nalokasi and Tagilali.

At the hospital Genenai stayed outside, which surprised me, but I didn't say anything. The hospital was just a thatched building, but it had a big table and cabinets with equipment and medicine in them. A true bush hospital, but the important thing was that it was Bagarap's own hospital.

Bagarap lit a pressure lantern and looked at the wound. Of course he spoke his name, bagarap. He was using his poor pidgin and he said, "How happen?"

Kakata started to explain, but Bagarap stopped him and said, "I like wounded man tell," and so Tagilali explained about the broken beer bottle. Tagilali's pidgin wasn't good because he was still drunk and not thinking clearly from pain and losing blood, and although I didn't laugh, I thought it was funny.

Anything is funnier when the danger's over. Here was the doctor with his terrible pidgin and the wounded man with excellent pidgin but too confused to use it—beer and the wound dragged Tagilali down to Bagarap's level.

I looked at Kakata and he shrugged his shoulders. I could tell that he was relieved and therefore he was relaxing a little bit.

Bagarap looked at Nalokasi and shook his fist at him. "Stupid boy! Bad drink! You make trouble! Be good now!"

Kakata said, "In the village we will take him to court, don't worry."

Bagarap got a needle and shot Tagilali with it. Tagilali didn't gasp or suck in air or grab Bagarap's arm when that little needle walked all around the big cut. I would have. Maybe he was more drunk than we knew. Bagarap started sewing it up.

Kakata said, "We thought about a tourniquet but we weren't sure how to use it. The blood wasn't spurting." He was talking clear pidgin. It's better for people who don't speak pidgin well to hear good pidgin because it's easier to understand.

Bagarap said, "You know pressure bandage?" and Kakata said, "Sorry, no."

He said *pressure bandage* in English. I knew *bandage* but not *pressure.*

Bagarap made a noise and waved his arms. "Live bush, not know pressure bandage, very bad."

Kakata said, "It's true, I'm sorry. Show me."

Bagarap took some cloth and folded it into a thick square, a little bigger than Tagilali's cut. It was about as thick as a finger. Then he took a strip of cloth and tied that pad down tight on the wound. *Ah,* I thought, *that's easy,* and as soon as I had that thought, Kakata spoke it.

Bagarap said, "Easy, now you see, another time you fix cut this way." Then he took a big penicillin injection from the cupboard, told Tagilali to turn over, pulled down his shorts, and stuck it into him.

Kakata said, "Yes, thank you very much for fixing Tagilali and teaching me about pressure bandages. I think Lalaga knows about pressure bandages."

Bagarap said, "Lalaga very good doctor, you ask him teach you more. You take this man Lalaga penicillin shoot, all day, one week."

Kakata asked if we could leave. Bagarap asked if he was going all the way home with Tagilali, and he said yes, Tagilali lived in his village. Bagarap said, "Yes, if you with, OK, if others here only, maybe no."

I looked at Kakata. I knew he was thinking, *I don't want to fight about anything more tonight.* He let Bagarap's insult pass, and that was the right thing. It wasn't really an insult. Bagarap is not polite but the first thing, for him, is the sick person. Maybe he's right and maybe he's wrong about how carefully somebody's going to look after the sick person, but I believe that's all he's thinking about, that the sick person should be looked after.

Bagarap didn't know who we were and so he didn't know if any of us could look after Tagilali's wound, so he chose the white man, even though the white man already showed Bagarap that he hadn't known how to look after a bleeding wound. That's how it is. It's like Genenai said about the dog. It's only barking.

Kakata asked, "Pay?" and Bagarap said, "Two shillings," and Kakata reached in his bag and found two shillings and gave it to him. "No extra for late night?" he asked, and Bagarap laughed and slapped Kakata on his shoulder. "No," he said.

Bagarap pointed his finger at Nalokasi again and said, "You no more drink," and he nodded at me, and turned to leave. Tagilali said, "Wait, Dakta, I have to say Thank You," and he did say "Thank you very much" in pidgin, and Bagarap said, "Not big thing," and stood by the door waiting for us to go out.

Kakata and I used our arms to make a chair and we carried him outside. Genenai and Nalokasi climbed into the trailer and we handed Tagilali up to them. They put him on the bloody rice bag. Tagilali said, "Not on the bloody bag," and Genenai said, "It's your blood, be quiet or Elliot will make you cook the bloody rice and eat it."

Kakata said, "I will, I will. Nobody told me that I would eat bloody rice in Nagovisi, and I don't want to. I can float insects out of my rice but how can I get blood off?"

We all laughed. It sounded to me like easy laughing. The worst part of the trip was over, I thought, and I'm sure we all felt relief. We didn't know what to do but we were lucky.

Kakata and I climbed up into the trailer and sat on clean rice bags. Dakta Bagarap closed and locked the hospital door, we all called "Good Night" to him, he waved his hand at us, and we started for home.

After we went through the Puriaka, which is close to Boku, we all relaxed. It was the last big river and there was still enough moon so we could see each other and the road. Kakata asked me if I knew why Genenai had stayed outside at Boku, and I said, "I don't know, why don't you ask him?" and he said, "No, you."

So I called out to him and asked. He said he was hoping Bagarap wouldn't see that he was the driver, in case Bagarap told the Kiap or the Didiman that he'd allowed his passengers to get drunk and into trouble.

Kakata said he didn't think the Kiap or Didiman would care, and Genenai said, "No, they do care because they know I'm in charge of the passengers and if anything goes wrong, it's my fault. Everybody knows that people drink on the way back from Buin, but the Kiap and Didiman don't like it. If somebody starts talking about it, the talk sticks to me. I'm like the Captain of a ship."

Kakata didn't say anything, but I'm sure we were all thinking the same thing, *If a white man's on the trailer, then the whites will say the white man was in charge, so he should be blamed for not making us do what the other whites wanted, except the white man can't be blamed because he's white so therefore One Eye Genenai must take the blame.*

Sometimes Kakata tells me this kind of thinking makes his head hurt and he is right.

Kakata said, "If we can't get into any more trouble, then let's drink."

I said, "Nalokasi?" meaning to ask if we should let Nalokasi drink more.

Kakata said, "American cowboys say, 'Get back on the horse that threw you off,' so I think Nalokasi should get back on the South Pacific Brown horse."

Kakata was laughing, we were all laughing, and we started drinking again, even Tagilali. Kakata said, "All the blood you lost, Tagilali, you can fill up with beer but you must pray to Jesus Christ, who turned water into wine."

Tagilali aimed a little kick at Kakata. "Elliot!" he said, "I don't need wine, I need blood, so let's do Holy Communion, where Padre turns the wine into Christ's blood," and Nalokasi said, "Don't insult Padre," but Tagilali continued, "You better bless the beer and ring the little bell and turn SP into blood for me."

We all yelled and screamed. "God will strike you."

We kept drinking. Before when we were drinking, we were unhappy because Kakata was angry about something and wasn't saying what it was. This time, we were relieved because Tagilali didn't die. And soon we were drunk again.

Kakata said to Tagilali, "Looks like Dakta Bagarap made me your mother now, so I have to look after you, my little baby." And he reached over and pinched Tagilali's cheek.

Tagilali said, "I'm too old to be your baby," but Kakata said nothing, so he continued, "Never mind. Mother, give me food and fix my wound," and Kakata said, "Yes, my son," and I said, "Now you're talking like Padre," and Genenai called back, "I'll tell Padre all your insults to the church."

Nalokasi said, "Not me. I didn't insult the church."

Kakata said, "That's because you were a good little boy in school." We were having a good time laughing and telling him that he was Padre's houseboy, his little altar boy, that maybe he could be the nun's workboy as well, not thinking much of it because what's wrong with teasing a boy drunk for the first time?

Kakata said something to Tagilali about how Nalokasi loved Padre so much he ought to become a nun and serve him, and Nalokasi must have heard it because he stood up and pointed his finger at Kakata and said, "Never mind nuns. Elliot, you're being Tagilali's mother because you *are* a woman, yes, working in Siuwako's garden digging sweet potatoes like her sister."

Kakata said, "What?" and looked at me. I thought he was asking what to do. I shrugged my shoulders. It was up to him.

Tagilali was laughing at Nalokasi, because his insult was wasted. Not one of us cares that Kakata's learning women's work from my wife. Therefore what Nalokasi said was a stupid thing, and indeed he stood there stupidly, drunk, swaying back and forth and trying to point his finger at Kakata, who had turned away and wouldn't look at him. Tagilali kept calling him a little boy who knew nothing.

It all irritated me. Nalokasi had caused Tagilali's trouble, and here he was causing trouble again. The first trouble was an accident but this was not. Kakata and Tagilali were having a small joke and it was a funny one, and Nalokasi wrecked it.

I said, "Little boy, shut up. Stupid. What do you know? You hardly know what a woman is except a breast to suck on."

I imitated sucking and nursing.

He said, "You shut your mouth," which annoyed me more than it should have. Even so I spoke as if I were teaching a child. I said, "You don't know enough to tell me to shut up. You only know what a child knows, that your mother and father do different work. You think that's what makes a man or a woman? When you grow up we'll talk about men's work and women's work, puppy dog boy. Idiot."

I wasn't angry enough to strike him. I didn't like what he said about Kakata, but I didn't think Kakata would do anything about it. The whole thing annoyed me, so I picked up a betel husk from the floor and threw it at Nalokasi the way I would throw it at a rooster crowing under my house.

Nalokasi wasn't looking, and it hit him in the eye. He started to cry, a child surprised by pain. Kakata put down his beer and started to get up. I think he was going over to Nalokasi to tell him not to worry, it was nothing, just calm down.

But Nalokasi was drunk and angry and hurt, which was bad, and feeling insulted, which made it worse. He shook his fist at me and screamed, "Know nothing? You think Elliot's a woman too. If you thought he was a man, you wouldn't let him walk out with Siuwako."

He said that to me! I was going to get up and slap him but before I could move Kakata jumped over and grabbed him by the arm and started shaking him. "Pig fucker!" he said, and Nalokasi hit him on his arm and kicked his leg. Kakata twisted away but was off-balance and Nalokasi gave him a good one on his arm and he fell down on Tagilali's foot and Tagilali started screaming "Stop it you fucking bastards" in English.

I got up to go over there and pull them apart but before I could, Nalokasi screamed at Kakata, "Know nothing? Know nothing? Everybody knows you fuck Siuwako," and it was quiet for a moment while we all thought about what we had just heard.

Into that silence Kakata pulled himself up, cleared his throat, spit, pointed at Nalokasi and said loudly, "You. You fuck your sister Miheru!"

Nalokasi began backing away from Kakata, his mouth opening and closing but making no sound. Genenai throttled down the tractor and stopped. Tagilali turned on his belly and put his hands over his ears.

I looked at Kakata in disbelief. He said the worst thing a Nagovisi can say. His arm went to his side. Nalokasi backed into Mesiamo's cartons, lost his balance, fell to his knees and began vomiting on the trailer floor.

Kakata said, "Oh shit," and started towards him but I shoved him down on his rice bag. I said, "Don't you move."

I turned to Nalokasi and told him to stay down. "I don't care if you sit in vomit," I said, "just sit and shut up."

I turned back to Kakata and grabbed his shoulder and shook him. I yelled at him, "You said the thing you cannot say!" and he shook his head helplessly. "Why did you do that? Why? You're proud you know that curse?"

He said, "No, not proud."

I stood there, breathing heavily. Only a moment ago we were laughing and joking. Then suddenly, this.

"Fucking bastard!" I said, and kicked Kakata's rice bag. So much joking talk about a white man in charge, and now this. How did it happen? The great masta did a stupid, reckless thing and now it was up to me to get us out of it.

I knew I couldn't let this thing linger in the air. Yes, like a terrible fart.

I kept my voice hard. I said to Kakata, "You turned a drunk fight into something so bad I don't know what we can do."

Kakata didn't say anything. None of us said anything. The only sound was the tractor's engine idling. He closed his eyes. I knew he was thinking, *What have I done, what have I done?*

Kakata was like the child who's been told not to touch something or not to open it but doesn't understand why he shouldn't. So he touches it and breaks it or opens it and sees something he shouldn't.

Or says something. Maybe nobody ever told him, "These are the words you must never speak," but he knew about brothers and sisters and he knew that curse had started fights and people had died. What he said wasn't something that slips out like a fart and you wave your hands in the air and apologize. You can't take it back. You can't take a fart back, but it's soon gone. That's the difference. His curse wasn't just foul, it was *dangerous* because it might linger as hidden anger, even for years.

These days knives don't come out, but there are other ways this could hurt Kakata and I was wondering if his thinking could run forward quickly enough to see what they were. Probably not, but mine could. Nothing but trouble, bad trouble, could come from this.

I reached down and pushed Kakata's shoulder. I said quietly, "You should have let the woman insult pass by," and he said, "I did, but what he said about..." and I didn't want him to continue so I said, "Never mind, you know what I mean." I leaned down and said, "If Nalokasi talks about what you said I don't know what will happen."

I went over to Nalokasi, sitting in his vomit and trying not to cry and shook him. "Drink made you both stupid. Kakata didn't know what he was saying. You too. You can't talk about this," I repeated myself, "Don't talk about it."

I was hoping that Nalokasi didn't realize the power Kakata had given him. I was hoping he was feeling ashamed of himself for talking about my wife and Kakata and was fearing what we might do to him and not thinking about what he could do to Kakata.

I knew I had to frighten him into silence, but it felt very strange. Nalokasi was the seriously-wronged one, not Kakata and not me.

I grabbed his chin and forced him to look at me. I put on an angry face and said, "If you talk about what Kakata said, I'll accuse you of cutting Tagilali on purpose and your mother will have to pay Tagilali's father. And I'll accuse you of insulting Siuwako, more court, more money."

I let go of his chin and gave him a small slap on his face. Now real anger was bubbling up in me and spilling out. "You know I'll do it! I'm angry at you for talking about my wife and Kakata and about me, as if I didn't care about my wife and if you say one dog fucking word about this you will be in so much trouble that you'll have to run away to the copper mine and Sepiks will steal you and fuck you up the ass and I will tell everybody about it, how you let redskins fuck you."

I shook him more. I said, "Tell me you understand," and he said, "Yes, I understand," and I pushed him down and stood for a moment not saying anything. Everybody was quiet.

I said, "It's finished. Everybody's been insulted. Everybody's behaved badly. Now everybody shuts up," and I turned to Kakata and said, "Including you, Kakata. You shut up too. If you're one of us, you keep your mouth shut."

Kakata nodded, Yes, and so did Nalokasi. Tagilali waved his hand.

I looked around the trailer. In the moonlight I saw bloody rice bags, vomit on the floor, cartons of beer and tinned meat ripped open. SP caps and bottles. Three drunks sprawled in the mess, one with his wound bound and two of them with theirs still open. That's what came into my head. Wounds. And me, trying to keep us all out of worse trouble. I could only shake my head. I hoped they saw me shaking it.

At least there was no vomit or blood on Mesiamo's cargo. Kakata wouldn't have to explain anything, which meant he wouldn't have to talk about the trip.

I thought, *What a drunken mess we're in.* I thought about how it might go if Nalokasi accused Kakata and then I realized that if it came to court it would be one drunken boy's story against those of grown men, one of whom was white. If Kakata, Tagilali, and I denied the story, and stood by our denials, it would come to nothing.

Mesiamo would make short work of the case and not only because Nalokasi would have no evidence beyond his drunken memory. As Kakata understood about Mesiamo—*in the end, he pays.*

"Genenai," I said, "Genenai! Let's go. It's nothing. Just a drunk fight." I knew Genenai would never talk about what happened. He was probably thinking it was his fault.

One Eye Genenai waved his hand, put the tractor in gear, and started up with a lurch. The night wind blew away some of the stench and the tractor exhaust replaced most of the rest. I felt sure I could deal with what remained.

We got down from the trailer near the Iada. Genenai helped unload all the cargo, which was unusual. The driver isn't the loader, but I'm sure he was thinking that we were in a kind of peace that could easily be broken and therefore we should take care to be helpful to each other.

We put it in the bushes where the trail goes down to the Iada. There aren't many thieves in Nagovisi, but if some boys happened on the cases of Ox & Palm they would take a few tins and then there would be one more thing to explain.

Kakata and I put bolts of cloth on our shoulders and supported Tagilali between us. Nalokasi walked behind us, carrying a bag of bloody rice.

There was no light in Mesiamo's house so we didn't have to stop and talk, which was good. If you don't want him to know that something's wrong, you had better not go near him. We could bring his cargo over in the morning.

In Pomalate, Semana was sitting on her steps, smoking.

Kakata said, "We almost had to have a funeral pyre for Tagilali," and she said, "Really?"

We all said, "Really!" and went to our houses.

I left the tins of dog food in my bag. I wasn't in a mood to explain anything to Siuwako.

Sigalagun Tavena

I'm called Tagilali.

Although my speech is Nagovisi, much of my thinking is Nagovisi, and I do know Nagovisi culture at least as well as anybody my age and better than some, I'm not like the other young men in Pomalate and Biroi. And I'm not like the young women either. I don't have the same memories, and I don't know as much village history as they do.

Why?

I'm a half-breed. That's why.

My mother was a Rotokas, one of the people up the coast behind Numa Numa plantation, my father is a Nagovisi, and I'm as black as both of them. Numa Numa is on the other side of Bougainville. My father was an overseer, working for the white man who owned the plantation. My mother came down to Numa Numa with her first husband, and they lived in married housing. Then he died in an accident. The Rotokas came and took his body up, and she went along but after the mourning was over she came back down. The plantation owner didn't allow single women in married housing, and my mother didn't want to live in the dormitory with the young girls, and she didn't want to live in Rotokas anymore. She told my father it was boring and backwards up there. When she asked my father to marry her, he said yes. My mother was very beautiful and a hard worker as well.

She died when I was four or five. Tuberculosis, and my father and I don't know how we escaped being infected. She got on a mission boat and went to the TB hospital in Buin, and we never saw her alive again. She died quickly, I think, but I'm not sure because I was just a boy. All I remember is that about the time I got used to having no mother, that same boat brought her body back to Numa Numa. My father told me the Rotokas wouldn't come down to get her so we buried her at Numa Numa.

I remember the crying and how the coffin was lowered into the ground with ropes. I remember the smell. I was dressed in new clothes. There must have been some kind of religion, but I can't remember any of that. I remember crying.

Going to Nagovisi—as far back as I can remember—was a trip to a strange place where I didn't feel comfortable. In Biroi village, I felt like an outsider. My mother taught me a few words of Rotokas and because my father taught me some Nagovisi I could talk to the other kids. But every time we went back I'd have forgotten their names, and I never knew what was going on among them.

And at first I didn't know how to behave. I didn't know place names. I didn't know the names of plants and animals. I didn't know very many kin terms. I made mistakes, but I learned.

Numa Numa was the place where I understood things. The culture I learned as a child was Numa Numa Plantation culture. This shouldn't surprise you. In a place where all the adults are *outsiders* the *insiders* are the children.

On the plantation, everybody spoke pidgin most of the time—the kids, always. Some kids knew only a few words of their ancestral language. Or I should say *languages* because there were kids whose mother and father belonged to different cultures and spoke different languages and the child could speak neither one, not really. So that kid's first language was pidgin and sometimes the only shared language his parents had was pidgin.

We children had our own little society there, and we all knew our places in it, whether our ancestry was Nagovisi or Rotokas or Nasioi or Telei or Rorovana or Tolai or Highlanders (none of us ever knew the names of Highland cultures, so we just called them Highlanders, which was rude). How to behave. What you could ask for. Who not to anger. And then, of course, as we got older, what girl you could try to get to go into the forest with you. And sometimes succeed.

Yes, getting girls to go into the forest with you. Or behind the storehouses or down at the river—it's all the same thing but in Nagovisi we like to say *go into the forest* whether that's accurate or not.

Among the Numa Numa children nobody had a clan and nobody had a marriage group and nobody was forbidden from fooling around with anybody else. At least not because of kinship.

When I was about 15, my father left the plantation and brought me back to Nagovisi. He did that knowing he'd be in a difficult position. In Nagovisi, everything flows through the mother, the women, and after a man is married he doesn't live with his sisters in the village where he grew up. Instead he goes to his wife's people, her clan, because that's where their children belong and that's where his wife has land rights.

I was talking about this with Elliot once, and he told me that although Americans have no rules about where a married couple should live, they do have a word for our way, and when he spoke that word—*uxorilocal*—I laughed. We don't have an *x* sound in our language, so when he said *ux* it sounded so strange I had to try that word for myself. It wasn't too hard but in truth I have no use for it.

Because my father had no Nagovisi wife he had no land rights. He didn't want to marry into another clan, the way he should have, and in any case he had me, a young man belonging to no clan, to look after. His sisters let him use some land for food gardening, and asked the older unmarried girls to help him. It was irregular, because an adult man, especially one with a child, ought not to be gardening with women of his own clan. People gardening together are supposed to be married. My father ended up knowing food gardening well—almost as well as Elliot does.

The women also told him—and me, because I was old enough to understand—that they would treat me as a Biroi clan member, even though I had no Biroi mother. And they called me Tagilali, which is the name of a piece of land the Biroi women control, downstream along the Wetu River. When I was born at Numa Numa, my father didn't give me a Nagovisi name, and my mother never gave me a Rotokas one. They named me Michael David, which meant I grew up with a double white name that meant nothing to me except that's what everybody called me. It wasn't connected to anything, so when the Biroi women gave me a place name I was happy.

When Lalaga told me that lineage names are taken from place names, I remember asking him if that meant there might be a lineage named after me. He widened his eyes and gave me a little slap on my arm. "Have you forgotten that you're a man?" he said, and I was ashamed because in my hunger to be a Biroi I had. No man founds a lineage.

Although I never asked him directly, Lalaga became my teacher. I walked to the Aid Post as often as I could, and sat with him and talked. He knew what I was doing, but never said anything. When I climbed the trail up out of the Tavera River he never asked why I'd come. He would say, "Here you are," and that was all.

And now the person who climbs up to see Lalaga is Elliot.

Lalaga's important to me. I want to understand Nagovisi culture as deeply as he and Mesiamo do. When we came here to live I knew I had a lot to learn just to get along. Beyond that, I wanted to *understand* Nagovisi. I was old enough to realize there was a difference between just *living* a culture, doing what other people do, not thinking hard about anything but daily life, and truly understanding how that culture functions—its bones, its skeleton, as Lalaga says.

And its heart. If Nagovisi has a heart it's what we call *aparito,* the idea that everything must even out, must balance. Elliot told me in his work they call that *reciprocity.* It may take a long time to balance some things. No one is saying it will happen in weeks or months or even a few years. But everybody understands it must happen.

Once I asked Elliot if the Americans practiced aparito. He gave a short laugh and said no. He said the Americans and the Australians were not very different, and had I ever seen aparito operating at Numa Numa or how the Australian Adminstration treated Bougainvilleans, or at the copper mine? That would give me my answer.

I gave a short laugh and said no.

He said he didn't believe in God or Jesus Christ but if you looked closely at what Jesus said, there was aparito there. "Do unto others," he said, "that's a kind of aparito."

I started my study of Nagovisi culture long before Elliot turned up. And I had a language head start, a big one. Even so, there are parts of our language that are difficult for me. For example, Nagovisi has sixty-three pronouns. I know only a handful, and make do with them, just as Elliot does. He wrote down all of them, which is why I know how many there are. My accent is much better than his. I almost never stumble, but he does. But yes, if you ignore those things we're not very different.

I get on well with the other young men, but they didn't *grow up somewhere else*. I did, and so did Elliot. Whatever it is that's put into you when you're a child and then a young person, I only got some of it, and Elliot didn't get any. I mean Nagovisi culture. We both got a big dose of another culture and have had to mix it in with Nagovisi.

I am sure Elliot's aware of this, but we never talk about it directly. Talking about how we *seem to be the same* would get in the way of actually *being the same*, or similar anyway. We are easy with each other.

I haven't forgotten how he helped get me out of danger the time were were all drunk on the road and Nalokasi cut me. And I haven't forgotten what happened afterwards, the business about the insult. I never bring it up because it would remind him that even though he thought he knew enough about Nagovisi culture to behave correctly, he didn't. Or else, maybe worse, that when he was drunk and angry he *forgot* what he knew. Either way it's not worth talking about. We both know what happened. He learned an important lesson. And we both know that if there's trouble because of it, Mesiamo will decide how the aparito will go. And it won't be simple.

One day Elliot came looking for me. My father sent him up to Na'alaada, where I was helping make thatching. He sat with us in the meeting house, where it was cool and dry. I picked up a sheaf of partly-finished thatching and tossed it in his lap.

"As long as you're here, why don't you finish this," I said.

He picked up the sheaf and made a face. "I don't know how."

"What do you know how to do, then?"

He put it down. "To offer you betel and pepper and lime," he said, "and I have enough for everyone." He reached in his bag and sure enough, he pulled out five or six nuts.

"From?"

"Kavibura!"

"No! We don't want to get dizzy."

"Hah," he said, "she told me they weren't too strong."

"And you believed her?"

"Yes, older brother, I did."

"We'll all be sorry, but let's chew."

And we did. And the betel was as strong as Kavibura's always is. Her palms bear the strongest; everybody knows that, but nobody knows why. If you're not used to them, sometimes you have to lie down after you chew.

After we chewed and spit, Elliot said to me, "I wonder if you have work tomorrow, because if you don't, I'll ask you to come to the big bush with me, down to Olapa Tavena, into the Tavera River, and then over to where the Sabosa River meets the trail to Birosi."

"I can, but why? That's just big bush."

"You really want to know?

"Why did I ask, White Man?"

"Hah, White Man says it's because he needs to join two places where he stopped surveying."

He picked up two sago palm leaves, the thatching, and put them together at one end and apart at the other. It was like a person's legs. We were all watching him. There's never any hurry when you're making thatching unless somebody's paying you by the piece. And not even then, really.

"Remember we surveyed the trail to Olapa Tavena, and stopped and came back?"

"Yes."

"And we surveyed down the big trail to the Sabosa and stopped and came back?"

"I remember that too."

"It's like this," he said, "what if we made a mistake going to Olapa Tavena, or we made a mistake going to Sabosa?"

"We?"

"Hah, am I the only one who makes mistakes? I'm saying that if the end's in the wrong place," and he moved one of the leaves away from the other, "when I go to work out how much land the Biroi have in the big bush, like between these two leaves, my answer will be wrong."

I worked with a surveyor at the copper mine and I learned about getting all sides of a triangle, that it was a good thing, or going around boundaries and coming back to where you started, so I understood immediately what Elliot was saying. I said, "If we join those two ends, then we have all sides, right?"

He said, "Right. Closed. And that means I can work out the track here and if it doesn't close up right I can find out where I made the mistake, and fix it. But not if I'm back in America, so it needs doing now."

I said, "Just the two of us? Who will hold the backsight rod?"

"Nobody else can come, so we'll use long black palm stakes instead of the backsight rod, and leave them there. I made them yesterday, and if we run out, we'll use whatever we can cut."

The other thatchers agreed. Mika said, "If you just want to join those ends, you can go part way in the Tavera River, that's easy, to the trail at Sigalagun Tavena and follow that trail to the Menara River, then along the Menara to the big trail, then up to Sabosa."

When one river runs into another, the place where they join, where one flows into the other, is called *tavena*. Nagovisi use tavena to locate places on a river all the time. If you think about it, how else could you do it? Rivers are long and if you say "meet me along the Wetu" how will I know where? But the Wetu, like the Tavera, has many small streams flowing into it, and these streams are all named. So I might say, "Meet me at Pumaia Tavena," and you know exactly where that is, because there's only one place where the Pumaia meets a larger river, and that's at the Wetu. In a river like the Tavera, which is a big river and not near where most of us live, people like me and Elliot only know the names of the tavena where large streams join the Tavera. We don't know the names of the little ones. Somebody does. Not us.

Once I asked Elliot the English word for tavena, and he said *confluence* was the only one he knew. We agreed that tavena was easier to say.

I thought Mika's plan would work, but I said, "I've never walked in the Tavera downstream from Olapa Tavena, so I don't know how long it's going to take, or what we'll see, or whether the river's easy or not."

"The Tavera River's wide so we'll see where we're going. Mika, can we do this in one day?" Elliot asked.

Mika and the others laughed. "One day if the Tavera crocodiles don't get you. If they do, you won't be coming home that night, not our Rotokas halfbreed and not our White Man either."

"Crocodiles?" Elliot and I said, almost together, "But we'll be above Sinsiluai!" meaning that everybody says there are no crocodiles in the Tavera upstream of Sinsiluai village.

Laughter and shaking of thatching.

Kalia said "That's what people say. Probably it's true —and he waved his hands in the air as if writing—"but I never saw a sign at Sinsiluai saying *Crocodiles Forbidden Above This Village*," and we all laughed and shouted.

Elliot shouted "Crocodiles forbidden! Forbidden!"

Mika said, "Tagilali. Elliot. Listen. I'm saying a true thing. You don't know that part of the Tavera. And it's not far from Sinsiluai. Be careful. They'll be on the banks if they're there but sometimes they're in the deep pools or tavena. If something seems wrong, Tagilali, find a place to scramble up. Call back to Elliot. Crocodiles won't follow you up a steep bank. You too, Elliot. You've been here long enough. Feel the air. If it's suddenly heavy or seems thick, or smells different, pay attention to everything around you. Sounds, too. If it's suddenly quiet, be alert."

Kalia said, "You cannot outrun a crocodile that surprises you on the sandbars or in shallow water. You have to get up, up, up as fast as you can."

Elliot said, "Maybe we should take Siro's dog Koria with us and hope the crocodiles eat him instead of us."

Everybody made faces because everybody knows about Siro's problems with Koria.

I said, "Koria won't go anywhere with you, Elliot," and he made a face and said he knew that, but was only thinking about helping out Siro.

I said, "I'll come to your house early in the morning if it's not raining. It's going to be a long day."

Then I went back to making thatching.

That night I lay on my bed thinking.

We could go at high speed. Nobody on the backsight rod, just leave it there, nothing much to write down, because the big bush is the big bush, and it's not divided up the way the land we put our gardens on is. So no boundaries to pay attention to, no place names to write down.

As for the crocodiles, I didn't think we'd see any. True, I've never walked in that part of the Tavera and I was a little worried about that. I knew Mika was right. I knew I'd have to try to listen and look and smell and sense everything I could. And of course the lead man always carries a machete. Not that a machete's much good against a crocodile.

And there would only be the two of us. More work, yes, but easier because we wouldn't be paying attention to what we said, who we went close to or even touched, or any of the other things that happen when you have a mixed group. I am talking about people from different clans, and also having girls, because we often worked with the two girls Lakabula and Wiare, Biroi clan girls.

There have to be two girls. Neither girl's mother would let her go alone into the bush with us. Elliot wasn't the problem as much as Siro was, which brings me back to where I always land. Siro's a Bero clan man, which means that if he went into the forest with Lakabula or Wiare it would be a bad thing because he'd be cheating on his wife, but otherwise not. It wouldn't be clan incest. Bero and Biroi can marry.

Elliot and I are in between—I think that's the way to put it. Maybe we're two things at once. We are said to be Biroi, Elliot even has a Biroi name, a namesake and a set of kin, and my name comes from a piece of Biroi land. Except we're not, truly neither of us is really a Biroi. Except in some ways, we are. We are, we aren't. We aren't, we are. It's endless.

What would happen if I went into the forest with a Biroi girl, was caught, and angry people shouted at me, "Bad enough but worse because you're a Biroi!" Then would I say, "No I'm not." But I am. Or I'm not. You see what I mean.

And what of Elliot, what if he went into the forest with a Biroi woman? It's against his own rules and it's against our rules if the woman's a Biroi. And worse if she's a married woman, then that's three rules broken: his, clan incest, adultery. If it was me, just one. Or two.

Elliot was ready when I went to his house early in the morning. He had the theodolite—I know its name, from the copper mine—in his pack, and was ready to put the heavy wooden tripod on his shoulder. I took the foresight rod, the tape in its big canvas cover, and the black palm stakes, which he had tied up with vines—one of things we taught him was to tie up things with vines. You can always find vines but you can't always find string. I slid my machete in between the vines and the stakes. I wouldn't be needing it until later. Elliot keeps his in his backpack.

"Careful not to cut the vines when you grab your machete," Elliot said.

"If I grab it in a hurry you know what that means, and who cares if the stakes scatter," I said, "and you had better leave your pack's flap open."

"If I'm attacked, I'll shove a tripod leg down its throat and run away."

"That might work."

"Betel?"

"Five. Peppers and lime."

Five might not be enough, but I had four myself. On these trips, we don't eat because what would we eat? Nobody wants to carry cooked sweet potatoes and there's little to eat in the big bush. Somebody always knows where there's water, meaning which little stream you can drink from. Sometimes there are tall coconuts, meaning that a very long time ago, somebody lived there. Nobody owns those old ones. We might send one of us to climb that coconut and get some green ones, if there are any, and we drink the water and eat the soft flesh.

Otherwise we chew betel, which takes away hunger.

The first part was through the gardens, and then we entered the big bush. It's cool there, because the tall trees block the sun. And yet because there's usually not much wind, you can get hot if you're walking fast or working. It's quiet, except for the birds.

We were walking along, not saying much. Elliot likes to look at the forest while he's walking, and on an easy trail that's not difficult. You don't have to look where you're stepping. If we're on trails, Elliot never wears shoes, but if we're going to go crashing through the bush off the trails, he does. The big bush has thorny vines that grow along its floor, and those thorns push right through even our tough soles. On this day he wore no shoes.

I wondered whether he'd want to stop and play slit gong. I am talking about striking the large keels of the maikui or mai trees with the butt of a machete, which makes a noise that's almost as loud as a slit gong makes when it's struck. The birds screech and scream and fly away, and I suppose if any flying foxes are hanging nearby they too are startled, but it takes more than that to get a flying fox hanging upside down and sleeping to fly in the daytime.

Now that I've told you that, I had better also say that if the birds are singing and making noise when a keel's struck, they will stop. I am saying that a loud noise will make them stop what they're doing. Or not doing, I suppose, it not-doing something is the same as doing something. You know what I mean.

Sometimes another person is in the big bush not far away, and that person will also hammer a keel. Then we answer, but because almost no one knows the slit gong language anymore, we just hammer back and forth until somebody tires of the game.

Elliot was walking behind me. He called out, saying he had to piss.

"Why do I care?"

"I have to put down the tripod and stop and I'm afraid you'll run away from me and I'll get lost in the big bush."

"Are you pretending you don't know this trail? You know this one." Maybe he just wanted to talk.

"Stop talking. I can't talk and piss at the same time."

I heard him zip his pants, and then grunt as he shouldered the tripod. He called to me, "I'll tell you an American song about pissing. I'll say it in English first so you can hear the sounds. 'No matter how much you shake and dance, the last three drops go down your pants.'" Then he translated.

I only understood *shake*, *dance*, and *pants* in English, and that's what I told him while I was laughing. I told him it was good. Every man who wears trousers knows that. The old people who don't wear trousers, not them. And the really old people, they didn't wear any clothes at all. Nothing to them.

We started walking again. I tried saying his little English song. I wanted to remember it, in case I was with another white man I liked, because it's a friendly thing. It's a joke, and I was thinking it was another way to say, *We're all men here, black or white.*

Elliot said, "Are you going to keep saying that until we start working?"

"No, only until I can say it perfectly."

"All day, then."

We both laughed. Elliot knows I understand more English than I let on, even to him. It makes us even, really, because he knows more Nagovisi than he lets on. Like most people with a new language, he understands what he hears better than he can speak. Same with me and English, which is why I was teasing him about learning to speak his little song.

I stayed in the lead, even though the trail was clear and indeed Elliot would have followed it easily. I was thinking about what I just said, that probably men all over the world think the same things about their penises. As far as I know, the only difference between penises, besides their size, is whether the foreskins are cut or not cut. I've worked with enough white men to know that some white penises are cut and some are not, and you never know which until you see it. Elliot is cut.

I stopped and turned back to tell Elliot what I'd been thinking, to see what he would say. He put down the tripod and leaned on it. When he did that I saw that he was a little tired. When there's a big group working, somebody else carries the tripod until we get to where we're going to start, and carries it home when we're finished. When we're surveying, he carries it. He wasn't out of breath but I was sure his shoulder was hurting him. His legs are as strong as anybody's. He can walk as far as any of us but he's no good at shouldering heavy loads.

"Men are the same everywhere," I said, "but I've been walking along wondering whether the uncut men have to shake and dance more than the cut men."

"The song says 'no matter how much,' but I know what you're saying. Too bad we cremated old Laumo," he said, "otherwise we could have asked him."

He was talking about during the Japan War when many Nagovisi were up at Torokina with the Americans, and

Laumo—a grown man—convinced an American doctor to cut his penis. Nobody had any reason to tell Elliot that Laumo's penis was cut like his, but when his body was being washed before it went into the fire, everyone could see that he was a cut man.

Later, Elliot told me that if someone had told him that Laumo had his penis cut at Torokina, he wouldn't have believed it. But there it was, and because Laumo spent half his life pissing from an uncut penis, and half of it pissing from a cut one he could have told us. But the pyre made ashes of him and his cut penis.

About the penises, Elliot asked, had I ever heard of people called Jews? I said I had, from the Bible, although I never had met one that I knew of, not even in Rabaul. He said that if you saw a Jew you wouldn't know he was a Jew unless he was wearing his special hat, but if you knew he was a Jew then you knew his foreskin had been cut off, because that's what Jews always do to their baby boys.

In America, he said, mostly men were cut, but in Europe, he thought mostly not, but he didn't know for sure because no one ever made all the European men line up and show their penises for counting.

That was funny to think about. I imagined lines and lines of European white men standing and holding out their penises, and men walking among them with paper and pencil, counting and writing down.

Cut, cut, not-cut, cut, not-cut, not-cut.

I would like to see that sight, although I don't care to see hundreds of white penises any more than I'd like to see hundreds of black penises. I did like thinking about lines of men standing and other men walking past them and looking at their penises. It would be something no one had ever seen before, the Day of Penis Counting. The world would be a strange place if what we think about could be made to happen.

When we started walking again I was still thinking about penises, about different kinds of penises. A duck's penis, which I saw in Rabaul, and it's very long and all twisted like the corkscrews that the whites use to open their bottles of wine. Dog penises aren't interesting apart from how they emerge for no good reason, and neither is a pig penis, although when it emerges it's very small and thin, even on a big pig—but then there's the donkey's penis, which is very human-like, except enormous, so enormous that when one of the old Padres brought a donkey to Sovele and the women saw its penis hanging out they screamed and laughed and at that moment a new oath was born, *by the donkey's long penis!* Everybody knows that story but only the women use the oath.

We kept walking. I thought Elliot was probably getting tired of carrying the tripod. I decided that the next time we stopped, I'd carry it. He'd complain a little but I knew he'd let me have it. I'd give him the bundle of stakes, which was much lighter.

Because we were moving quickly and would get to the Tavera in plenty of time, I thought we should stop and rest. I didn't want to say "Let's stop and rest" because I know he doesn't like to be reminded that he can't carry as much as we can. He doesn't like to be treated as the weak man—who does?

So I thought I'd start him talking again, about something complicated and interesting, something that he'd probably want to sit and talk about. And it would take time, longer than he'd be willing to sit if we were just resting. I told you we were easy with each other, and we are, but it's also true that he doesn't like to admit to getting tired more quickly than I do. I believe he tries to be the first one to say, "Let's go!"

Because we'd been joking about penises I decided to get him talking about the old story called Red Woman, because to me even though the word penis is not spoken in it, it's a story about penises.

Red Woman is a *kobonala*, "like a stone," a story from the old days. A kobonala, Lalaga told me, is anything that nobody alive has seen.

Some kobonala are like lessons. They tell us what should and shouldn't be done. For example, there's the one about Sipita, the demon ancestress who gave birth to Crocodile, then hid him so her husband, Crocodile's father, wouldn't know what she had birthed. She hid Crocodile in a basket, told her husband not to look in the basket, and went to the river. Her husband disobeyed her, saw Crocodile, and cut him into pieces. Sipita cried, and was angry. Crocodile wasn't really dead, so Sipita told him to go to the river, wait for his father to cross, and kill him. And that's what Crocodile did—he killed his father. I don't know whether he ate his father or not.

I think this story says "Do not disobey." Am I saying that when I first heard this one, I said to myself, "Ah, disobeying is bad?" No, of course not. Perhaps a small child would think that. Or perhaps a parent would say, "and this story shows that. . ." but adults I think just listen, and take in the meaning as a reminder.

I didn't hear about Sipita and Crocodile until I was grown, and as for Elliot, it was the same. The children, though, they heard it when they were small and I suppose they learned a lesson from it.

Red Woman is an important kobonala. I was there when Tupuua spoke it into Elliot's tape recorder. I was watching Elliot's face as Tupuua spoke and it had a look on it that I've rarely seen. Tupuua can't speak pidgin, so when he was telling the story Elliot was on his own. I could tell that he was trying hard to keep up, even though he knew he was getting it on tape and could take his time listening to it later.

I turned around, walking backwards. "Elliot," I said, "if I say 'Red Woman' and 'penis' then what will you reply?"

"Ha ha!" he said, "I thought we were done with penises, but all right. Red Woman is my favorite kobonala. Every part of it is strong and filled with meaning. Including penises."

"Go ahead, then. Tell me Red Woman."

He walked a few steps, clearing his throat.

"A red woman was crying," he said, and then he stopped. "When Tupuua spoke those words, just those first words, I knew, I don't know how I knew, but I did, that I was about to hear something very powerful."

"Why?"

"Because I never heard a story that started like that. And he was speaking slowly, I don't know it that was for me or the way he tells the story."

"It was the first time I heard it too. I don't think it was for you."

"To me it was immediately a mystery, a red woman, what could a red woman be? And why was she crying, and why all this at the beginning? It was like being suddenly pushed into a deep pool, Tagilali, that's what I felt. Even now sometimes I speak those words to myself because they are so beautiful and mysterious."

He shifted the tripod from one shoulder to another.

"Fuck a dog, this is getting heavy."

"The stakes are heavy, too."

"I see a keeled tree ahead," he said, "let's sit there and lean against them and chew."

I didn't expect him to say "and let's rest."

"Good."

When he was settled he began.

"I know we're having fun with this penis talk, but it's hard for me to take this serious story and make it into a joke."

"I'm not asking you to make a joke."

"Good. I'll be serious about the penises. A red woman was crying." He paused and shook his head. "Her name was Koso and she was hungry. She thought she could eat some things she saw on the ground, but they were leaf spines, not flying fox bones."

He stopped. "This is why I love the story so much. We never learn why she was red, and although the thing about flying fox bones sounds good, she couldn't eat flying fox bones. Nobody eats flying fox bones! So this part isn't really about looking for food, it's about seeing something that stands for something else, and being wrong."

I said, "Maybe. But what if she thought people were walking along eating flying fox, and they might feed her? But continue."

"I will," he said. "Some men came and said to Koso, 'You had better go to Sekentu's house. Perhaps a pig's been killed there, and you can eat it.' Koso didn't know who Sekentu was. Koso's father took her to Sekentu's, and left her there."

I said, "Who were 'some men?'"

"Truly," he said, "it's like that all the way through, isn't it? Indeed who were these men? Where did they come from? And why did they tell her to go to Sekentu's house? And then her father, yes her father just appears and takes her there. And we never see him again, the father. It's very strange. No mother?"

He continued. "Sekentu's mother was Makunai, the demon ancestress of the Eagles. Makunai sat Koso down on a bed made of black palm planks and told her she was now married to Sekentu. In this way, Makunai became her mother-in-law."

He laughed and shook his head, and spit. "Koso still doesn't know who Sekentu is, but she doesn't ask. She didn't say, 'What husband? Who?' Makunai tells her to stay on the bed until Sekentu comes back from hunting pigs, and she talks about how the bushes will shake. If you're hearing this for the first time, you say what? What? Shaking the bushes?"

"What did *you* think, Elliot?"

"I didn't think anything, because I knew it was a kobonala and its world wasn't our world. Also I was struggling to keep up and didn't have time to think."

I said, "I like the part about the snake making the bushes shake, because what snake ever did that? It's another way for the story to tell us Sekentu was not like the snakes we know. Sure enough, Koso looked up and saw the bushes shaking. When she saw her husband, he had a pig tied to his tail," and I punched Elliot's arm and said, "How does a snake tie anything to his tail?"

Elliot said, "Or to the pig! Or did he wrap his tail around the pig? I'll continue. Koso saw he was a snake, not a man. And what I like is that she doesn't scream and try to run away. She only says, 'What kind of husband is this?' It's like she was disappointed, not terrified. Then she begins to cry, who wouldn't, but Sekentu goes to sleep and doesn't see her. And he goes to sleep under the bed. Why does a snake have a bed and if he does, why does he sleep underneath it?"

I said, "He sleeps on the ground like a snake! But no, he curled up on a basketry platter. Why? The only reason I can think of is that the platter is made by coiling a thick vine, so maybe the vine is like a coiled snake, like his mirror."

"Hah, I never heard that, but, true, that's what it looks like."

"So here we have the snake coiled up on the platter with his new wife that he doesn't know about just above him, crying. Don't snakes have ears?"

"It's a kobonala!"

"True, true. Sekentu wakes up because he's getting wet from a few tears. It's not like rain, but it's enough."

"I think that's all right. Maybe a teardrop hit him in the eye."

"He's sleeping! His eyes would have been closed!"

"All right, so we don't understand that part."

Elliot said, "And it gets worse. Here's the giant talking snake under the bed and instead of looking to see what's above him, he asks his mother."

"That's what mothers are for."

"Makunai tells him that Koso's his wife, and he doesn't say anything like 'why can't I have a *snake* wife?' instead he coils around her, puts his tail in her vagina, and ejaculates."

I said, laughing, "*Why can't I have a snake wife*, truly. Remember the platter Sekentu was sleeping on? Where the coiling begins, there's a hole. Some people call that the platter's asshole. Hah, I think vagina, not asshole."

"And we return to penises," Elliot said, "Indeed. Snake tail penis. Or, as if I had to tell you, Sekentu himself is a giant penis, but no balls, so where did the semen come from?"

We laughed. Elliot eased his machete out. "Let's see if anybody's in the big bush with us." He struck the keel a good one. The bird noises stopped.

"Perhaps that's why many women fear snakes," I said, and Elliot laughed and shook his head, "Do women fear penises? Not many, I think."

"And we know who they are!"

"I don't, but I'm sure you do. Some men fear snakes," he said, "I've seen it."

"I'm not afraid of snakes. Remember when I caught that snake in the garden at Tutueo-go and the women were screaming at me to kill it, so I took the black tar from my pipe and put it in the snake's mouth? You were there."

Elliot said, "It died soon enough, and that was before I heard the Sekentu story or I might have said to the young girls, 'here's your husband.'"

I said, "No, you wouldn't have. No. You're too polite."

"Or scared of saying something wrong, in truth."

So we chewed and spit red on the tree's keels. It ran down, making long red trails.

"Red Woman's tears," Elliot said, and I said, "True."

We sat for a moment without talking. Then we heard somebody striking a keel twice. Elliot struck again, three strikes. Then we heard four.

I said, "If we start adding to each other's count, we'll be here a long time. Don't reply."

"All right. I'll continue," Elliot said, "I was thinking about Sekentu and how he never talks except to ask his mother why he's getting wet. The whole story is about Sekentu and that's all he ever says. I can't think why that is."

"I can't either, except later on the only people he *could* talk to are her brothers, and you know a husband has to be careful around his wife's brothers."

"True, yes, maybe," Elliot said, "and now I'll jump to the part where they went to Koso's village so that Sekentu could meet her brothers. The part about how Sekentu went hunting and caught pigs for Koso because she was thin, and they smoked them…I don't see much to talk about there, do you?"

"No, but we're probably missing something. We should ask Lalaga. As for going to the brothers, it was Makunai who sent them, so maybe Koso was happy and didn't want to go back to her people. And in the story she has no sisters, why not?"

"I don't know. Eating smoked pig every day instead of only when there were feasts, maybe she liked that."

"Does that make up for having a snake husband?"

Elliot laughed and waved his hands. "I don't know, so I'll continue. I like this part because it's so very strange, that her brothers did not know what happened to their sister."

"It's true," I said, "why didn't her father tell them?"

Elliot said, "Maybe he was ashamed of what he did," and I said, "Maybe, but also where is Koso's mother in this story? Nowhere! If you think about it, there are no women except Koso and the demon woman Makunai."

"Ah, that's true, so maybe this is a story made up by men to tell other men."

"You know we don't have men secrets and women secrets, so maybe it's a story made up by women, to show what happens if men control everything."

"Hah, could be." Elliot continued, "At Koso's village, Sekentu went to the feasting house and Koso went to a cookhouse, where people asked whether her husband had come, and Koso said yes, that he was at the feasting house. Her brothers went to the feasting house, filled with slit gongs, but they didn't see anybody there. They went back and said, 'Nobody's there,' and Koso said, 'Ah, you think he's a man, do you? Did you look inside the slit gongs? You killed me by sending me to Sekentu.'"

I said, "And who was *you*? It was her father, not her brothers."

Elliot said, "So they went back, looked inside one of the slit gongs, and saw a snake. They said to each other, 'What kind of thing has married our sister?'"

I spit a loud *kuioto* spit. "Why didn't they say 'what the bloody fucking hell is a giant snake doing inside our slit gong?' but no. They only looked at him. I would have run away."

Elliot shook his head. "True! I think this is when Sekentu becomes a penis-snake or maybe a snake-penis. Slit gongs! What is more like fucking than pounding on a slit-gong? And the sticks to beat them with," and he hit the tree keel with his machete one, two, three, four, five times.

I said, "Now we'll have to wait and answer."

"Ah, it doesn't matter. Sticks are like penises and then the giant snake penis has already fucked the slit-gong… the whole thing is like fucking, maybe that's why only men beat slit gongs…except Sekentu was all the way inside, so maybe the slit gong vagina captured him…there are stories in the world about vaginas that have teeth and eat penises, or the penis can't get out, but no teeth in this kobonala so maybe not."

And he laughed. And so did I. We spit red. Vaginas with teeth? I never heard of that.

I said, "And the brothers, 'what kind of thing has married our sister?' and why didn't they know that, considering it was their father who sent Koso to Makunai's house to marry a snake? In this story everybody talks like idiots."

"You see that in European stories, too. Idiots, I mean. And Koso says 'You killed me,' except that she's still alive."

I said, "You can skip over the next part if you like."

"I will. The brothers hid in the bush as Sekentu and Koso passed by, and they measured how long Sekentu was. Koso and Sekentu said they would return and when the brothers knew they were coming, they put logs across the trail so that Sekentu's body would be draped on the logs"— he made motions with his hand—"and then jumped out with axes and chopped him to bits."

Again he shook his head and laughed. "It's the only part of the kobonala that makes sense in our world. If you want to cut a big snake on a trail, it's soft ground so your ax won't go through on the first strike, but if you're chopping against a log, it will. Right? I've tried and tried to think of a meaning for waiting until Sekentu drapes himself over the logs, and I can't."

"Yes, that's true," I said, "cutting up the penis . . . into what, more penises? Short ones? And the logs are like penises themselves, so a giant snake penis is being cut up on top of wooden penises."

Elliot gave me a shove. "Like the kobonala where the woman has a *thing* that goes up a breadfruit tree and brings down fruit, and the man catches her doing it and chops her thing into pieces that become women's decorations? In the old days people must have liked to chop up penises."

"Hah, yes. I was thinking about that one, too. Was the thing a penis? Perhaps that's why women don't have penises."

Elliot said, "But what was that thing, really. It climbed the tree! The kobonala just calls it a thing. It could be her clitoris or it could be that the woman actually had a penis."

"We can't know!"

"True, but if it were a penis, then what we have are women who put pieces of that woman's chopped-up penis into their ears and noses. Not a man's penis. So when a woman put one into her ear is she thinking, 'this is why I have clitoris and not a penis,' or is she thinking, 'this is in memory of when we women had huge long things,' and not worrying about that the thing was?"

"I could ask some of the old women," I said, "but so could you. Your grandmother Warabai would tell you. She would shout and laugh, but she would tell you."

Elliot said, "I have an idea about the brothers and how they killed Sekentu."

"Tell me."

"Suppose that the meaning comes from how brothers aren't supposed to hear anything sexual about their sisters, and if Sekentu is a penis, then every time the brothers see him, they have to think about their sister and her husband's penis, and this shames and enrages them because Sekentu is doing and showing them what must not be done, so they have to kill him."

"Maybe," I said, "or Sekentu makes them think about sex in the presence of their sister, which they must not do, so they kill him to keep themselves from thinking bad thoughts."

"Both our ideas could be true. What do you think the brothers did with the pieces, then?"

"I don't know. I can't think of anything. They disappear. Like the brothers. No, wait. The salt water kills the brothers. Aparito. Now for the end of Red Woman, yes?"

"All right," Elliot said, "The last part. Makunai had tied a vine to Sekentu's tail, and she pulled the last bit of him home after he was chopped up, and now we get to the part where Sekentu isn't even a snake anymore, but something that makes salt."

"I wonder whether the piece Makunai pulled back included the snake's asshole?"

"Asshole!" He paused. "I'll give you an English word, which is *cloaca*, and that's what you're calling the snake's asshole, but it's not like a human asshole. Everything comes out of that one hole: piss, shit, and semen. There's a penis in there somewhere but I don't think it comes out. Maybe."

I said, "Cloaca, cloaca. Good word. And about what it is, I didn't know that. I never saw snakes fucking. I'm glad people aren't like that."

Elliot said, "Indeed. Especially that our women aren't."

I shouted, "Shut up! We're talking about penises"

"So we are, but listen to this. Long ago, a European man wrote, 'we are born between piss and shit,' but at least women have three holes, and not a cloaca."

I hit him on the arm. "I don't want to think about that. We're not talking about women, you and I, neither of us has a woman, so why talk about them?"

"We're talking about Koso, though."

"She's not a real woman. Kobonala."

"True." He sighed. "Even so, talking about real women makes me sad."

"And me," I said, "as you know. When the crocodile has you in his jaws you'll be thinking, 'I'm being killed and I never screwed a Nagovisi woman.'"

"Tagilali! Stop!"

"All right. Continue."

"We're back at Makunai's house. She put the tail into the thatching above her fire and when she wanted to season the food she was cooking for Koso and Sekentu's children she would command it to come alive and spill out salt water."

I said, "So now it's a cut penis and it ejaculates salt water, not semen."

"Yes, but only when a woman tells it to. How can 'come to life' not mean 'get hard?'"

"What mother tells her son's penis to get hard and ejaculate?"

"A demon woman, I suppose. I wish the Sekentu penis was still tied to a vine, so Makunai would just have to pull on it."

I said, "Like turning on an electric light in town. On, off, on, off. Also she has complete control over the penis, like it's her child. Ah, Sekentu *is* her child. Maybe this is about how women control their young sons."

"But what's the lesson, then? It's not like 'mother knows best,' because it was Makunai who sent him off to be cut into pieces."

"If she was human, but she's a demon so we're meant to believe she had some plan."

Elliot said, "And now we come to the end, which is like a famous story from Europe and probably everywhere in the world, where the children start something but cannot stop it. They command Sekentu's tail to make salt water and it makes so much that it covers the land and kills Koso's brothers and becomes the sea."

I said, "Did you ever notice that Koso is the only named woman in the story? Except for Makunai, and she's a spirit. There's only Koso and her brothers and her father. Everybody else is just *people* so we don't know what they are."

"True. I did notice it but I didn't think carefully about that."

I said, "And about red. I think maybe Koso is a red woman because of blood, that she menstruates."

Elliot hit the keel again and said, "I never thought of that. You must be right. But that would mean at the beginning, that would mean that Sekentu screwed her when she was menstruating."

"He was a snake. What do you expect?"

We laughed. Snakes don't care about anything.

We sat for a moment, thinking about the story. Nobody answered Elliot's keel strike.

"Another thing," Elliot said, "Koso disappears from the story when Sekentu is chopped up. Where did she go? She got pregnant by Sekentu before they killed him, but there's more than one child, so who was the father? And we never heard about any children until then. By the donkey's long penis, I love this story. It's perfect, because it's not a story of our time. But we don't care. All the things that don't make sense are what please me."

I said, "I won't tell anybody that you swore a woman's oath," and Elliot laughed.

"We had better go," he said, and got up and put his machete back in his pack on but before he could put the tripod on his shoulder, I grabbed it and handed him the bundle of stakes. He nodded his head and said nothing.

It wasn't long before we reached the cliff overlooking the Tavera, where Polanara's old taro garden was, before the Japan War, at Olapa Tavena, where the Olapa river joins the Tavera. That's where Elliot had stopped his surveying.

"Here's the place where Polanara cut the bush so we could see," he said, "I'll make a triangle so we don't have to tape down the cliff. I'll set up here and then you help me with the baseline, and then you go down and put a mark …" and he looked at me and said, "but what do you think, for down there—in that sandbar? On the other side?"

"I like the sandbar. Easy to place the stake. And I don't have to cross."

"Do you really think there are crocodiles here?"

"I don't think so, but it's possible."

"That's what I think, possible. So we'll be careful."

"I'm glad I'm not Sipita's husband."

"Good one."

When Elliot came down to the Tavera the sun was high. We wanted to finish the river section before late afternoon. If there were any crocodiles that's when they would be active. And in low light they would be hard to see.

Elliot and I worked our way downstream, usually without meeting. This was because pulling the tape was easy. There was little for it to catch on. I stood at my stake until I saw him fold the tripod and put it on his shoulder, and when he picked up his end of the tape I would move ahead to the next place I'd decided to drive a stake. Elliot knew I was good at placing stakes. If I didn't feel him jerk on the tape I just kept walking until I got where I meant to go, or he stopped me. The tape is 100 meters long. Then I'd shove in a new black palm stake, and wait for him to finish, then do the same thing, and the same thing and the same thing again.

The Tavera twists and turns but sometimes there's a long straight stretch, then a tight turn, and another long stretch. The first time Elliot called these *hairpin bends* I didn't know what a hairpin was. Then when he described one, I remembered that a Chinese woman I worked for in Rabaul had them. I hadn't known what they were called.

The long stretches are easy but the hairpin turns are hard because unless I wait for Elliot I have to begin dragging the tape without knowing where he is. I can't see him until he gets to the stake I left behind.

As the Tavera goes towards Sinsiluai, its banks are lower and lower. I knew the trail we were looking for, the one Kalia said we should use, but I wasn't sure I'd recognize it. I only walked it where it crossed the river so I didn't know what it would look like from upstream. At least it was a tavena, so that would help. I didn't want to miss it because there was no other trail until we got to the big road at Sinsiluai. And that's where the crocodiles might be.

I set a stake on a sandbar at a hairpin turn where there was a tavena. The small stream entering at that point was tangled with vegetation, and dark. Trees had fallen over it. The stream looked wide and and shallow. I felt uneasy so while I was standing there waiting for Elliot to turn the theodolite I didn't turn my back on it.

When I saw Elliot fold the tripod I headed downstream and after I planted my next stake, I turned back to look for him. When he came into view I watched him put down his pack, set up the tripod over my stake, and then wade out to look for the end of the tape. I suppose I was 50 meters away, half a tape. I saw him suddenly run for the bank, away from the tavena and I heard him yell "Tagilali, up, up, up." And I saw him reach and grab the branches of a small tree and pull himself up.

So I crossed over to his side and climbed. Of course I did. "What?" I shouted.

"Something! I don't know! Crocodile! Come!"

Where we were, the Tavera was terraced on both sides. I made my way along the terrace to where he was.

"I heard noises like moving branches, something walking in shallow water, and a splash in there," and he pointed to the tavena. His voice was uncertain.

"Fuck a dog. And we can't see anything."

"I didn't like that splash, I was thinking crocodile belly, what should we do? Wait?"

I looked carefully. There was the tripod, the pack on the gravel and I could see the end of the tape. I couldn't think what to do. I said, "How long do we wait? What if it doesn't come out?"

"Don't know."

"If it comes out, it's better. We can see it and we'll know what to do. We can wait for it."

"I can't lose my theodolite! But I grabbed my notebook"— he showed it to me—"so I haven't lost our work. I want my theodolite. I can't lose it."

"I know, I know."

We stood for a moment, looking. I was thinking that Kalia and Mika would know what to do but they were nowhere near us, the newcomers who knew nothing about crocodiles.

Elliot grabbed my arm and shook it. "I have an idea. Let's *make* it show itself. Not wait, make it happen."

"Good idea."

Elliot released my arm and breathed out, *hah*. "Tagilali, it could work. What if you go downstream and I go upstream and cross over to the tavena side, and we climb the bank and creep along the terrace, staying high up, and when we got close we make noise and throw anything we can throw and if it's in there, maybe it'll come out and then we'll know."

I thought that was a good idea. I said, "I come upstream and you come downstream and that way one of us can see where it goes, even if the other one can't."

"That's true."

"Better anger it than scare it, right? If it's angry it'll come all the way out."

It was possible. I could see that. The only danger was getting down and across the water to the other side, but we could run. Getting up wouldn't be hard and moving along didn't look like it would be too hard either.

"I have my machete, but yours is in your pack."

"Nothing can make me go to my pack! I have my small knife in my pocket. I can stab it in the eye."

"Elliot, do you really think there's one in there?"

"By the donkey's long penis, I don't know." He laughed but it was a nervous laugh. "I don't know. Something made that noise, I know what I heard. Truth, I don't think one's down there but I'm frightened to go down to my tripod and keep working. I turn my back and it rushes out and I'm dead. So I think, I think let's do something else."

"Do it."

"Do it!"

We shook hands, and clapped each other on the shoulder.

I've heard Mesiamo say it's best if you can see your enemy and I think Elliot was remembering that. Therefore our goal was to make the crocodile come out, if it was there.

The problem would be if it never showed itself. If we decided it *wasn't* there and went down to keep working but it *was* there we might be killed. If we decided it *was* there and went home Elliot might lose his theodolite. No matter whether it was or wasn't there. A very big problem for him. And that's why Elliot's idea was a good one. Instead of waiting, we would take action.

I was thinking all this as I went back to where I'd been, dropped down, and threw the tape's canvas cover up on the bank. If we had to run home, we could at least roll it up and it wouldn't be lost. Then I crossed and scrambled up the other bank. It was as we'd seen—not hard to move along, staying higher up than I thought a crocodile could reach.

When I saw Elliot, he was doing the same, approaching me and the tavena.

I will say that I shook my head at what we were doing. At what it would look like if anybody was watching: two young men, one black and one white, creeping like possums along a narrow terrace, hanging on to small trees, heading for the same place intending to make noise and throw things in case there was a crocodile hiding. I thought of how it would be in a movie, because in a movie there *would* be a crocodile, a big one and we would fight it. But this was no movie.

Finally we were close. We couldn't see the water in the small stream. Small trees and tangles were in the way.

"Ready?" I called.

"Ready."

We began yelling loudly. Elliot shook his tree and shouted in English "Bastard crocodile! Bastard crocodile!"

I shouted "Come out, come out you bush demon," and chopped off a branch and threw it down like a spear into the tangled vegetation. Then another.

There was a noise, a crashing. Something was moving.

"Moving!"

"Something!"

"Fuck a dog!"

"Aiiiiiii!"

Then a grunt, and the crashing moved up the small stream, not down.

"Pig!"

"Pig!"

And we both started to laugh.

"It was just a pig!"

"Or two pigs."

"Or three!"

"Fucking pigs!"

"Let's go down carefully."

"Carefully."

At the tripod Elliot said, "At the first crash I almost shit my pants."

I said, "I almost lost my grip and fell."

Again we shook hands.

"Fuck," Elliot said, "Fuck."

I said, "We never saw that pig, you know. Truly I think it was a pig but let's finish and get up from this dog fucking river."

"Pig fucking river."

"Crocodile fucking river, yes. Let's hurry."

And that's what we did. I almost ran from mark to mark and Elliot walked very fast. Usually he measures the angle twice but it looked to me like he was turning his theodolite only once, then recording. I would have done the same. I didn't want to be down in the Tavera any longer than I had to be. We lost time when we were frightened, so it was mid-afternoon by the time I spotted Sigalagun Tavena and the trail. The bank was easy and we were able to tape up it. No need to lay out a triangle.

At the top we leaned against a big tree and then slid down and sat. I was feeling a combination of excitement and left-over fear. I asked Elliot about it and he told me that was exactly how he was feeling.

"Maybe relief, too, but…what a story we'd have to take back if it had been a crocodile, so I'm a little sorry that it wasn't one, and we didn't fight it and defeat it. We were frightened and excited for nothing."

"Nothing?"

"You know what I mean."

"You must mean that you want us to go back down and run your line to Sinsiluai, as it gets dark, so we can find some crocodiles."

"Hah, no. As if I had to say. But tell me you know what I mean."

"I do."

And I did. We two were still young enough to seek danger so we could feel proud of ourselves.

"Why didn't the pig make noise when you were staking, I wonder. Or when I walked up with the tripod and opened it?"

"I didn't have to pound it in, but with a pig, who knows? Maybe it was so busy rooting that it didn't hear me. Or you."

"Maybe there were two pigs and they were fucking."

We sat for a moment shaking our heads and chuckling. Either a crocodile or two pigs fucking. Big difference. *One is dangerous and the other isn't*, I thought, and that made me think of the last time I'd been in danger.

"Remember in the trailer?" I said.

"Which thing?"

"When I was bleeding."

"We were frightened, yes. It was dangerous for you."

"I think this crocodile fear was different."

"How?"

"Because we were working together against danger but we didn't know whether it was truly a danger. With the wound we saw the blood. We knew what was happening. We understood the danger and even though you and Siro didn't know what to do, you did know that stopping the bleeding was important. You could see it."

"Yes. True. There it was, nothing hidden."

I spit. "Today we escaped from something we never saw or maybe it wasn't what we thought it was. Does that mean we weren't in danger?"

"We were! What we *felt* was real, and we can't truly say that it wasn't a crocodile.

"Are we going to tell people about this?"

"We could make it a funny story."

I imitated a pig. "The grunting."

"We don't have to talk about that. Maybe it was only branches breaking."

"Nobody will believe that."

"So we never tell anybody it was a pig, not a crocodile? And that makes it a story about escaping danger? If so, I agree."

"That's what I mean," I said. "We can have a lot of fun with this, and it doesn't hurt anybody."

"Shall we say we saw the crocodile, but it didn't chase us? That I saw it back in the stream so I did my angle quickly and then ran to you? That makes me seem foolishly-brave, even stupid."

"Let's say that it happened the way it really did, including climbing and going back to the tavena, making noise, and all the rest, but we'll say that no crocodile came out, you climbed down, did the angle, walked to my mark and then when we looked back, there was a big crocodile walking out of the tavena, but slowly, so we went on as fast as we could because it didn't seem interested in us."

"Like that, but how about on the backsight I saw into the crocodile's open mouth. It was eating the stake. And it was so far away we didn't think it would chase us."

"Yes, yes, yes. That's a good story. Let's tell it that way."

Elliot nodded his head. "Yes, that's good. That's our story." Then he started laughing. In truth we were both still laughing nervously.

He said, "I'm remembering an American joke. Do you know what a bear is?"

"Yes, from movies. They can kill you."

"That's it. All right, two guys are in the forest, and a bear chases them. One says to the other, 'I hope you can run faster than the bear' and the other says, 'I don't have to run faster than the bear, I only have to run faster than you.'"

"Faster than you," I said, spitting and laughing. "That's very good. I wonder who can run faster, you or me?"

"Someday we'll race."

"Someday."

"Before I go back to America."

"Before you go home."

"This is my home now," he said, and punched my arm.

We grinned at each other.

I said, "Elliot. Truly, if the crocodile took you, I would have fought. I would have tried for its eyes with my machete."

Elliot said, "Truly, if it took you, I would have shoved a tripod leg in its mouth and tried to pry it open, to free you."

I said, "If it was small. A big one, I don't think so."

Elliot shivered, and pushed against me with his shoulder. "Tagilali, I was really scared."

I said, "I was too."

We stood up and started surveying again. There wasn't much light in the big bush, but we thought we could get to the Menara before it was too dark to work. The trail was mostly straight. After a while we stopped to rest. We split the last betel nut.

"Hungry?" I asked.

"Yes, hungry. Thirsty, too."

"There's a small stream not too far from here. We can drink."

Elliot cleared his throat. "I've been thinking about something, here in the big bush and now that you talk about a stream, and because we've been talking about being chased, I'm thinking about something but I don't know whether I should tell you."

"Unfair! Don't tell me you're thinking about telling me something and then don't."

"You're right." He sighed. "It's about Maniku and it happened on the other trail from Olapa Tavena to Sabosa."

"Tell me!"

"I was measuring Maniku's garden. She was there with her husband. When I finished, I said I was going on to Sabosa, and she said, right in front of her husband she said, 'I'll walk with you.'"

"Elliot, you wouldn't have been the first."

"Yes, I suppose, I've heard stories, but you know I can't screw any women, my rule, and we're in the same clan, too. Both Biroi. And she's married. It's like baseball, three strikes and you're out. Maybe I'd be kicked out of Nagovisi."

I interrupted. "No, you wouldn't. People would be angry, is all."

"I suppose. But what I don't like is that people think I don't care about women, that I don't want to go into the forest and it's not true but what can I do?"

"Not everybody. Nevermind. Tell me your story."

"I knew if I came out of the bush into the gardens at Sabosa with all the women there, and Maniku with me… impossible. We would be accused of screwing even if we hadn't but I could tell she wanted to screw. The way she looked at me. I saw so much trouble ahead, a mountain of trouble, a river filling with trouble, so I had to think fast."

"Did you think you might be wrong, that she didn't want to screw you? Just wanted to walk?"

"No. I was sure I was correct. If it hadn't been Maniku, maybe not. And how could I say anything? I didn't want to refuse to walk with her because what reason could I give? I already said I was going there. Because I knew the trail, I said 'Let me go first, because I have an itch or something is bothering me so I want to be in the water, and I can use that first small stream to wash. Wait and then come along. I'll be there.'"

"And?"

"And when I was out of sight, I ran as if she were chasing me, a bush demon was chasing me, a crocodile. I ran to that stream but instead of washing I left my footprints in the mud, stirred up the water, and then I carefully went upstream and hid. I lay on the ground behind a keeled tree and I waited. Maniku came to the stream and called my name, but I didn't answer."

"Of course you didn't."

"I heard her say, 'not today, then' and I waited and then crept out near the trail, and she was gone."

"What then?"

"I went back to Olapa Tavena, where her husband was, except he was in the garden house and I didn't think he could see me, so I carefully crept around the clearing to the other trail and then I went back to the big road as fast as I could. I didn't turn down and go to those gardens at Sabosa. I went ahead to Lalaga's."

"Did you tell him?"

"Yes. When he saw me he said, 'What's wrong?' and instead of telling him I said 'You've taught me well,' then of course he made me talk about it."

"His way," I said."

"His way. I told him I was confused because never in my life had I run away from a women who wanted to screw me and although I was proud of myself, at the same time I wanted to weep in frustration. And it was like today, Tagilali, it was fear and excitement because I avoided bad trouble but unlike today I was wanting that trouble to find me. I said that to Lalaga. I admitted it."

I said, "We both know we can tell Lalaga anything," and Elliot nodded his head and smiled.

"In Lalaga's meeting house I bent over on a bench and I was almost crying. He made me get up and walk around with him. He said, 'Don't sit, keep moving until you're yourself again.' He kept saying, 'Don't despair,' and 'Don't worry,' and 'You've done a hard thing well, you should be proud,' and he kept saying, 'I am the one who understands you entirely, you can always talk to me.'"

"I will say I understand you too. As you understand me."

"It's true, Tagilali. I'll continue. In the late afternoon the women and Maniku came along the trail and saw me talking to Lalaga. I didn't think Maniku would say anything, and she didn't. The women asked why I hadn't come, and I said that I was tired and would join them another day. Then we all started back to Pomalate. Maniku was ahead of me and I kept looking at her and thinking, *we could have screwed in the big bush*, and again I'll say it was like the two of us today. Fear, excitement, nothing happened and here we are."

"That's it," I said.

But I was thinking, *Elliot's crocodile was what our women wanted to do with him. Ever since he came to us it's been hiding, maybe there, maybe not there. And he never knew which. Then Maniku made it show itself. When Elliot saw it was truly there he knew what he had to do. And he did it.*

I had nothing to offer him. He understood everything he needed to understand. I thought he had made the connection I made, himself. I wanted to praise him, but I didn't. He didn't need that from me. Understanding, yes.

I didn't think he would ever go into the forest with anybody. His own rule was too strong.

But I knew what he was feeling, considering that I was a Biroi man in a village where all the women were Biroi. There were crocodiles hidden from me, too, or not. True, at feasts when the singing and dancing lasted all night and nobody watched the young people closely, I sometimes went into the forest with Bero or Lavali girls.

I thought about telling him, sharing a secret, but I didn't because I knew it would sadden him. He would think about it when he went to feasts.

So I only said, "I understand. You know I understand."

"Yes, my friend."

I said we had better get started again or it would be completely dark before I set the last mark.

Elliot said, "If we can get to Lalaga's before they eat, they'll feed us."

I said, "We'll tell him it was a pig."

"A pig, yes."

I Don't Kill People Anymore

Most people call me Mesiamo, but I like to be called *Kerasi*—Old One—because it reminds me that I used to be young, strong, and dangerous. I was the one people feared, and they still do, even though I don't kill people anymore.

You know those church people who say they've changed their ways and aren't going to sin, aren't going to do the devil's work? I'm not like them and that's not because I don't worship those Catholic spirits. It's because I haven't changed my ways at all and even now I'd kill anybody I had reason to.

As for our white man, I always call him "White Man," even though I know his name and have no trouble saying it. I've known many white men and ours is nothing like them and that's why calling him White Man suits me.

White Man turned up out of nowhere one day and asked to live with us. He came like a flash flood. If you live in a place where the rivers flood you know that a river in flood is dangerous not because of the rushing water but because of what it's hiding—big logs, branches. If you try to cross that river, it's not the water itself that's dangerous. It's what the water's hiding—something that knocks you down or tangles you, and you're swept away and drown.

If White Man was a flood, I asked myself, then what hidden dangers might he be carrying? I worried about that, because white men are never alone. Even if he seems to be alone, there's always somebody behind him giving orders, or perhaps making trouble with what he tells them. Here in the bush we can never know who those hidden people are. We only know that they're bound to be there.

I thought having him live near me would be best. I made sure he was shown villages I knew he wouldn't like— wide hard-packed dirt spaces, slippery in the rain, hot in the sun, houses all in a line with their cookhouses behind them, not many shade trees, no river nearby—and only after that to be shown Pomalate Village, which is very different.

Pomalate has grass, the houses are widely-spaced, there's plenty of shade, it's on a cliff overlooking a river, you can see the mountains—I knew he'd want to live there. It's the kind of place white people like. And Pomalate's close enough to Biroi, my village, so that I could watch him.

It's best to keep potential danger near you, if you can, and although I didn't think White Man himself was dangerous to us, I couldn't be sure. What was he going to do with what he learned about us? Who would read this book he says he's going to write? Will there be things in it that people or companies or other countries can use against us?

It's better if people who don't wish you well don't know much about you.

I don't believe all those other countries are intending us harm. Perhaps some are. But how would we know which ones? We have no way to know what they might come to steal from us. We have no way to learn which other countries wish us well, but that's less of a problem.

The Australians and the copper company wanted the copper and gold at Panguna, so they took it. They didn't ask. They took it, and there's no way for any of us to know what else they might decide to take, also without asking.

And fighting. There's no way to know about that. I had no reason to think that the Japanese and Americans and Australians were going to have their war on top of us. And yet they did, and many of us died in the middle of bloody fighting we didn't ask to join.

The Americans starved the Japanese. They dumped poison from airplanes on gardens, mostly Japanese ones, and what were the Japanese to do but steal our food and kill us if we resisted? That's when I began killing Japanese, but you could say it was the Americans who made me do it.

I'm telling you so you understand I've learned to be on my guard, to be wary about what comes our way unexpectedly, not to believe everything outsiders say, and that I'm willing to kill people if I have to. As I've said.

All of this applies to White Man. He's an easy man, but an easy man can be dangerous. I didn't kill Japanese with my axe by rushing at them. No, I acted like a harmless man, anxious to help. The trick was to get the soldier's guard down. The rest was striking quickly.

I was wary but that didn't keep me from sitting easily and talking with him, smoking his tobacco, chewing betel. It's impossible to learn what anybody's like if you're aggressive to them, or seem frightening. I learned that long ago, and so at the beginning I acted mildly towards White Man. Not submissive. I mean only friendly, a little reserved, courteous, helpful, but not like a servant. Of course he quickly learned who I was, and some of the things I'd done years ago. At the beginning, I let other people tell him about me. I knew they would.

More men have tried to kill me than you can count on all your fingers and toes and the fingers and toes of the man sitting next to you in the cookhouse, even if that man is White Man, who has as many fingers and toes as I do.

I never thought he'd try to kill me and I never thought I'd try to kill him. These days, you can't kill somebody just because it seems like a good idea. But you can make people cautious. You can make them believe they had better think carefully about doing something against me—against us— because they can't be certain how I might react.

After I began to know White Man's ways, after we'd spent many days talking, I was less and less worried about him. Although I'm not easily tricked, and I rarely make dangerous errors—these days, danger would be something like an angry boar rather than an angry man who wanted to kill me—indeed I am old now, and indeed I don't know as much about White Man's American world as I wish I did, which takes me back to the White Man flood.

I began thinking would be good to remind White Man that I was dangerous, in case he was beginning to think I wasn't. I wouldn't do that by sticking my finger in his chest and saying, "Watch what you do, White Man. Betray me and die."

Thinking about doing that makes me laugh. I don't know what he would do. Treat it as a joke, I suppose, so it would be wasted. A threat does lose its force if you have to explain it. Would I stand there saying, "No, White Man, I really mean it?"

In any event that's not my way. It's never been my way. Even when I was young and reckless I didn't puff myself up like a rooster and threaten people, even my enemies. What a waste of effort! People knew that every man who attacked me was dead by my hand, and that was enough.

I didn't want him to be terrified of me, no. I didn't want him to look at me the way he'd look at a crocodile that suddenly rose up from the Tavera, mouth open, when he wasn't expecting it.

I wanted him to look at me and see a crocodile basking in the sun, seemingly not paying attention, and understand that this crocodile was watching him closely and would attack if it saw the need.

So I decided to talk about blood and death sometimes in detail and sometimes lightly, as if they were small things. I'll tell you that's not what I believe. If there's any place in the world where killing isn't serious, I wouldn't want to live there. But I know White Man well enough to know that if I only talk about something that's like a heavy load for him to carry he'll try to put that load on his shoulders and he'll get so tired that he'll stop paying attention. He'll be thinking *killing, killing, killing, blood, blood, blood,* and he'll stop paying attention and he won't understand what I'm trying to teach him. Or make him think about.

I did want him to understand that only a fool would believe that a man who's stopped doing something of his own accord would never start doing it again. And White Man is no fool.

One day I yelled at old Lunta to go over to Pomalate and ask White Man to come and chew betel with me. I knew he'd come, and not just because he loves chewing betel.

White Man's been with us long enough to know that "why don't you?" from me means "you had better."

It was a rainy day, and cold. After we'd been sitting at the fire, talking about one thing and another for long enough, falling silent when the rain on the thatching was so loud we couldn't hear each other, I told him I'd been thinking about the Japan War. We talk about it often, so that didn't surprise him.

I've shown him many things from the war—papers, pictures, clothing, things I got from the Americans at Torokina and later from the Australian Commandos I fought alongside—but it's true I haven't showed him the guns, ammunition and grenades I have stored in a secret place.

I got up and went over to a metal box, opened it, and took out a Japanese cloth hat. As I walked back to where he was sitting I said, "I was thinking about the Japan War because one of the children asked to wear this hat, but I didn't allow it," which was a lie.

White Man looked at me with a puzzled expression. He knows I'm always gentle with children. I had the hat lying flat in my hand.

"Is it an important hat?" he asked, and I answered, "In a way."

I handed it to him and he stroked the brown cloth before he turned it over and saw the tear and the blood stain. He didn't seem startled, but his expression changed. Perhaps it was excitement. Certainly not disgust or horror, which was good. I wanted to draw him in, not repel him.

He said, "This must be what it looks like," and I said, "It is," and stopped, so that the rip and the stain could speak for themselves. He put a finger into the tear and said, "This must also be what I think it is, because people have told me how you killed Japanese soldiers, but it's one thing to hear about it and it's another to hold…" and his voice trailed off.

I said, "I keep it to remind me of when I had no gun and killed soldiers who did." That was closer to boasting than I like to get.

He blew out through his nose. "Indeed," he said, "indeed."

I said, "It put me in mind of the Japan War, this hat did, and I thought you might be interested in some things I haven't told you about," and he said, "About fighting?" and I said, "Yes, but not about soldiers. About an Australian Kiap who arrived with the Army, and ordered me to kill men who weren't soldiers." I paused.

He handed the hat back to me. He said, "The Kiap ordered you to kill Nagovisi?" and I said, "No, he wanted me to go down into Siwai and kill a man there."

I acted as if there had been nothing much to it. I told White Man the Kiap said a Siwai named Uta—a man I knew well—was helping the Japanese. He told me to go there and kill him. What White Man might find interesting about this story, I said, was that although I didn't like being *ordered* to do anything, I did kill Uta.

I paused, and then said, "With my knife."

"A knife fight?"

"No, no," I said, shaking my head. "I didn't want a fight. I just wanted to kill him. We talked and ate and smoked and chewed betel in his feasting house and then at night when everyone was sleeping I took my small knife, rolled over and slid it between his ribs into his heart."

I made the motion although I had no knife in my hand.

"I had shoved my forearm into his mouth so he couldn't scream. I could feel his teeth, his tongue, his lips. He made some noise but it could have been the noise of a man having a bad dream. No one woke. I didn't pull out my knife, so there was almost no blood. I lay on him until he died and then I picked him up and put his arm over my shoulder and walked outside with him as if we were two men going together into the forest to piss. If any of his men saw us leave, they said nothing."

White Man's eyes widened. He shifted on his seat. "And then?"

"And then?" I laughed and slapped his shoulder. "And then I threw his body into the Hupai and either the crocodiles ate him there or he washed down to the coast and they ate him in the mangroves."

White Man was quiet for a moment. Then he said, "Yes, the Hupai carries a lot of water, yes, I can see that would work." I knew he was searching for a good response. He knew crocodiles didn't range far up the Hupai, but he said nothing about that.

I laughed again. "Yes," I said, "Yes, crocodiles can be useful."

Then I twisted him a little more. I told him that I came back to Nagovisi and told the Kiap I hadn't been able to find Uta, but that I'd sent word to the Japanese commander that Uta was working for the Australians, and so the Japanese killed him. Even now I'm not sure he believed me, but Uta disappeared, as the Australians wanted. They never knew I killed him.

White Man was shaking his head and making noises in his throat. Then he took a stick and poked around in the fire. I said nothing.

He said, "Can tell me why, if you didn't want to obey the Kiap, you killed Uta anyway?"

I gave him another push, again as if we were having a joke, and said, "I didn't want him to think I was his *boy*, and because along the Nagovisi-Siwai border Uta was my rival and"—I hesitated for a moment—"because I wanted one of his wives."

"One of his wives?" White Man said, and I said, "Yes, as I said. After I killed Uta she left Siwai and came up here." I pointed. "She's over there."

White Man was startled. "What?" he said, "Really?" and then he quickly said, "Ah, I don't mean 'really' because clearly it's true…Kavibura?" and his voice trailed off.

From the back of the house Kavibura called to him, "Elliot! Yes! That's how it was and I'm glad I came here, because otherwise I'd never have chewed betel with a white man."

We all laughed.

Before White Man composed himself I struck again. I said in the mildest tone, "After that, I killed Paramount Chief Kamanai, in the same way—with a knife—and got rid of his body in the same way—crocodiles—but this time in the Jaba, not the Hupai. I told everyone that the Japanese had attacked us and shot Kamanai but that I escaped. Yes," and White Man cleared his throat, and I said, "Before you ask, yes, he was another rival but he did work for the Japanese, and I didn't take his wife."

Kavibura called from the back, "Old One, you know you didn't *take me*. I wanted to come to you."

After a moment White Man said, "I'm confused. You hid these killings. Didn't you want people to remember you were a man who killed people?" and I put my leg up on the bench and turned towards him, to make sure he could see my face, and said, "It suited me to have people believe I was lying about Uta and Kamanai."

White Man widened his eyes.

I said, "Uncertainty and doubt are weapons. People didn't know what I'd do. Those who thought I killed Uta and Kamanai feared moving against me, the master of secret killings. And those who were unsure, the same. Keeping everybody uncertain is good."

"I suppose," White Man said, "I suppose that's true."

"The Uta and Kamanai business was complicated. The Japanese, the Australians, the Americans up at Torokina, Nagovisi who were so confused about what was happening that they'd believe anything…a leader has to act differently then. Nothing is simple, and even when it is, sometimes you *want* to make it seem complicated. It's more difficult."

Then we chewed some betel. After that, I smoked. White Man only smokes sometimes, and this time he didn't want to. The rain didn't stop but it was lighter and we could hear each other easily.

White Man cleared his throat and spit and said, "In America if you kill somebody you keep it secret, otherwise the government will put you in jail or execute you," and I said, "I suppose that's true, but I'm talking about a time when was no government, except for that Kiap who wanted me to kill Uta, and the armies. If you want to write it down, his name was Masta Clark."

White Man wrote in his notebook.

I said, "I wonder if he's still alive. I wonder what he'd think if he knew I tricked him."

White Man said, "Yes, perhaps I could find him in Australia and ask," and then he wrote in his notebook. I thought I'd probably worked on White Man enough, so I told him he ought to go back to Pomalate while the rain was still light.

The next afternoon I went to his house when I knew he'd be back from Siuwako's garden. I was sure that he'd been thinking about what I'd told him. I was again intending to talk to him about fighting and killing. What I'd told him about in Biroi happened during the Japan War, and even he knows that in wartime people do what they must. But what about when there's no war? I mean war the way the whites understand it. I wanted to tell him about something that happened even before the Australians put their Patrol Post at Boku. Even before the first Padre came.

I went up his steps and inside and sat down in his false cookhouse, and called to him. I was already lighting the cigarette I'd rolled when he came from his office in back.

"Old One!" he said, "I heard you come in," and I said, "I was sure you would."

He was holding some kind of newspaper. I could see pictures of soldiers and a village with houses something like ours. He looked troubled—uneasy, perhaps even angry, although if he was angry he was controlling it. He sat across the fire from me on his other bench, and tossed the magazine on it.

I pointed to the picture and said, "You never wanted to be a soldier?" and he said "No!" loudly and then he said it again. "Never," and then he said, "I'm a student," and I didn't know why he said that. I knew he was a student. I raised my eyebrows and he said, "Ah, I have to explain that students aren't made to be soldiers. Otherwise, I'd be fighting in a place called Vietnam, which is near Japan and China."

I'd heard the name of that place on the radio, but as for the other thing—it surprised me. I said, "They would force you to fight?" and he said the government would put you in the army whether you wanted it or not.

I thought that in America, people did as they pleased, and I said that. He said he was only talking about the young men, which didn't surprise me because the soldiers in the Japan War were mostly young. The leaders were older but it was the young men who were killed. That wasn't true of our own fighting, which is why I took note of it.

Then he told me that by being a student he was *excused* from fighting. I laughed and got up, walked around the fire and sat next to him. I punched him on the arm. "Here," I said, "here, not everybody fought, but nobody was excused from being killed."

He said, "I'm sure you'll tell me what you mean."

I asked him if he had any betel. He did, so we started chewing. We talked about nothing much while we chewed— the weather, whether Otoloi would ever corral his troublesome pig, who would kill Siro's dog for him, whether the cocoa flush would be bigger than usual—ordinary things two men with nothing much to do would talk about. I wanted to know what was bothering him. But I wasn't going to grab his arm and say, "What's bothering you, White Man?"

I'd heard about the war in the place Vietnam, so I motioned towards the newspaper. "Those soldiers," I said, "I suppose they're good fighters. Is America winning?"

I wasn't expecting the reaction I got.

He spit forcefully and said, "Winning?" His voice was tight. "Winning?" he said again, and I said, "Yes, winning. Your Army defeated the Japanese, so I suppose you can defeat the Vietnamese."

"Fuck winning," he said loudly, "and fuck the Army and fuck Nixon too."

We know how to use the English curse *fuck*, but he was using it more angrily than our young men do.

I looked over at him. His arms were tense, his shoulders hunched. I'd sat with him many times, and I knew how he carried himself. This was not the White Man I was used to.

I said mildly, "Yes, Nixon is your president. You're angry at him?"

He picked up his newspaper and opened it. "Look at this," he said loudly, "look!" and held it out to me and I saw naked people dead, blood, American soldiers. He pointed from picture to picture, turning pages, saying "Look! Look at this!"

I caught my breath. I've seen many bad things, but nothing like what I was seeing. Soldiers in battle, yes. Certainly. Wounded, dead, burned, rotten, bleeding. But in the Japan War soldiers didn't turn their guns and bayonets on women and children.

All I could say was, "White Man, what is this?"

"It's the fucking war in Vietnam," he shouted, "we Americans are like wild dogs now, as you see. As you see!"

I said, "As I see," and then I said, "Explain, if you can."

He breathed out through his nose, and tossed the newspaper onto the bench. "Here," he said, "Old One, what happened was that American soldiers in Vietnam went to a village and started killing everybody in it, men, women, children, putting fire to the houses—that's what you're seeing." He raised his voice, "No one was excused! Those soldiers excused no one!"

White Man got up from his bench and went into his kitchen. He walked slowly. I heard the sound of a storage tin opening, and he came back with two Navy Biscuits. He carefully handed me one.

He said, "Old One, let's eat something."

I nodded, and before I bit into my cracker I said, "I suppose that everywhere in the world things happen that should not, but that"—I gestured at the newspaper—"that's the worst thing I've ever seen," and then I said, "What reason can there be for something like this?"

He took a bite of his, and chewed. "These are dry," he said, "Shall I get some water?" but I said I didn't need any, and he said in that case he wouldn't take any either. He broke off some pieces and tossed them at the hen sitting in the corner, who stood up and scratched around, pecking at them.

I said, "I'll hear what you have to say, White Man," and he pointed to the newspaper and said, "You see it there," and I said, "Pictures don't tell me *why* something happened," and he sighed and said, "I'll tell you what I know. Indeed some of the village men were enemies and the soldiers believed they had killed some Americans, but they didn't know which villagers had, so they began killing them all, and as for why they started killing women and children, I don't know, then other American soldiers pointed their guns at the killer Americans and said they would shoot them if they didn't stop, and those killers did stop, the helicopters came and saved some villagers, and the commanders tried to keep what happened a secret, which is very bad. All these things are bad."

He said all that in a rush, his words spilling out. He had picked up the newspaper and was hitting it on his thigh as he talked.

I said, "What caused this, then? Were the soldiers ordered to do this?"

He said, "Ordered? I suppose somebody did, but it's not who ordered it that's bad, it's everything"—he was raising his voice again—"from the soldiers up to the officers and then President Fucking Nixon," and he started shouting and cursing Nixon again.

He made a big noise—*Baah*—and stood up. He waved his arms around without speaking. Then he shouted that his President was a dog fucker, the vagina of a sow who's just given birth, a human turd. I was surprised, because although I knew the young men taught him to curse, people rarely curse around me.

While White Man was shouting I saw his grandmother Warabai come out from her cookhouse, machete in hand, probably thinking she needed to defend her grandson. Most women will sing and dance in anger and brandish ginger stalks, but Warabai will fight with whatever weapon's at hand, which is why no wife accused her when the demon Topegina was using her shape and tempting men into the forest.

Siro's dog Koria started barking. "Shut up, you dog-fucking dog," White Man screamed, and then he made a strangled noise and said "I can't even curse a dog properly," and collapsed down on his bench. Then he bent over and put his head on his knees and his hands behind his neck.

I looked out and saw Warabai go back into her cookhouse. She probably decided it had to do with Koria.

You can imagine how strange all this was to me, because White Man lost control of himself only that one time coming back from Buin Town, when they were all drunk and fought and he cursed Nalokasi. News of that fight made it to me quickly. I decided to do nothing about it.

When he sat up and looked at me I was surprised to see sadness. "I'm sorry," he said quietly, "I'm not myself, Old One."

I said, "I can see that," and slid over next to him. "White Man," I said, giving him some gentle pushes, "you were shouting and angry, but now you're sad and I'm wondering why. For your country? Or those Vietnamese?"

He folded his arms and bent over the fire. He exhaled strongly through his mouth, and then again through his nose. Then he put his hands on his face and rubbed his eyes.

"Old One..." he said, and I said, "Go ahead and talk about it." He was quiet for a moment and then cleared his throat and said, "Some say that fear is anger's mother, and I suppose that anger could be sadness's father." His voice trailed off. He was tapping his hand on the bench.

"White Man," I said, raising my voice. "You're trying to talk about how one thing is another thing, the way you and Lalaga like to do." He shook his head, but I continued, "Don't say no. You're talking to *me*, not Lalaga and telling me why this"—I picked up the newspaper and waved it at him—"made you sad is the best thing."

He shook his head but I didn't think he meant "No."

I said, "Do you think I don't know what you're like? Did you arrive yesterday? You don't show anger but just now you did, and now you're sad. This is a new thing and you had better tell me about it."

He was silent. A light rain was beginning, and its sound on the thatching filled the silence. I thought he would probably tell me what was troubling him but not if he could avoid it, so I didn't slow. I didn't want him getting lost in the rain.

I motioned at the newspaper. I said, "Is this why you wanted to be excused from fighting?" and he said it was, but not only that.

"What else?" I said, to keep it moving, "Tell me what else."

He said that the Americans went to Vietnam because the Vietnamese were fighting against each other, the Communists against the people who were not Communists, and the ones who were not Communists asked the Americans to help.

I didn't know that war had to do with Communists. The catechists say Communists don't believe in God and Jesus. That makes me a Communist, but there must be more to it than that.

He coughed and spit. "I'll tell you, Old One. I'll say it in a simple way and then I'll try to explain," and I said, "I'm listening."

He took a stick and poked the fire. He said, "Yes." He cleared his throat. "Yes, I'm sad because I'm here in Nagovisi far away from America, which means I can do nothing to stop this war"—he picked up the newspaper and struck a picture of dead people with his fingers—"to stop this, nothing."

I didn't understand. I understood what he said, because he spoke clearly, but I didn't see what being in Nagovisi had to do with that war, or stopping it, and I said so.

He said, "There are ways to make the government stop doing something, but I can't act when I'm here."

I thought he was talking about going to meetings and speaking, or perhaps voting. We do those things. You can imagine how greatly he surprised me by saying that there were people fighting the American government in

America, and that some of them were his friends. I tell you, I don't know what he could have said that surprised me more.

I said, "Fighting? Fighting?" I swung my arms in a fighting gesture.

He slapped his palms on both thighs and said loudly, "Fighting. Old One, fighting. I'm talking about blowing things up, cutting power lines, crowding into the streets, fighting with the police." He made fists. "And shooting police, even soldiers. Yes. Old One, it's true, what I'm saying."

He might as well have told me he was Chinese or that his mother was a spirit. That's how strange it was to me. I had no idea white people fought in their own countries, but then I thought, *Why would they tell us if they did? They wouldn't want us to know. They want us to think they're better than we are.*

I said to him, and I could hear the surprise in my own voice, "No idea. I had no idea." Then I said the part about his being Chinese or having a spirit mother.

He said, "It's complicated," and I laughed.

It was a genuine laugh although if I'd thought that a false laugh would keep him talking I'd have laughed a false laugh. I didn't like the sound of this. Learning that there was fighting in a place I thought was peaceful—that was a surprise, because it meant that something was wrong in America. I again wondered what might be hidden in the White Man flood.

I asked him if he'd fought before he came to us. Hearing that question come from my mouth was very strange. I was watching him closely when I asked. He closed his eyes. He held his mouth in an odd way, and then I realized he looked ashamed. Ashamed? What was happening here? Shame? He didn't answer me.

"You did, or you didn't?" I said.

He shook his head and said that he hadn't done anything except marching in the road, what he called a *demonstration.* He explained that was like what the Rorovana women did when the mining company was trying to take their land. He looked at me, but then looked away, out the window.

He said, "All I did was demonstrate but even so I might have been put in prison and I couldn't have come here," and I still didn't understand, because he was saying that he hadn't done anything wrong, so why prison? And what could he be ashamed about?

I said, "What's this about prison?" and he said that sometimes the police attacked people who were demonstrating, and if the demonstrators fought back they were beaten and locked up. And in court the police would lie, saying that the demonstrators attacked *them.* And if that happened to him, the court, the Australians would learn what he had done and call him a Communist and not let him come to Bougainville.

I said, "White Man, I've been beaten by the police, and in the same way you're talking about. I never attacked them but they said I did—it's the same, except it had nothing to do with war."

White Man looked at me, "With what, then?" he said.

"They wanted me to confess to something I had not done, so they beat me and took me to court and lied about it and I went to prison in Lae, as you must know," and he said, "I do know, yes."

He turned away from me. I could hear him swallowing.

I said, "It's not the same thing. I'm only telling you that's their nature, the police. Clearly the American police aren't different."

I stopped. We could talk about police another time. I said, "White Man, why would the Australians care what you did in America? Communist or not? What trouble could you cause here?" and he said, "They would think I was coming to make you angry about the copper mine, and start you thinking about being free from the Australians."

I said, "We stay free by keeping out of their way. As for the copper mine, we don't know enough about it yet."

In truth I'm aware of the talk about *secession* and *independence* but there's no fighting in the talk that comes my way, and I know what I need to know about the copper mine, except whether he's connected to it or not. I saw no reason to say anything just then.

White Man stood up and went to a window and leaned against the wall and looked out. He was silent for a moment. When he turned back to me, he said "I've been unclear. I wanted to fight against the war, but I also wanted to come here, and I had to choose. You know what I chose, and I'm ashamed about that."

I didn't see why. Coming here was his work. So why wouldn't he take care not to spoil it? I said that to him.

He put his hand on my arm. "Old One," he said, "suppose it was the Japan War, and Nagovisi were dying from no food and the fighting, and Masta Clark said, 'Mesiamo, how about going to Australia and learning about us instead of staying here fighting for your people,' what would you do? You would stay!" and he looked startled, I suppose because he'd told *me* what *I'd* do, but he was correct and I said so.

"Well," he said, "now you can see that I chose to look after myself rather than looking after my country, trying to make Nixon stop the war so that this"—he pointed to the newspaper—"wouldn't have happened."

Even so I didn't see why he was *ashamed.* I said, "White Man, it's not as if your government was killing your family or your friends and you didn't try to protect them," and he said, "That's true," and I said, "Certainly it's true. I understand you're talking about something else, but I don't think it's different. Trying to resist something that you can't resist is foolish and no reason for shame." I gave him a gentle push and said, "You were right to come here."

White Man kicked the fire. "Yes," he said, "I don't know. Perhaps. I suppose that's true. You would know," and I said, "Indeed I would know," and he said, "Yes, but it feels as though I ran away."

I sighed and started rearranging the fire. Among us this is a signal that talking should stop for a moment. It's as if we believe that no one can speak and poke a fire at the same time.

I've been saying "He surprised me," or "I was shocked," because I'm moving my story along, but what was really happening in my head was complicated, and distressing. I don't like being surprised when I never imagined there *could be* a surprise. I've been surprised many times—some dangerous, most not—but it was always when I knew very well that I *might be.*

White Man's surprises came from nowhere. If he said to me, "Old One, I'm working for the copper miners," that wouldn't be a big surprise because it's something I thought could be true. But what he told me truly were surprises.

White Man took a stick and pushed the fire around himself. When two people are rearranging the fire they both are careful. Moving a stick that the other person's moved is rude, because it's the same as saying "you've done it wrong," or "I know better."

White Man pushed around sticks I hadn't moved. Finally he said, "Old One, for me, these are hard things," but instead of going on he started with the fire again. He cleared his throat. "As for shame," he said, "I'll tell you what's truly shamed me. What I told you is the smallest part. You may as well hear it."

I said, "Tell me."

He cleared his throat again, and said "In America I only went to demonstrations where I thought there wouldn't be trouble," and I said, "A good idea," and he cleared his throat and said, "Yes, but one of my friends was demonstrating when the police attacked with clubs and dogs, and another time when the police killed people, and was not afraid. She's very brave," he said, shaking his head, "she wrote me letters about it, and I said to myself, 'Here I am in Nagovisi, safe and happy but the war continues and she's fighting against it, putting herself in danger, and I'm not.' And this is shaming to me."

I shook my head. Killing, not just beating! And more surprising, a woman fighter. I thought I knew her name.

I said, "I wonder if this friend could be the woman Anna who wrote you letters?" and he said, "Ah, the same. I know people look at my letters," in an unsurprised tone, but I didn't respond directly.

I said, "The children say there are no letters with Anna's name on them anymore," and he said, "It's true."

I said, "Perhaps she's in prison?"

He said, "No, not prison. Her anger pushed her beyond demonstrating. She's joined a group of fighters. They have weapons, and I believe they've killed soldiers or police, I can't say because she's hiding and fighting and I don't know where she is," and his voice trailed off and he started again with his stick.

I was beginning to understand. Part of his shame was because he thought his woman was braver than he was. That's no cause for shame. There's always someone braver than you and if that were a reason for shame people would be ashamed all the time. I do think that an Australian man would feel shamed by a brave woman, but White Man never puts himself above women, so I didn't think that was it.

I put my hand on his thigh and gave him a small push. "White Man," I said, "I don't see why you're ashamed. I already said opposing something you cannot change is foolish."

He moved on the bench. His body said he didn't accept what I was saying. I can tell you that it felt very strange to be trying to make him feel better about his feelings of shame on the day I'd planned to put fear into him.

He said, "Yes, but as I said, here I am far away and safe and doing nothing to help and even worse, yes even worse, here I am talking to you about it, you, the man who fought against an army. So there's my friend over there"—he stretched out one arm—"and there's you over there"—doing the same with the other—"risking death and in between"—he hugged himself—"there's useless me, talking, talking, talking."

A lot of movement and not a lot of sense. His voice was heavy with sorrow and also, it seemed to me, with self-pity. We know self-pity. Usually it's a waste, as I thought that White Man's was.

I tapped on his stick with my own and said, "I told you what I think and I haven't changed my mind, but I'll say it again. You've done nothing to be ashamed of."

We sat. I poked the fire. He poked the fire. White Man sighed and shifted around on his bench as if he couldn't find a comfortable position. The hen clucked. The rain had stopped. The children were trickling home from school and the people were coming back from their gardens. Pomalate was filling with little noises and probably had been for a time, but I had been so intent I hadn't noticed.

I decided to go ahead and talk about what I'd intended to, but it came to me that beyond making sure he feared me—in the ways I've been telling you—this talk of doing things or not doing them, of shame, could be useful.

I asked him if he had tobacco and newspaper. We both rolled a cigarette and started smoking. He reached over to the hen at the end of a bench and poked her. She clucked and puffed up.

"Yours?" I asked and he said, "Mine." A hen doesn't know who owns her, and will lay in anybody's house. I said that when the chicks were big Kavibura might trade her strong betel for some chicks. That made him laugh, but his sad face returned.

I said, "Because we've been talking about fighting and killing I'll tell you about something that happened on the trail up beyond Lopali."

White Man put off his sorry look. I'm sure it was because he thought he was about to learn something. We all know that having something new to learn makes him happy. When he reaches for his notebook and pencil, he's as happy as a man reaching for his wife.

I drew on my cigarette and exhaled. I said, "I'll begin, if you want to get your notebook."

He said, "Wait," and went to get it.

When he came back and was ready to write I said, "It was like this. When I was a boy, there was a fight between the mountain men and our people—Wapola and Lopali both. Arrows and spears and knives were everywhere, White Man, and although I was only a boy I was in the middle of it. That fight was so big and confusing that although we killed five of the mountain men, we killed two of our own clan-mates by mistake."

White Man said, "What caused this fight?"

I pushed his thigh and said, "Later. For now I'll say that after my father Kanabi died and was cremated at Lopali, his village, the mountain men came to mourn, and on their way back to the mountains, we attacked them."

White Man said, "I'll wait for you to explain."

I gave him a little push and said, "It won't be hard for you to understand. The mountain men knew there might be trouble, so they were ready. They saw one of our men moving in the forest, and raised the alarm and this takes us to the fight, where men were running everywhere, in the forest and on the trail, as I said."

White Man leaned forward. "Just on a trail like the ones now?" he asked, and his voice was excited.

"No," I said, "not as wide. My elder brother Tanno cut through a garden and there was the mountain man Leau, running away. When Tanno chased him he threw away his spear, so Tanno threw away *his* spear."

"To make it equal?" White Man asked.

I wanted to laugh, but I didn't. I said, "No, so he could run faster, and that's why Tanno did the same."

White Man made a noise.

I said, "Tanno caught Leau and held him. Lunta had an axe and he picked up Tanno's spear and ran up to them. Tanno pushed Leau away"—I made a pushing motion with my hands—"and Lunta threw down the spear and hit Leau in the head with the axe, which knocked him down. Then

Tanno picked up his spear and speared him. Nobody can survive an axe hit and a spearing, so Leau died there on the trail."

"Our old Lunta?" White Man asked, and I said, "He was young then."

I paused, and turned to look at him. "Then I ran up, meaning to take Leau's head."

"You!" White Man said, "A boy!"

I said, "Taking a head, yes, it's called *winato*, we didn't do it often, and yes, I was a boy."

I could see he didn't care what it was called because he didn't write it down. He was looking at me with something like shock, or wonder. He didn't look at me that way when I told him about Uta. I understood. He had no trouble with an adults fighting, but as for a boy—this must have surprised him. And the head.

The day before I wanted to remind him that I was a dangerous man. But after *his* story I was thinking differently about *my* story. I'd known nothing about the Vietnam killings and White Man's shame. But now I did and I decided to tell the story differently.

I said, "Our men gathered around Leau's body. Some of them were shaking, some were laughing, some were weeping. Some did not favor taking the head, even when there was a death to be avenged," and White Man interrupted me, "Your father's?" and I said "Yes, but we'll get to that later. I was the right person to take the head, although this was true of Tanno as well."

I paused. "I didn't take it. I should have, but I didn't."

White Man said nothing for a moment. Then he put down his notebook and took a deep breath and said, "Old One, about the head," and he laughed the kind of laugh people laugh when they're uncertain and said "Why didn't you take it?" Before I could answer he said, "It's odd. I feel I shouldn't be asking about this," and I asked him why and he said because it felt like asking me about sex, or something else people didn't talk about.

I laughed. "I'll tell you," I said, making a motion with my hand, "It's no secret. I stood there wanting to do it, but I had no knife. Everyone was looking at me and all I could think was *I have no knife*, even though I could have made a bamboo knife. I was paralyzed."

White Man shook his head. "Bamboo knife," he said, as if he'd never heard that word before.

I said, "Bamboo knife. I stood, unable to act, while Tanno was offering me a bamboo knife." I paused. "I couldn't take it."

White Man shifted on his seat and said, "But why?" and I said, "Because I'd faltered. Because I lost my chance. If I'd shouted 'Give me a knife!' and someone had handed me one I would have immediately cut off Leau's head. But that moment passed. When Tanno was holding the knife out to me it was as if he was *allowing* his little brother to do a man's job."

White Man said, "I see, yes," and then he shook his head and said, "I understand what you're saying and what you thought, and I can imagine men running and spearing and shooting arrows, but in truth, Old One, I can't imagine cutting off a head with a bamboo knife."

I decided to act as I had about Uta and Kamanai, so I said, "Cutting off a head isn't difficult, even with a bamboo knife. It's only slicing. You're cutting through skin and muscle, although the windpipe is slippery and you have to pinch with your fingers"—I reached over and gently pinched his throat, and he flinched—"and at the end you do have to cut between the vertebrae."

White Man nodded his head, and wrote in his notebook. I don't know what he wrote but I'll tell you I thought he was writing to calm himself. He shifted his feet and reached to the fire but pulled back. He cleared his throat and said, "Ah, how did you carry the head back?"

I laughed, and reached over to push him. I said, "I did what anybody who has to carry something like that does, even you. I went into the bush and cut some broad leaves and wrapped Leau's head in them and tied it with vines."

"I see," White Man said, "Yes, that's what everybody does. Leaves. Vines, yes, even me," and he paused and shook his head. He wrote. I sat, saying nothing. If he couldn't imagine cutting off a head, he probably couldn't imagine wrapping that head up and carrying it home. I thought I'd let him think about it.

After a moment he said, "About not taking the bamboo knife. I suppose it was the same when the Kiap wanted you to kill Uta."

I made an approving noise, and he said, "But it's not exactly the same, is it?" and I said, "Not exactly, but as you've seen, I don't like being told what to do and I don't like being *allowed* to do something," and he nodded his head and was silent.

I was hoping he wouldn't say the thing that didn't need saying, that the black boy standing over the dead body, unable to act, was not unlike the older white boy turning away from a fight. And he didn't.

White Man likes to summarize things, to wrap them up nicely, and when he's doing his work that's a good thing. But just at this point it wouldn't have been a good thing because it would have made him think he understood everything. I was pleased with him for not doing it.

After a moment he said, "And the bodies, what about the bodies? Did you leave them where they fell?"

"No," I said, "the custom was to put bodies side by side on the trail, because their kin would return for them, and there was no reason to make them search for the bodies."

"That's kind," he said, and again he was shaking his head, but writing. He asked, "How many people died, then?"

I said, "Five of the mountain men, and four of us, even though two of our dead, we caused their deaths."

White Man started tapping his fingers on my bench. I don't know that he'd ever stopped moving some part of his body since I started about the head. He said, "So it wasn't even?"

I said, "That's it." Indeed it was even, but I hadn't told him everything.

He nodded his head.

I said, "Perhaps it was a good thing that we mistakenly killed two of our own, because that made the deaths even and we had no more trouble with the mountain men."

I drew on my cigarette and blew smoke out my nose.

"Four against five," he said, "you said it wasn't even and then you said it was."

"Later," I said, although I did think he'd already worked it out. He should have, because that part was simple.

"Yes," he said, "I'll wait. Dead men on the trail, one with no head, even or not even, and I don't know yet what caused the fight." He looked at me and raised his eyebrows. He was seeming himself again.

I said, "White Man, yes. I told you it had to do with my father, but not in a simple way, and now I'll take us to *no one was excused.*"

He said nothing, so I continued.

I said, "It was like this. My older brother Andeko sickened and died over there at Wapola," and I pointed out his window to Wapola, never mind it was a place he saw every day, "and many of us believed it was from sorcery. We did something called *pekupeku,* which happens when there's a death from sorcery. You have to kill someone."

He said, "Someone? The sorcerer? I never heard that word."

I said, "Pekupeku, pekupeku. The word's not used much these days. Yes, the sorcerer, or anybody in the sorcerer's clan or village."

He said, "Anybody?"

"Yes, anybody," I said, "My uncles Nawa and Kuiai believed the Lopali poisoned Andeko because they were envious of him, even though his father—my father—was one of their own. They went to Lopali and the first person they saw was a woman named Madiawa, so they speared her."

White Man started shaking his head again. "Speared her," he said, "Yes."

I said, "Speared her, and when Madiawa was screaming and coughing and dying her little daughter Wanga ran to her. Kuiai grabbed Wanga by her feet and bashed her head against an almond tree until she died. All this took only a moment. Kuiai and Nawa came back to Wapola, and that was the end of pekupeku."

I paused, but he said nothing, so I continued. "With only one death to avenge they should have stopped with

Madiawa, but we and the Lopali quickly agreed about compensation and the matter of Andeko's death by sorcery was put to rest."

White Man looked as though he was trying not to show his shock and unhappiness. I was sure he understood the reasoning, that one person was as good as another, and I was sure he understood me when I said that no one was excused from being killed, but even so hearing about a child bashed to death against a tree in a place he knew was hard for him. Our young people would not be happy hearing the story either.

He spit and said, "The head-taking made sense to me and the idea of pekupeku makes sense to me, but a woman standing innocent in her village, suddenly speared doesn't seem right to me. I have to say."

He looked as though he'd said something he should not have, and in his way he had. He never says "this is right," or "this is wrong," except about his own people.

All I said was, "According to pekupeku she wasn't innocent," and when he said nothing I said "I think you're unhappy because of Wanga, the child."

He made a face and said, "It's true, and made worse because when you came I was sad about the Vietnamese children, but it's also because of the way Kuiai killed her," and I said, "Why?" and he said, "As if she wasn't important enough to waste a spear thrust on, and also because the child did nothing to anybody."

I reached over and took his forearm gently and shook it. "She didn't, but her people killed my brother with sorcery. I've already said that killing Madiawa should have been enough, or killing Wanga but not Madiawa."

He didn't speak, so I said, "White Man, these things happened a long time ago, before the Japan War, before the

Kiaps. It's not the same as what your soldiers did," and White Man said, "No?" and I said, "No, because everyone knew who killed Madiawa and Wanga, and they knew why, and there were only the two of them."

White Man didn't respond.

I thought he might have gone about as far as he could without a rest. He had stopped writing, and I thought he was overwhelmed. I leaned over the fire and pulled a burning stick towards my feet.

I said, "I'll take more tobacco, if you have any, and some of that American newspaper, unless you have something better."

He said, "Here's different newspaper," and took a sheet from under the bench. "This one is called *Rolling Stone*," he said, "Maybe it's a better smoking paper than the other one," and I said, "What's the other one called again?" and he said, "*The New York Times*." I rolled a long cigarette and lit it from the burning stick. Both American papers were bad but the Stone one was better.

I smoked. White Man didn't.

He said, "About your brother Andeko, yes, it's clear. But you said the fight with the mountain people was about your father."

I thought White Man needed more betel. I said, "I'll explain, but let's chew first."

I had some of the especially strong ones Kavibura grows. She likes chewing with White Man, and sometimes gives him a strong one, to see if he'll faint. He always pretends to, then gets up immediately, laughing. He knows better than to joke about how he's been poisoned.

I reached in my bag for one and tossed it to White Man, who put it in his mouth and husked it with his teeth, as we've taught him. Even with our sorcery talk I didn't worry about not licking it all over, the way men like Lunta still do. He pulled his machete from its place in the thatching, cut the kernel into halves, and tossed one back to me.

White Man shifted his body and looked out his window and spit through his floorboards and then turned back to me and said, "I'll speak because you aren't. Vietnam, Old One. What I told you. I don't want to hear about a child's head smashed but Vietnam was worse because it was my people and I feel responsible," and I said, "We're not arguing about which was worse. Certainly it was worse but you weren't responsible," and he said, "I mean, if we could have stopped the war it would not have happened," and I said, "That would be true if you could have, but your people couldn't," and he said, "Not fighting against the war means I helped kill those people in that village and again I'll say I'm ashamed."

Then he sat down and slumped over. He didn't bother getting his stick and poking the fire, although he did spit into it several times and seemed to be paying attention to how the spit sizzled on the burning wood.

When he seemed finished spitting I leaned over the fire, took a stick, and relit my cigarette. I took a deep drag and exhaled through my nose.

I looked at him, cigarette in my mouth, and said, "We won't talk about your shame, because you know what I think," and he nodded. I said, "About pekupeku—these were people we knew. Do you see? There's the difference. I'm talking about the fight and pekupeku both. When Tanno cut off Leau's head and I wrapped it in leaves and vines and carried it to Wapola we knew what we were doing, and who we were doing it to, and when Kuiai smashed

Wanga against the almond tree, the same. That girl was no stranger to him."

White Man said nothing. He nodded his head. Indeed, what could he have said?

I continued. "From what you're saying, White Man, your soldiers in Vietnam wanted to kill people, but they didn't know *who* those people were and they killed as many as they could."

He said, "It's true, it's true."

I picked up his newspaper and hit it gently on his thigh. I said, "Madiawa and Wanga's people understood pekupeku, and it was put right quickly," and I opened the newspaper to those pictures and said, "and so here are your soldiers, and I expect they were saying the same thing we *and* the Lopali said after my father died—Someone will pay for this!"

He turned to me and said, "You mean pay for your father's death?" and I said, "Yes. I haven't finished my story. He sickened and died soon after Andeko did. The Lopali could have accused *us*, the Wapola, of having poisoned *him*, and made pekupeku against us. But they didn't want to, so the Lopali and Wapola leaders agreed to blame the mountain people for his death. That's why we attacked them on the trail, and because the four fighting deaths plus my father's equalled the five they lost, it was made even and there was no more fighting."

White Man was nodding his head and writing in his notebook. He said, "Ah, I see. That's why you said that you and your brother were the right ones to take the head," and I said, "That's it, and I think you know that whether they truly believe it or not, people will find someone to accuse. As we did."

White Man said, "I understand."

Neither of us said anything for a time.

I thought he understood everything I'd told him about balancing deaths, but I didn't think he understood about things can be stopped and those that can't.

"Another thing, White Man," I said, "No one's tried to kill you, and you've never been with men intending to kill people. You don't know how it feels," and he said in a low voice, "I don't, no," and I said, "There's a lust for blood, or a rage and when it spreads among men, more people die than ought to die."

He started shaking his head again.

I said, "I'm talking about groups of men. If it's just one man, he may be able to master this rage, or he may not. When I was young I could not master it, but later I could and I never killed more men than I intended to. And I controlled my group of fighters entirely."

He said, "I understand what you're saying."

I breathed out heavily and said, "Do you? Perhaps. When we were fighting along the trail we had no leader either to push us or stop us, and it was only luck that the right number of men died. No one was giving orders. Certainly no one was counting."

"Counting," he said, "I'm still not used to thinking about counting how many people you need to kill, the ones who aren't excused."

"You aren't," I said, "and you never will be, because it isn't your way."

I was silent and so was he. I could hear him breathing. After a moment I said, "When you talk about this in America, don't forget to say that nobody has been killed here since the end of the Japan War."

He shook his head and slumped down again. He said, "I won't."

It was already getting dark. The schoolchildren had walked by while we were talking about killing children, but neither one of us said anything. I think it would have brought it too close for him. Next door, Siuwako's children were banging on pots and smoke from her cooking fire drifted over to where we were sitting.

I was satisfied.

"Don't be ashamed about not fighting against the war with your Anna," I said, "Let the others carry that fight, White Man. I don't think it's one they can win. The important thing is that you didn't *abandon them*, which would have been shameful. Yes. You decided *not to join them*, which is something else entirely."

He said, "Perhaps," which was probably the best he could do. He'd need time to think about what he'd learned. As for me, the same. I would have thought less of him if he'd said "You're right."

I said, "I'm going to Biroi," and he said, "Go."

I shook his hand, which normally I wouldn't have.

"Good," he said as he shook mine, and I said, "Good."

That night I lay on my bench thinking about what had happened. I was the only one awake, and the fire was low. I've told you that White Man likes to summarize what he's learned, that he likes to wrap things up neatly. I do it myself, and so there on my bench, with my wives snoring, listening to the night sounds and the Wetu, I thought about what this all meant, and whether there was any danger to us.

I had gotten over my surprise about the war in America, and if I'd understood him correctly it wasn't really a war.

In the place Vietnam, yes, a real war. But young people fighting against their government? I saw no way that would affect us, especially because White Man never joined that army and didn't know where the fighters were or what they were doing. So there was no connection that might draw that fight to us. I wouldn't forget how surprised I was but I saw no danger there.

As for my plan, indeed I was sure I'd put some fear into him and—although I never intended this—made him wonder who was the fiercer and more bloodthirsty, his people or mine. Perhaps that gave him something to think about, that his people took no care to make killings even, and ours did. If he did something that caused his people to fall upon us he knew they would not stop until they killed as many of us as they pleased.

And as for his friend Anna and her fighters? I thought they were probably like the group of foolishly-brave mountain men—no guns, no leader, no experience—who came wanting me to tell them how to attack a Japanese camp. I asked them if they were prepared to die. I'd say the same to Anna's fighters.

As for White Man, this Vietnam and Anna business has bound him to me, which is better than having him fear me.

If I'd planned this and made it happen I'd be pleased with my cleverness, but I planned something else. I told him everything I meant to tell him, but what happened in his false cookhouse was not what I expected.

He started us down a different trail by showing me what his people had done and I kept us walking. When I was counselling him about his shame I said nothing I didn't believe.

White Man and I had no secret between us, and now we do. The two of us were like a man and woman who unexpectedly found themselves together in the forest, did what men and women do, and were bound by it. I'm sure that seems a strange thing to say, but that's how I felt it.

White Man couldn't have known that he'd bring us to that hidden forest place where he could expose his secret, and yet when he found himself there, he did. If what I exposed was carefully chosen I exposed it nonetheless, and there the two of us were, as exposed as a man and woman who had taken off their clothes. He won't forget that, and in truth neither will I.

White Man always asks other people about what he's been told. I know he'll ask Lunta about that fight and Lunta will tell him that on that day I did cut off Leau's head, wrap it in leaves, and carry it to Wapola.

MY WHITE MAN

MY NAME IS SIUWAKO. I'm a Hornbill, born into the Biroi clan, Waina lineage, and I live in Pomalate Village.

When the white man Elliot Lyman lived with us, I was his woman friend and his teacher, and that's the story I'm going to tell you. It's a small story, I suppose, not as exciting as those that men like Mesiamo tell, but for all that it's not an easy one. It does have pain and blood in it, but not much danger, if we're talking about the kind of danger that might kill you.

We all taught him different things. I didn't teach him the things that the men did, but I taught him what women know because that's what he wanted to learn.

When he walked into Pomalate Village for the first time, I stayed in my house. I was nursing Nuai, and although we don't hide our infants like some people do, we don't take them out into the direct sun for no good reason.

It isn't good when white people come to our village. They are always after something, and nowadays it's never clear what it is. The old people say that before the Mission came, and before there was a Patrol Post at Boku, when a white man came it was easy to know what he wanted. He wanted workers. He wanted men to go to the other side of Bougainville and work on the plantations. White men never wanted anything else.

Now, there's no way for us to know, because there are different kinds of white men. So when one of them comes to the village, we wait to see what it's all about, what thing the white man wants. There's always something.

Our men deal with the whites. This is because the men have gone out into the towns and other islands to work, and they know far more about whites and their ways than we stay-at-home women do.

This is true even though we women own the land, the houses, the crops, the pigs, the shell valuables, and the children. A man leaves his own people and goes to his wife's village when they marry, and lives there surrounded by her people. Not his.

Does this mean that among us, the women are the bosses? No, it doesn't—but it doesn't mean that the men are, either. It means we cooperate, because if we didn't, how could anything be done?

And so you can see why we women don't feel small or worthless just because when somebody has to deal with white people, it's the men. It's the best way. True, if that white man who has to be dealt with comes to your village, comes and has a house built next to yours, close enough so that if he blows his nose or sighs when he's in his office you hear it, then you have to learn to deal with that white man in your own way.

Mostly I'm going to tell you what happened in my garden or on the trail to it, and there won't be many people in my story except Elliot and me and my children. This story's about how a white man and a black woman became something neither of them had ever been, or seen, or heard about.

That last thing—*heard about*—I suppose has only to do with me, a village woman who doesn't know much about the outside world. I'm sure that in America men and women have different ways to be with one another. But here, there aren't many. Indeed there are hardly any beyond being clan-mates or being married, and Elliot and I were neither of these except, as you'll see, he was in an unusual way both my brother and my sister.

It was four moons before I had my first serious talk with Elliot. I am not talking about passing the time in my cookhouse, or down at the Wetu washing clothes or getting drinking water. I am talking about a conversation where both people speak and listen carefully because what they're talking about is important, where somebody wants to know something the other person knows.

You've noticed I said "moons." Most of us use the pidgin *mun* when talking about the white *months*, which I know from school. January, February, March, and the others. But we women know very well that the white months don't match what *pegia*, the moon in the night sky, does. I suppose the men know, but I don't think they care.

If you're dealing with church or school or the Co-Op, you have to use *months*, but if you're dealing with women's things then the moon itself is the best guide. That can't be a surprise to any woman.

My husband Siro told me that white women bleed with the moon as we do. In Rabaul he worked for a woman named Missus Alice. He knew that if she was bleeding at one full moon, she would be bleeding at the next full moon, and he knew this because, as her houseboy, he knew about the things she kept between her legs when she was bleeding. He had to burn them.

We Nagovisi women don't put anything between our legs when we're bleeding. True, some of the young girls do, because they are modern and the store at Sovele sells the things. I think it's silly. When we older women are bleeding we wear a black wrap and that's enough. Anything that comes out goes into the cloth. Sister Mary Agnes says that white women lose more blood than we do. I think it must be true, because we don't need those things and the white women do.

I'm telling you about me and Elliot and I started with moons not because I like to talk about women and how they bleed, but because it was talk about blood that first made me feel close to Elliot. It was the start of my feeling that Elliot was a friend to me, a woman, and that I knew things he wanted to know, and could talk about them.

I was bleeding, with the new moon. That's my time. I was wearing my black wrap. Siro and I had come back from the garden, and Elliot was at his house. We went into our cookhouse. I sat on one of my cane benches, which I like better than the black palm ones. They look nicer, and they're flexible and pleasant to sit on. So I sat on it, and my blood ran into my wrap and then, although I didn't know it, some of it went on the cane and turned it red. I sat there and then I got up to look after the fire, and Elliot came over to talk.

He saw the blood and said, "Siro, Siro, someone is bleeding, someone has a cut, I hope it's not Nuai or Nema, maybe I should go to my house and get a bandage."

Siro knew what it was and he said, "No, White, you're looking at the moon, and I wonder if you know what I mean?"

Elliot shook his head, No, and Siro said, "White, think hard. Blood, moon…"

And Elliot said, "Oh." That was all he said, "Oh."

I was watching him and I saw he was feeling shame, which was normal because although we don't hide our bleeding, there's no reason to talk about it, either. It's like farts. Everybody farts, but that doesn't mean we always want to be talking about farting. It's a thing our bodies do, and so is bleeding with the moon.

I didn't want Elliot to feel shame for his mistake. He was worried that one of us was hurt and wanted to fix it—what's wrong with that? I did think it was funny, but I didn't laugh.

I thought it was stupid for us to stand around looking at blood on a cane bench as if there was nothing to do but look at it. So I said to Elliot, "Yes, Elliot, that blood there is what you think it is, and now because the men are always telling you about the name of this and the name of that, I'm going to tell you that what you're looking at has a name, and its name is the same as the name for moon."

"Pegia," he said.

"Indeed," I said, "If you see blood like that, you say pegia for those two reasons that Siro said but didn't explain. One is that it's shaped like a moon and the other is that it has to do with women and their bleeding. And now I'll tell you that you can say pegia when you look at the back of a woman's wrap and you see a dark moon-shaped spot there, too."

I could tell he was surprised to hear me talk about this. His eyes widened. He said, "Does everybody say pegia when they see these things?"

Siro started to answer him, but I motioned to him to be still. This was my time to explain, and I was liking it. I told him that it's not wrong to notice it or to talk about it, but that usually there's no reason, so most men don't. And then I said to him, "The men are always telling you men do this and women do the other thing, so I'm telling you that women tease each other about pegia especially if the woman has been surprised and is wearing a light-colored wrap, perhaps even a white one. If that happens, then we'll tease the woman who didn't notice. We'll say, 'Don't you know how to look at the moon?'"

Elliot said, "I understand. I'm happy that you told me this. In America men don't talk much about these things with women."

I said, "I have more to tell you," because I did.

Even now I remember how much I liked what I was doing because it was what Lalaga and Siro and Mesiamo did with Elliot. And it was my first time.

I said, "When I said 'look at the moon' in Nagovisi, the women meant truly 'look at the moon in the sky, to see whether it's reminding you that you're going to bleed soon,' so it really means 'look' in the same way we would say 'Look at what's on my cane bench.' That's true, but it's also true that when we're speaking pidgin, as Siro was, and we want to talk about this kind of bleeding, we say *meri ilukim mun,* which can mean "the woman sees the moon" but usually means 'she's bleeding.'"

Elliot clapped his hands together and gave me a big smile. He said, "That makes me happy," and I could tell that it did, and it made me happy, too. And then he began to ask *me* questions, which made me even happier.

He said, "South Solomons men, Malaita men, they're afraid of that blood. To them it's like poison. They say it's dangerous to men, that if a man comes near a bleeding woman, he loses his power. My question is, do Nagovisi men believe this?"

Again Siro started to answer but again I shut him up. "Husband," I said, "I heard you talking about women and so now it's my time to talk about men." Siro laughed and turned his head away. "I won't listen," he said, "so if White asks me the same question I won't give your woman-answer."

I told Elliot that Nagovisi men didn't care about it, and would never say that it was dangerous. And then I said that just because that was so, it didn't mean that men *wanted* to touch our blood, or have it on them. It only meant that it wasn't important. I said, "A man will not scream and run away if somehow he gets blood on him, even if he doesn't like it. He might say, *giu! giu!* which is what we say when we touch something that seems disgusting, but that doesn't mean anything."

Elliot repeated those words, giu, giu, and said he hadn't known them. Nuai began trying to say them. Then he said he thought he knew the answer already, but if a woman was bleeding, did she try to hide it?

I said, "She wears a black wrap, but women wear black whenever they want to."

"So it's not a sign?" he said, and I said, "No, only a pegia is a sign," and all of us laughed.

And he said, "And are there people who must not know when it's happening?" which is a different question and a good one because I saw that I'd forgotten to tell him something. I was talking about how nobody cared very much, and although that's true, I was so interested in talking about other things I forgot about a woman's brothers.

I said, "Oh, you know that brothers and sisters are not supposed to know that sort of thing about each other, and I forgot to say that a brother should not know his sister's bleeding."

Elliot said, "I wonder if you think you're the only person who's forgotten to tell me something, or left part of something out?"

I shook my head and smiled at him, although I lowered my eyes.

Siro started to laugh again. He said, "I like this very much, what's happening in our cookhouse today. White's been talking to men and talking to men and talking to men and now finally he's talking to a woman and that woman is my wife and it's all because of that pegia there on the bench."

And Elliot said, "Good, good, yes, very good," and I could tell that he was pleased and happy. And I said to myself, *I like this very much, how it makes me feel, that I am somebody who knows things and can explain them properly to Elliot,* but what I said was, "Perhaps Siro will take some water and clean my bench," and Elliot looked at me as if to say, "I'll do it," and I shook my head just enough for him to see. Siro got up and went to the water bucket.

It took me a long time to understand that Elliot wanted to work in my garden. He never said, "Will you let me go with you to your garden and work next to you?" Instead, he hinted, but his hints flew by me like the play arrows children shoot. I thought he was being indirect because he was still learning our language.

Another reason I was slow to understand is that Nagovisi men know very little about gardening. Men do the heavy clearing and other work that takes strength we women don't have, but they don't know how to *manage* a garden. I can't think of a man who does, except Tagilali's father.

So when Elliot kept saying that he wanted to garden with me, I thought he was teasing, the way some men will. I admit that believing that he was teasing me felt good, because I thought he was doing the kind of teasing that happens between men and women who are interested in each other.

No, no. He was never crude. He never said anything he shouldn't have said, never. It's that talking to a woman about working in her garden is the same as saying that they should get married because we Nagovisi say that a man and a woman are not married until they begin working in the garden together. So you can see that when Elliot started talking about working in my garden with me I thought he was joking.

Finally I understood. That night, when we were all sitting in my cookhouse chewing betel and Elliot was playing with my daughter Nuai, he said, "I wonder if I'll ever go to the garden with you."

Then Siro said, "Yes, wife, you should answer Elliot. I think it would be all right, but you'll decide."

"Wait," I said, "I thought you were joking."

"No," Elliot said, "I'm not joking."

I felt stupid. I felt like a small child. I asked Elliot what he wanted to do, and he said he wanted to learn everything about gardening. I was still worried about understanding him, so I said, "Tell me why? I never heard that any white man wanted to learn about gardens before, not even the Didiman."

He said it was clear that Nagovisi was changing, and changing fast. Every year there were more and more babies, every year Nagovisi were planting more cacao trees where they used to garden for food, Nagovisi were planting sweet potato instead of taro, Nagovisi were making money and using that money for things like tinned meat and rice and sugar. He said nobody knew how much land it took to feed people and pigs.

"Nobody knows!" he said, and therefore how could anybody decide whether to plant cash crops or food gardens? Was there enough land? He said that the only way to find out was for him to take his scale and weigh all the sweet potatos that I dug out, and take his tape and measure how much land I used to grow those potatoes, so he could learn how these things all change over a year.

I gave Siro a look that said, "Does Elliot know how hard this is going to be? Is he crazy? Are you crazy? Am I crazy?"

The teaching part, I thought right away I could do that. My mother taught me, my older sister taught me, when it's time to teach Nuai I'll teach her, and so I thought I could teach Elliot by talking to him and showing him things.

Elliot said, "I have to learn what Siro does, too."

Siro spit and moved around on the bench. He kicked the fire, and said to Elliot, "Maybe you didn't notice this, but I don't go with Siuwako every day. If there's no clearing to do, I don't go. Instead I go to our cacao orchard."

Elliot knew Siro didn't go every time I went, so I thought Siro had already decided what he was going to say, and was only waiting for the right time to say it. Even now I'm not sure whether Elliot and Siro had planned what happened that night. In my cookhouse that night with one man kicking the fire, the other squirming in his seat as if he were a small boy needing to piss, and one surprised woman—though less surprised than she had been a moment before—nobody was talking about the biggest problem, which was sex.

We Nagovisi believe that if a man and woman are where they *can* screw, they *will*, and therefore a man and woman who can screw if they want to must never be alone on the trail or in the forest, never mind in a garden house with walls. True, if the man and woman are in the same clan they won't, because of incest, but if they're in marriageable clans then anybody who wants to accuse them of adultery can say "You two were together with no one around," and the couple will have no defense. We've all seen this happen and by that time so had Elliot.

Elliot had already done name-sharing with a Biroi boy, which made him a Biroi, and my clan mate, therefore forbidding us to each other. So the rule about *can screw* wouldn't apply, and we could have walked out unaccompanied. The baby he shared his name with will call me sister when he's old enough, even though we have different mothers, and that meant if Elliot wanted to call me by a kin term, it could only be *sister*.

The first thing—sex between clanmates who don't call each other brother and sister, which does indeed sometimes happen—only makes people angry. The clan brother-clan sister thing horrifies them, disgusts them, and if it happened it would cause enormous trouble even today. In the old days, the two would have been killed.

Making him a Biroi by name-sharing was a way to fit him in and give him some kin. It didn't change his being an outsider who might screw Nagovisi women. The whole thing was an example of the problem we all had: what *was* Elliot's position here? It was easy to say he was both one-of-us and not-one-of-us, but saying that solved no problems. So which would Elliot be? Or I should say, "Which way would *we* be—a woman walking out with her brother, or a woman walking out with a white man?" There never was an easy answer.

If Siro knew about this plan, it meant that he was at ease with having Elliot walking in the bush with his wife. I gave him a strong look. I think Elliot saw that look, because he quickly said, "Siuwako, there won't be any talk, because Nema will always be with us," and that's when I knew that he'd been talking about the problem with other men, probably Lalaga and Mesiamo, and they had explained to him that if there's always a child who can talk about what happened or didn't happen, then it's all right.

I thought, *So they're made a plan about this.* I was annoyed. Had everyone decided what I was to do, and they were now asking me in the same way you ask your child "Shall we go wash at the Wetu?" when you mean, "We're going to go wash at the Wetu."

I reached over and took Nuai and put her at my breast. She didn't want to nurse, but I held her there. I did it to remind those two men who the mother was, and what the gardening was for.

I wondered if Elliot would like studying how husbands and wives fought. If so, I thought, here was his chance.

Those two knew better than to push me on this—once they'd seen that I was not pleased—so nobody talked for a while. Nuai started nursing quietly, and I cooled off. This new idea was an exciting one, and indeed nobody *was* saying, "Siuwako, you must do this thing."

I didn't answer right away, because I didn't want to seem anxious for this to happen. So I gave Nuai back to Elliot and busied myself with the fire. I said that it was an interesting idea but that I would have to think about it. I'll tell you that I had already decided.

Yes, already decided to *do* something with Elliot. That's how I thought about it. *Doing* something besides talking and having him look after my daughter. I thought of many reasons why I wanted to do this thing, but I decided to behave as if it were uncomplicated. If they wanted to pretend it was simple, so would I.

I said, "I'll teach you gardening, Elliot," and he gave me a big smile, and hugged Nuai to his chest, "even if it might turn you into a woman," and he widened his eyes.

Siro gave me an odd look. "Yes, husband," I wanted to say, "Did you start this without wondering whether Elliot interests me? Are you so sure of yourself? Perhaps you should wonder why I said that last thing." Of course I didn't.

Even now I like thinking about the time I asked Elliot if there was any place in the world where people did things for only one reason. He laughed so much that he started to cough. Because he and I were very close friends by then, I knew he wasn't making fun of my question. I started laughing along with him.

I said, "I think your answer must be no," and he said, "Nuai's mother, the answer is not just no, but no no and no again."

At first it was very strange to have Elliot following me around my garden, watching everything I did, asking questions and writing things down. Kneeling down beside me and working with his own knife, saying "Like this? Or like this?" Hoeing. Cleaning. Harvesting, planting.

Everything else we'd done together had been in the village or at the Wetu, but in the garden it was different. Not only having him with me all the time, but getting used to what he wanted from me, which was to do everything in the way I always did. That became easier, but at first it was hard. When I'm working alone, I don't say to myself, "Well, I've done this, and so now I'll go and do that, or maybe stop for no reason, or just harvest some food and go home because I don't feel much like working." I decide what needs doing as I work.

I understood what he wanted, but because he was paying attention to what I was doing I didn't feel as free as when I was by myself. That part wasn't because he was a man, or a white man. It was because I wasn't used to telling anybody what I was doing while I was doing it.

After less than two moons we were easy with each other, almost as easy as Siro and I had been. With Elliot coming all the time, Siro came to the garden less often. Elliot began doing some of Siro's work. At first, heavy clearing was hard for him. He got better, but he never was as good as Siro.

He was always wanting to try the trick of chopping nearly though six or eight trees in a cluster, and then chopping all the way through one, which causes them all to go down with a huge noise, kakatas screaming and flying around, possums running away, leaves and branches everywhere. Children and adults screaming. Dogs barking.

Men love doing this but Siro told Elliot he wasn't ready. He might hurt himself. Elliot knew this, but when it was heavy-clearing time he always asked me if I thought he should. And I always said, "I don't want to write a letter apologizing to your mother because I let you kill yourself."

Adjusting to the stakes he drove in the ground took me longer than two moons. Always he connected them with string and sometimes he left it. I'll tell you I didn't like those stakes. I kicked them sometimes and it hurt.

In a garden, among all the hills and mounds and sweet potato vines you don't think much about where you're walking, because everything around you is soft. It took me a long time to remember to walk carefully where I never had to walk carefully before.

Elliot didn't curse when he kicked his stakes himself. That amused me, but I said nothing about it. Elliot had learned to curse the way we do, and he knew that when he hit his foot it would be all right for him to use bad language, but he never did. Elliot was being careful to make no sexual remarks at all, even curses that most of us will use anywhere.

After a few moons, most of the teaching was finished and all we did was work together. And I liked it. I know I already said that, but I'm saying it again because it was a strange thing. I realized I liked working in my garden with a white man who understood what I was doing, and helped me do it. It was like having a sister.

After his second Christmas with us—not long before he left us—I became aware that something was wrong. I think I was the only person who sensed the change in him, not only because it was a small one, but because no one spent as much time as close to him as I did.

I was working next to him all the time, sometimes so close that our arms brushed against each other. If his stomach made noises, I heard them. Sniffling, the same. Every kind of noise that a person makes, that a person's body makes, I heard and that meant I was used to everything about him. I suppose he was used to everything about me, but I'm not talking about me.

It wasn't from anything he said. He and I were never chattering sisters in the garden, and when we settled into hard work there were long periods during which the only sounds were sounds from the forest, whatever noise Nema and Nuai were making, and the sounds of our tools. My hoe, the sound of the sweet potatoes striking his scale's metal tray, the sound of the old stone adze he found and used to drive his stakes into the ground.

When I watch other people, I can always tell from their movements what their mood is. They don't have to talk to me. I don't believe that's a hard thing to do. Paying attention is all it takes, paying attention and then being able to recognize a change.

What I'm talking about is that sometimes he pounded in his stakes and stretched the cord very slowly, as if it was an effort for him. But it shouldn't have been, because he'd been doing that for moons and when he was himself, he was quick about it and his body moved in ways that said he was happy.

Most days he was as he'd been, but I thought he was having more not-himself days than before. He still had his quick smile, and he never changed the way he treated Nuai and Nema, with patience and care that even some mothers among us don't show.

I thought maybe he'd learned something that was bothering him. Perhaps something about America. I knew he had people in America, at his school, his mother and father, someone named Anna—they wrote him letters and he wrote back.

Siro noticed there were no letters from Anna after January. We didn't know Anna's second name, because all she wrote on the envelope was "Anna," and the address. Siro said that the last letter had no address at all. Only "Anna." Elliot never talked about Anna, so we didn't know who she was.

Siro thought it might have to do with his work. He said we couldn't know whether Elliot was doing the correct kind of work. Maybe Elliot was doing what he wanted to do—because it was clear to everybody, not just me, that he liked what he was doing—but it wasn't what he was sent here to do. And somebody in America was angry about it, and Elliot knew he didn't have enough time to do something completely different.

I thought that might be true, but I thought more likely he was troubled by something here. I could think of something that might be upsetting him. I was thinking about the young girls. I was thinking that he might be feeling more desire for them than was good for him. Nagovisi men feel desire and I never thought whites were any different.

Perhaps one of the girls let him know that she'd go into the forest with him, and his desire was disturbing him. If the women around you never tease you or give you reason to think that they'd like to go into the forest with you, then controlling your desire is your own affair and for Elliot it shouldn't have been difficult.

I was always careful never to do anything, give him looks, or move my body in any way that said to him, "I'm willing." But young girls aren't careful, and I thought maybe Elliot saw that and was bothered.

I was thinking that when the girls sat with him, they were always conscious of his being a man, a white man, a white man they could tempt into the forest if he would cooperate at all. Surely it was exciting for them to think about it. I didn't blame those girls, but if that's what was causing the change in Elliot, I wanted them to stop.

I will admit that I was jealous, at that time. If I was jealous of the way the girls were with Elliot, my jealousy was because in truth he was much closer to me than he was to any of them.

In one way I wasn't different from those girls. We all knew he was one of us and not-one of us. He was a Biroi Waina, except he wasn't. We women who were his clan sisters felt the power of our own beliefs—power that gave us completely new feelings when we thought about a man we called *brother* but we knew was *not* our brother. And that meant any desire we felt was exciting, dangerous, and also shameful.

And he was a man who could be sexual, but wasn't. It was clear that it wasn't his nature that kept him away from women. In this he was like many priests. With some priests it's clear they like women, girls, but they fight it and they control it and they don't break the promise they made to God, to Jesus, to Mary. With others, it's clear they are not interested in women.

When all you know about a person is what you see, then it's not surprising when you think about that person as a man first. When you don't know his ways, he's just a man to you. I think that's true of everybody. And because this person you don't know very well is just a man to you, you think of his maleness and when you think of that, how can you not think about him sexually? That's all you know! That's how I thought about Elliot at the beginning. I think that's how all the women did.

Then you get to know that man, to know him very well. You spend time with him, you do things together, you talk. When that happens the man-part of him becomes less important. He begins to be a person and he becomes part of your life. The fact that he's a man is less important.

And finally after a long time as not-only-a-man, it can happen that the person begins to seem like a sexual man to you. Again. When it reappears it's more powerful because it's emerged from something deeper.

That's what I'm trying to make sure you understand. You need to understand it, because when Elliot and I circled back again, our story became more complicated.

In those days I wondered how a white woman's life differed from mine. I wasn't interested in the lives of white women in the towns, like Missus Alice with her servant Siro. The Osileni women used to tease me about having Elliot for a servant, and sometimes my younger sister Inalamada teased me, saying that it was like looking in a mirror, because a white woman had black Siro for a servant, and me, a black woman, I had white Elliot for a servant. I never thought it was as funny as she did.

I really wanted to know about the lives of women living in their own places. That's the kind of life I wondered about—food, clothing, houses, children, which person does which job, who owns what, how it's different for young people and old people.

In those garden days, wondering about white women, my thoughts sometimes drifted over to imagining being his wife. What I'm saying is that sitting and dreaming in the garden house, or walking home from our garden at Wanawo-nami on the trail I knew so well I paid no attention to it, I imagined myself as Elliot's wife in America. Not in Nagovisi. America. And because that was impossible it was a safe thing to think about.

I wasn't a young girl. I could never leave Siro, leave my children, my clan, my village. So that's why it was safe for me to think about Elliot that way if I wanted to. It wasn't the same as thinking about going into the forest with him. I never daydreamed about that and I never nightdreamed about it either. All women have thoughts like that, so I don't understand why I didn't but I was glad of it.

I was young then but even a young woman knows that when you start to think about something that's possible—a good thing, a bad thing, it doesn't matter—you start planning for it. No matter how much you think you're not planning that thing you must not do, you are.

And I had better say that when I thought about going to America with Elliot, I thought of this Anna woman. I imagined being so far from my home that it took days to travel there, and when we arrived Anna rushed to Elliot at the airport shouting, "Who's this woman with you?" And what then? I couldn't turn and walk home.

If Anna said, "Elliot's mine!" then what dream-speech would come from my mouth? "No, he's mine?"

What a thing to think about! It was frightening but exciting. In any case there was no Anna claiming Elliot here.

In the time I'm talking about, something happened in our garden that shouldn't have happened, but it did. It's something that shouldn't have made trouble, but I think it did.

Elliot went down to the little stream that borders our garden. I was working on the far side of the older planting areas, away from the little trail to the stream, hoeing, when I decided to go down to the abandoned planting area and have a look at what remained there. When I got there and started looking, my wrap was slipping off. I turned away from where I thought Elliot was, and opened it up. I stood there a moment with it open, because it was hot and I was sweaty and the little wind on my legs and belly felt good.

And he was standing there looking at me. He'd used the old trail. He looked steadily at me. I don't wear a top when I'm working, so he saw all of me. He didn't turn his back, pretending he hadn't seen what he saw. But he did look away as he walked past me, headed for where he'd been working.

I finished rewrapping and went back to work. I didn't know whether this was the first time something like that had happened to him. I didn't ask. It's a common thing, really. Your wrap needs adjusting, you turn towards where you think nobody is, open it, and rewrap. If there's somebody you didn't know was there, it's only an accident. A small thing.

When we started home from the garden he didn't seem himself. His movements were slower when he swung Nuai up onto his shoulders. They were the movements of a person who wants to demonstrate that he's doing something properly. I hadn't seen him do that for a long time.

On the trail he was carrying Nuai as he always did, and she was sleeping and waking up and playing with his hair, all the things she normally does. And he wasn't treating her differently except that he seemed to be reaching back to settle her on his shoulders more than he usually did, as if he thought she might not be comfortable and safe.

Elliot was leading. We walked by Lopana's wife's garden and he was in it and he gave our greeting, which is, "Where are you coming from?"

Elliot could have said *Kasino kitai*, 'from the garden,' which says nothing about whose garden it is. He could have said, *Wakam kasino kitai*, 'from her garden,' but he didn't say that either. He said, *Nekam kasino kitai*, which means 'from our garden.'

And he used the dual form. If he'd used the plural, that would have included Siro. But he didn't. Perhaps that was what came into his mind, nothing more. I knew he thought of it as his garden and my garden and therefore ours, but he'd never used that form before.

I was wondering about what he'd said, and wondering why he'd returned to that way of moving. And I was wondering whether he'd been troubled by what he'd seen. As I've said, he should not have been, but as I've also been saying, he didn't seem himself.

A little way past Lopana's garden, I decided to talk. I thought I'd praise him, so I said that unlike Lopana, he'd do well gardening for himself because he could do everything. I said I didn't know any other man who could. And then, without thinking, I said he knew the woman's part better than the man's.

I still remember how surprised I was when he asked if that didn't make him a woman. I didn't expect that. I should have, because I knew from Siro that white men don't like being compared to women. And I was thinking that the business with the wrap was unimportant.

I wanted to talk about what he *knew*, not what he *was*, so I said that to me he was both. I should have known he wouldn't let that go.

He asked "In between?"

Now I was going to have to explain what I meant. I knew I hadn't meant *in between* because I'd never questioned that he was a man. I tried to think of what I'd felt that made me say that thing I was wishing I hadn't said. It was because I was thinking about what he *did*, rather than what he *was* and that's what I said.

His answer was, "I don't understand," and I heard unhappiness in his voice. I can still hear it. I didn't think I'd said a difficult thing. Perhaps he was not wanting to understand me.

I couldn't think what to say. Then a thought came to me the way an eel swims towards you in the Wetu and that thought-eel almost wiggled past me.

Now I laugh at myself for thinking about eels, because *walama*, the eel, is sacred to the Biroi, and we must not touch it or eat it. But the thought seemed like an eel and I supposed it was all right to grab a thought-eel.

I said, "I mean…in our garden, when I need man's work done, you work like a man, and when I need woman's work done, you work like a woman." That was the best I could do.

He stopped and turned towards me and when I saw his face it showed hurt surprise, as if he'd understood what I said and didn't like it. Not exactly anger. Surprise.

Nema walked into his legs, and fell down on purpose. Elliot squatted down and picked him up and held his hand. Nuai didn't wake up.

Before he turned and started walking again he said, "And when I'm not with you?"

Another thought-eel. "Then…I think it depends on who you're with. Yes. Maybe you aren't anything until you do something. No…maybe you're both until you do something."

I started towards him, thinking I might touch his arm, but he turned and started walking, still holding Nema's hand. That was good, because I shouldn't have been touching him along the trail. We might be seen. Perhaps he realized that, or perhaps he didn't want to be near me.

We adult Nagovisi don't touch each other much. We don't hug, as the whites do. We don't hold hands. If a man and a woman have their arms around each other, bodies close or touching, they're doing something no one's meant to see.

"It's hard to think about," I said to his back.

We walked without saying anything until we were beyond Osileni, where it started to rain, first lightly, then heavily.

The next thought-eel was a slow-swimming one and I grabbed it. It twisted but I held it fast and it didn't get away. I said, "It's hard to know what you are because you came to us like something floating down the river…unconnected."

When I said that—*unconnected*—I saw what those eels were. I'd been talking about two things at once. One was Elliot's nature, and the other was how he was with people, his own or us.

He slowed his pace and I didn't change mine and that brought me nearer to him. I said, "We've never seen you with your own people. And now you've lived with us a long time so *we* know the Elliot-who-lives-with-us, but I don't think he's the same as the Elliot-who-lives-in-America, who's the one *you* know best."

He said, "That may be. But what about the me who's myself, not with anybody, only a man?"

I sighed, because I wanted him to know that this was difficult for me. I said, "I don't know who that man is because I've never seen him except on the first day. I've only seen you with us. But if you're asking about your body, then certainly I know you're a man," and I thought he said "Good," so I continued, "I never thought you were a woman, although you grew your hair long like a white woman's. You never said why."

He raised his arms over his head and waved them around. Nuai was holding onto his hair, so it didn't matter. I think that meant he was annoyed, but I couldn't see his face.

He said, "Why? You never asked. I didn't want to look like the other whites."

That surprised me. I thought it might be because he didn't think any of us could cut his hair for him.

I said, "Elliot, I meant to say a simple thing. I know what you are in your body, Elliot, I have eyes, and I hear your voice, I have ears, but to me you aren't *only* a man. That's all I'm saying."

I paused in case he had something to say, but he was silent. He kept walking along the muddy trail in the rain, holding Nema's hand, carrying Nuai, wet with water running down, just like any Nagovisi man, except for his hair, which I couldn't see anyway.

I walked faster because I again had in mind to touch him and by then I wanted so much for him to understand me that I didn't care who might see us. I caught up to him and reached up and put my hand on his shoulder, which I had never done before. He stopped, and I held his shoulder and turned him around, facing me.

I looked straight at him, but he looked away, as if to tell me I shouldn't be doing this, and indeed now that I had put my hand on him, had turned him, I was afraid. Not of being seen, but of perhaps starting a thing I hadn't intended. He knew about touching and not touching. All I could think to do was repeat myself.

I said, "Elliot, my friend. I'll try again. I *know* you're a man." I swept my arm up and down, careful not to point at one part of his body but slowly enough to make sure he wouldn't miss that I was talking about his entire body.

I said, pointing straight at his chest, "I'm pointing at a man's body but I think of you as man *and* woman. It's because of what you've learned. That's what I'm telling you. That's a powerful thing. Before, you were just a white man, but now you've learned to be many people. Man or woman—too simple. Can't you understand? That's too simple. In this you're like Mesiamo, and if you don't see that and if it doesn't please you then I can't think what else to say."

He gave me a long look and then he nodded and turned around and started walking. All the while, Nema was tugging at his hand because he wanted to get home and be dry and eat something.

At our house he handed Nuai to me. She didn't wake up. I said, "You stopped talking. Are you angry? Don't be angry at me. Did I make you sad?"

"Nuai was asleep," he said, which was true, and "I didn't want to wake her," which perhaps was true, and then, "I understand what you said." I thought that last thing was true, and I still do.

I can't tell you why I didn't see something else that rainy afternoon, which is that for all my talk about how he should understand how *I* saw *him*, in truth I was pushing *him* to think about *me*—not as his sister, not as his garden partner or his teacher, but as a woman. And this not long after he'd seen me unclothed, although I had not meant for that to happen.

I was pushing him to treat me as if I were a white woman, as unconnected as he had been when he arrived. I'll tell you that it took me a long time to realize this. By the time I did, he was gone.

Late one afternoon it was raining, the way is usually does. Elliot splashed over to our cookhouse, settled down near me, and said that he wouldn't be going to the garden the next week. I was surprised and quickly unhappy. I thought maybe he didn't want to be there with me, or didn't want to be walking back and forth, and I thought it was maybe because of what we talked about. But I was only unhappy for as long as it took him to ask Siro to help him map every day for a week.

He said it was more important to finish all the mapping than to follow the garden, and then he asked me if I would take care to remember what areas I harvested, so he could measure them later.

I said, "Remember? I've done that all my life," and he said, "Ah, I've insulted you," and I laughed and said, "No, no. But what about the weighing?" and he said he would have to give up on the weighing for that week. I shook my head and picked up a small sweet potato and tossed it at him.

"I haven't watched you use your scale?" I asked.

He said, "Truly?" as if he'd never thought of it.

I said, "Truly," and then I told him that if I weighed every potato, as he did, and did all my work as well, that it would be dark every day before we got back from the garden. I said, "If I can weigh all the potatoes from one heap at the same time, that would be easy," and he said, "You would do that for me?" and I lowered my voice and imitated the way Siro sometimes talks to him, and said in English, "White Man, you help me I help you," which was not very good English, but it was good enough.

I said, "Elliot, you cut bush for me, you slash undergrowth, you make fires," and then I thought I would tease him a little, so I continued, "although you have to make them with matches because you've never mastered firesticks," and he laughed and said "Oh, so true, Grandmother," and I said, "Even though you have forgotten how to use our kinship terms, I'll work for you because you work for me."

Siro laughed and said, "And you, wife, you said a thing that doesn't need saying," and Elliot said, "So did I," and we all laughed, including Nuai, who was by then on Elliot's lap. She laughed because we were laughing. That's the way children are.

He said, "Will you really do that?" and I said, "Yes, truly. I'm not joking. I've watched you do it, but as I said, I want to put all the potatoes on the scale at one time, and then I'll write down that number for you. You can show me again about the thing you slide, to make sure I understand."

He said, "You know your name will be in my book, and Siro's, and Lalaga's, and Mesiamo's."

Siro said, "Too many names. No room on the cover," and Elliot said, "Wait," and went to his house.

He came back clutching a book to his chest. He brushed the water from it and pointed to the cover and said, "See, there's only one name here." Then he opened it, turned some pages, and showed us one with a long list of names.

He said, "This is what we do. Here are the people who helped with the study, because no one can do a study like this alone. The cover is for the person who wrote the words in the book, but this page is for the people who taught him and helped him. Mine will be the same, and your names will be on it."

I liked hearing that.

Because I wanted to know more, I asked, "And your people in America, will they be on this page also?" and he said, "Yes, my teacher, and my mother and father, and others who have helped me."

I had to say it. "And your friend Anna?"

He asked, as if to avoid saying anything, "Anna?" and I said, "Yes, we all know you have a friend named Anna, and if she didn't want us to know her name she should not have written it on letters that anybody bringing you your mail could read," and he said, as if he'd never thought about it, "Oh. Yes, it's true about the names on the letters. A friend. But in the book, no Anna, I think."

Siro said, "You had better make sure you tell us every place you might live in America. Otherwise we won't be able to write you." Siro had already written every address on a sheet of paper he kept locked in his metal strongbox.

"Yes," I said, "my writing is as good as Siro's. You'll see," and he said, "I'll see," and then he closed the book, said if he didn't start his rice boiling we would have to feed him, and left. It was still raining, and because I always liked seeing him walk under our eaves, quickly jump over the ditch between our houses, and hug the walls of his so he wouldn't get wet, I pretended I had to do something so I could move near the door and watch.

When I turned back to the fire, Siro made a noise and said, "Why did you say anything about Anna?"

I acted as though I needed to think for a moment, although I didn't. "Why not?" I said. "Many months with us, and from the beginning pretending we didn't see letters with a woman's name on them? Can he be thinking nobody noticed? Impossible," and Siro said, "True, but I didn't like the way you said it," and I said, "What can you mean?" and he said, "If it was me, I would have found a way to make a joke, to tease him, but you asked him straightaway, the way you could ask about his teacher or his mother," and I said "What of it?"

He stopped for a moment. He did look annoyed. He said, "Because that says to him that you've thought about Anna so much that you're used to thinking about her even though you've never used her name. You didn't even say, 'Oh, what about this person who writes you letters,' and then say her name wrong, or pretend you couldn't remember."

I said, "Husband, I don't tease Elliot about women," and then after a pause I said, "about his women or our women either, no, if I have something to ask I ask it plainly. Why are you acting as if you don't know that teasing is dangerous?

He said, "I was surprised. That's all," and then he said it was true that Anna had not been writing letters for a long time, and that made me think again that perhaps what was bothering Elliot might have to do with Anna. But there was no way to know.

What Siro said was true. I had become used to thinking about her. I'd been wondering if he'd go to Anna when he left me. Yes, by then I was thinking leaves *me*, instead of leaves *us*.

As for Anna—had she stopped writing because they were angry at each other? Or she went with another man? Maybe they did the same kind of work and she went to study some people somewhere, and it was impossible to write. Maybe she was in the big bush, the far last place, somewhere with no radios and no airplanes and no Kiap to bring bags of mail. There was no way to know.

During that week I've been talking about, I did Elliot's work for him. It wasn't difficult to work his scale and it wasn't difficult to write the numbers. It wasn't difficult to be there without him, but Nuai and Nema seemed to miss him.

It *was* difficult to walk home carrying the food and Nuai also. But I remembered that before Elliot I'd gone to the garden and back many times without Siro, each time carrying Nuai myself, although she was much smaller then. It was only that I'd become used to not carrying her, and not worrying about where Nema was, because Elliot looked after them.

During that week I became aware that Elliot was more important to me than I'd recognized. I'm admitting that even though it makes me sound as though I hadn't been paying attention. Had he been only a puff of wind or a trickle of water or a new moon until I had to do without him and then he turned into gale or a flood or the full moon?

Somebody comes to you, somebody stays, somebody goes. That person passes through your life and there's nothing wrong with thinking of that passage as brushing shoulders. There are many people who pass through a Nagovisi life and although most of them are Nagovisi, some aren't.

I think many of us thought of Elliot as the man who came to us, brushed shoulders, and left. Elliot could have passed through my life, and Siro's, and my children's, and everybody else's, in that way. Brushing up against, pleasant, good feelings, happy memories, nothing else.

I've tried to think about what changed that for me. Part of it was what happened on the trail, yes, those hard questions. But what happened during the week he wasn't with me was stronger.

As I was working with *his* tools in *our* garden I found myself looking around for *me*, who should have been just over at the other side doing *my* work with *my* tools. I'd catch a motion in the corner of my eye and I'd think it was me, although it was always Nema or Nuai. It was a strange feeling, as if my spirit had left me and was working by itself.

I began thinking that by doing Elliot's work I was somehow becoming him. But it wasn't that simple. Certainly I was still myself. Those were my hands working his scale, in the dirt pulling out sweet potatoes, loading the basket.

I tried to understand what was happening to me, and all I could think was that doing his work was *joining* us in a way I couldn't easily describe. The first day the feeling settled into me I felt a kind of peace. On another day, a kind of joy. On another, a kind of acceptance of what I knew, that he would soon be leaving me.

I will tell you what came into my head: *We are one person.*

I will tell you that thought was strange and powerful and came into my head not as words, but as a thought needing to be named, and I named it *weareoneperson.*

In the garden I could close my eyes and it would come into my head. One word. I can't explain any better than that.

When Elliot finished his mapping week with Siro I said to myself, *He's mine again.* I remember feeling happy to be back on the trail with him. Going to the garden or coming back it was the same. We were on the trail, in motion, and it seemed to me that if we stayed in motion there would be no end to our time together.

His first day back we were walking easily down the trail. Nema was happy, running ahead and running back to Elliot with whatever he found along the trail. He had something in his hand with legs that waved, and Elliot said, "Better not be a spider," and Nema said, "It's a poison spider!" and Elliot waved his machete and said, "I'm ready!"

Nema ran off again, saying "Only a beetle, only a beetle," and I saw that was true.

I said to Elliot, "Do you know the story about Rhinocerous Beetle and Firefly?"

He did, so I said we should tell it to Nema, each taking a part. He said he ought to be Rhinocerous Beetle because he was big and ugly. I laughed.

"All right," I said, "I'll be Firefly."

He called to Nema and said, "Your mother and I have a story to tell you. I'm Rhinocerous Beetle, like the one you caught, and she's Firefly."

Nema's eyes got big and he stood, waiting. Elliot said, "We'll walk while telling it, so you get between us," and Nema did.

Elliot said, "One night I was flying in the forest with Firefly, and I said, 'Firefly! Aren't we lucky to be flying along by my light?'"

Elliot walked faster. Nuai was pulling on his hair.

I said, "Stupid Rhinocerous Beetle! It's my light!"

Elliot said, "No, you're stupid. Even a child as small as Nema knows it's my light."

I said, "Not as stupid as you are," and we talked back and forth like that. When Nema turned to me, his eyes were shining. I don't think he'd ever seen us playing together. No one ever had, and that's the truth.

When it was my turn again, I said, "Rhinocerous Beetle, you lying, stupid bug, see what happens when I turn off my light."

Elliot said, "Go ahead! Go ahead! Oh no! Oh no! I can't see!" and he pretended to crash against a tree. Nuai wasn't afraid. She was laughing and screaming "Stupid! Stupid!" and hanging onto his hair. Nema was yelling "Look out, Rhinocerous Beetle."

Elliot turned away from the tree and put his hands in front of his face and said, "Now my nose is all smashed and my mouth is ruined and it's sticking out in front," and I said, "That's how Rhinocerous Beetle got his mouth!"

Nema ran and crashed against Elliot's legs, and fell down laughing. "It's true," Elliot said, "your mother—oh, Firefly— lights our way."

Nema got up and took Elliot's hand and in this way we walked to our garden at Wanawo-nami.

It had turned into a hot day, and clear. I thought it wouldn't rain until late afternoon, and we'd be headed home by then. Elliot was doing light clearing, a task he liked.

I started digging out potatoes. I was using my machete, holding it by the blade as we all do, working in an area Elliot staked long before. I wasn't paying attention, and as I pushed my machete forward, probing for sweet potatoes, its point struck a stake, my hand slid down the blade and I was cut.

I gasped and held my hand in the air. There was a lot of blood. I made a noise and then I called "Elliot!" He turned to me and saw what had happened.

He stuck his machete in the ground and started towards me.

"Don't leave your knife like that!" I said, "It's dangerous," and I started to laugh. We Nagovisi don't cry from pain very much, but I think laughing isn't very different from crying.

"Look what I've done," I said, and he said, "What did you hit?" and I said, "Your stake."

He made a face. He curled my fingers into a fist and wrapped his hand around mine, which surprised me. I wasn't gushing blood but it was flowing.

With his other hand on my shoulder he turned me towards the garden house. I could have gone by myself, but indeed I was confused. It was sudden, it hurt, and here was Elliot holding my hand tightly, moving me along with his other one. Even in pain I felt the strangeness of it.

In the garden house I sat on a bench. Nuai crawled over to me and climbed up. When Elliot opened his hand, there was mine, dripping blood.

"I squeezed your hand so it wouldn't bleed as much," he said, "Can you move your fingers?" and I moved them before saying "Yes." It was painful.

He said he would stop the bleeding by bandaging the cuts. He used his small knife to cut strips from the bottoms of his underpants and laid four on the bench, and then another which he cut into pieces.

"Dakta Bagarap taught me to do this," he said, "the time Tagilali was cut."

He put away his knife, and knelt in front of me. He had the drinking cup in his hand. "Wash out the dirt," he said,

"Ready?" and I said "Ready," and he poured the water. That hurt more than the machete did.

He said, "One by one, and I have to make them tight," and I reached my hand out to him. He said, "It will hurt when I tie them," and I said, "Go ahead," and indeed as he put a small pad on each and tightened and knotted, it did hurt. I sucked air through my teeth, but I didn't make any other sound. When he pulled the worst cut tight I couldn't help reaching out and grabbing his forearm and squeezing it.

"Aaah," I said. I couldn't help that, either.

He looked up from what he was doing and smiled at me and gave a little laugh.

"Sorry," he said, and I said, "It's nothing."

When he raised my hand up to look at his work he was gentle. He released my hand and I put it in my lap. Nuai had been watching. "El, El," she said, and held out her hand, fingers spread, so Elliot cut more little strips and tied them on her fingers.

When Nuai's fingers were play-bandaged Elliot said "Can you finish?" but without waiting for an answer he turned away and said "I'll do it for you."

I said, "Let me try," but when I followed him over to where I'd been and picked up my machete, the cuts were too painful. I started back to the garden house, but he said, "Stay and tell me how many to dig out."

I thought that meant he wanted to talk, because he didn't need to be told. Nuai toddled over to sit with me. I didn't know where Nema was, but he never goes far, so I wasn't worried about him.

Elliot started working.

He said, "I'll be you, the way you are when I'm here."

I made a noise.

Then he surprised me. He said, "Because if I'm man and woman both then I can be you *and* me," and I said, "But not at the same time!" and he said, "Not at the same time, no. Sometimes man, sometimes woman. Who knows which one?"

I do, I said to myself but I only gave a small laugh because I wasn't sure where this kind of talk might go.

He kept digging with his machete, pulling out potatoes and heaping them up to be weighed. I said, "If you don't care whether you're man or woman I'll ask you questions about Americans and you can answer like an American man or an American woman, as you wish."

He made a noise.

I was still wondering about Anna, so I said, "I don't know when Americans get married, if they're young or old. Is there a rule?"

He stopped digging and put his machete across his knees. He said, "It's different in different places, if we're talking about laws. Not young. If we're talking about when most people get married, I suppose between twenty and about twenty-five."

He started digging out again. The soft *shhhs shhhs* of his machete sliding into the dirt was the only sound, except for birds in the forest.

I said, "So, about your age. And your friends, your school friends, what about them? Are they married?"

He said, "Only a few," then he stopped digging, and cleared his throat. "Not many. Everybody is studying hard and has no time for marriage," which surprised me.

I said, "No time?" Perhaps American marriages were more different from ours than I knew. With two people doing what needs doing, there should be more time, and that's what I said.

"Ah," he said, "I'm being unclear. Usually students like me marry other students. Both of them have to study hard, and so who will do the marriage work? How can they look after each other when they're both busy?"

"I don't know," I said, thinking he'd explain more. "Couldn't they divide the tasks, the way we do?"

He said, "I suppose, but it's easier not to marry. If you live alone there's no need to worry about the other person. You eat when you want to, sleep when you want to, study without worrying that your wife needs your help."

He returned to digging out.

After a time I said, "You can't live that way here, or you won't have food," and he said, "I have my bag of rice, but if I don't harvest for you there won't be food in your house, so yes. Never mind my bag of rice. I understand what you're saying. That's what you've taught me," and I said, "It seems that today you're looking after us."

I had an urge to say "like a husband and father," but I didn't because I thought he was probably thinking it himself.

He didn't respond. He put his hands in the dirt he'd loosened and started pulling out potatoes. "Look at these," he said, holding one up, "for second-plantings, they're large," and I said, "Show me," and he tossed it over to me.

"Don't forget which heap it came from," I said, tossing it back, and then I said, "You're correct about how large it is, Elliot. Truly, you understand," and as if we hadn't moved away from the man-woman talk from the other day, hadn't put aside what he *was*, he said, his voice suddenly heavy, "Like a woman, is what you're saying."

I answered quickly. I'd started this and I wanted to stop it.

I said, "Elliot. Woman or not-woman isn't important because *understanding*"—I said that word louder and harder than the others—"isn't male or female. It's not a thing like a body, and you have it, it's what you have from working so hard, harder than those unmarried students in America you're telling me about."

He only made a throat-clearing noise and started again with his machete, but he was using it differently now, returning to that way of moving I'd seen before that worried me. I couldn't think how we'd gotten from happy Firefly to this. Even my wound should have lightened him, because he dealt with it so skillfully.

I gave Nuai a little nudge and gestured towards him with my head, when he wasn't looking. I wanted her to go to him, because she makes him happy. She came up behind him and tried to put her arms around him. He was startled and jerked, and she fell to one side, surprised, but she didn't cry. He turned, put down his machete, picked her up at the waist and put her on his knees.

"Nuai, Nuai," he said, "Nuai fall down!"

She looked him in the face and held up her bandaged fingers and said "Mother! Mother!" and wrapped her arms around his neck. He put his arms around her. I thought nothing of it, until I saw his back heaving and when he turned I saw tears glistening on his cheek. Not sweat, tears! I was shocked.

Nuai meant "bandages like Mother's," but Elliot must have thought she was calling him *Mother*. I heard him say, "Not your mother," and then he gave a great sob and said, "Someone's father." He held Nuai tight and she put her head under his chin and turned away from me and I heard her little voice say, "Crying."

We sat. Around Elliot and Nuai there were vines but I was sitting on dirt in the open. He was hugging Nuai and rocking back and forth, not looking at me. I didn't want to say "What are you talking about?" because he hadn't been talking to me.

So I waited.

Nuai peeked at me and waved bye-bye. He must have felt her move but he didn't look towards me. Whatever caused this was inside him, so I thought *weareoneperson* and said "Tell me."

I could hear him swallowing. He coughed. He wiped his nose with the back of his hand. He turned towards me, stretching his legs out in front of him and slid Nuai down into his lap. He kept one arm around her belly. He looked at me but said nothing.

I waited.

I thought how I'd always liked seeing them together. It pleased me very much to see their skins change together: Nuai was darkening, and so was Elliot. He was brown and she was black but their skins together were beautiful to me. Their skins should have reminded me of how different they were but instead they spoke to me of how close they were.

I wanted to say "Tell me" again, and I wanted to say "I'm listening," but I didn't say either thing. I was afraid that if I pushed him, he would control himself. I was afraid he might turn away, saying it was nothing, and I would never learn what *Someone's father* meant.

So I sat in the sun, my hand hurting, my daughter in Elliot's lap, waiting. I calmed myself. A cockatoo flew across the garden, yakking. I wanted to say we should go into the garden house, but I didn't want to interrupt whatever he was thinking. *Elliot, tell me, tell me.* I sent those words to him without speaking.

I was sure I would hear something different. Something in all ways different from what he'd told everybody about his life and how he was in America. And it came to me that this might be the source of his unhappiness, of what I'd been seeing in him—not a great secret like the ones the old people thought he might be keeping, but a simple one about men and women and children.

Nuai was quiet. I could heard Elliot breathing.

Finally he cleared his throat and said, "Anna."

I cleared my throat. "Anna."

He wiped his nose. He said, "It's not a new thing, about Anna, but this is"—he swung his hand around in an arc, pointed to my hand, held Nuai's, rubbed her stomach with the other—"this, what happened here, I thought, it felt to me…" and his voice trailed off.

He seemed surprised by his emotion. I didn't want him looking for an escape, so I said again, "Tell me," and then I said his name, and then without thinking I said, "Because we're in our garden."

He sighed a big sigh and rubbed Nuai's back. He said, "We are. Even so it's hard to talk about this. Maybe it's dangerous, or foolish, but I will." He stopped for a moment. "You said I was man and woman to you."

I nodded, *Yes*, hoping that we weren't headed back to that.

He said, "Now *I* say to *you* that you are many people to me, not just woman, and I am many people to you, as you've said. Today we walked to the garden, woman, man, children. Like a family."

I said, "We did."

He said, "Today we played with Nema on the trail, then you cut yourself, and I bound your cuts and made-believe with Nuai and then I came out here to do your work as well as mine, and I was so many people," and he waved his arm around, "I thought, truly this is my family but Siuwako isn't my wife and never can be, and Nuai isn't my child, and I became more and more confused, and then sad, and I started thinking about Anna," and he tugged at some sweet potato vines, pulled them loose and put them on Nuai's head, which made her giggle, but he wasn't laughing and I knew he was preparing himself for something, "and Nuai came to me and said *Mother, Mother* and it was like the bamboo water tube spilling over or a pot boiling over or the rain so heavy you think you can't breathe and you choke even though nothing's choking you, and I cried."

I felt a rush of emotion. Talking about how I could never be his wife? Exciting. Maybe dangerous. I thought that talking about Anna would be safer, so I said, wanting to push it away from me, "I can understand, yes, but about Anna—are you missing Anna and these things made you miss her more?"

He said, "Missing her, yes. But what made me sad was bigger than that, and I'll try to tell you." He looked away and said to the ground, "Some of it will make me ashamed."

I said again, "We're in our garden." I didn't know what he would say but I knew I would never shame him.

He said, "I told you Anna was a friend. We were students, but as I've said, had no time for marriage. We never wanted to marry but we wanted each other, so sometimes she slept at my house and sometimes I slept at hers. You know what I mean."

I said, "I do," but I was sure there had to be more.

He cleared his throat and coughed. "When I came here, she wrote me letters. As you know. And I wrote to her."

I said, "The letters stopped. Is that it? Did she run away from you?"

He sighed a huge sigh. "No. Yes. They stopped, and that was very hard. I was sad. There was no one I could talk to."

Elliot started pushing his machete in and out of a heap. I thought he was making up his mind what to tell me. Then he started. He said that around Christmas, a letter came from Anna. He picked up his mail at Bereteba and started walking home, looking at the letters. He wanted to save the Anna letter for last.

He said, "This is how it was. I crossed the Iada and climbed up our side and when I got to the demon Topegina's place I opened the letter. I wasn't trying to read it at Topegina's place. I was trying to wait as long as I could." Then he was silent.

I thought he was avoiding saying what was in that letter but he started again, "I opened it and the first words I saw were, 'Elliot, I'm pregnant.'"

When I heard that I gasped and put my hand to my chest.

"No!" I said, and Elliot said "Yes! Yes, and it was lucky I was alone because like you I was so surprised I said it out loud."

I said, "You said 'No?'"

"No," Elliot said, "I said 'Pregnant, what? What?' as if asking the question when I had the answer in my mouth would take it away."

I said again, "Tell me."

And he went on. "I stopped on the trail and read the letter out loud instead of thinking the words in my head, because if what she said was only in my head perhaps it couldn't be true. I heard my words as if someone else was speaking them. After I read it I could only say, 'Ah, ah.' I knew nothing of it and there I was reading, speaking that she was pregnant and about to have the baby and I looked at the date on the letter and it was a month old."

I said, "And that was all?"

"No, no," he said, "There was another letter." He paused. "This will seem strange to you."

"Tell me," I said.

He told me about the place where unmarried women went to hide and have their babies, so as not to shame their families. I was surprised because I never heard of such a place. I said, "An unmarried woman who has a baby—this is shameful in America?"

"Yes," he said, "usually. Sometimes not. Usually yes, so the girls go where no one knows them and have their babies. And they give their babies away so that where they live, the people never find out."

How could the people not find out? It wasn't the time to ask about it. So I said, "Give it away? Never see it again? That happens in America?" and he said that it did, but only for women who had no husbands and were ashamed to raise a child without one.

I was saddened. Giving your baby away, and not knowing who took it or where it went. That was very hard to think about.

I said, "That was the first time you knew, then, the letter?" and he said that it was. "And she was truly pregnant? And you're the father?"

He shrugged his shoulders and hugged Nuai to him. "She never said, 'You are the father.'"

I said, "Did you count the months?" and he said, "Yes, but she didn't say when she'd give birth. The months said that it could be true. I wrote her and asked. I think you can imagine how hard that was."

I said, "I can. And this was Christmas or New Year?" and he said it was, and I said, "An Anna letter came in January. Is that the one you're talking about?" and he shook his head and said, "It was, yes. You know everything," and I made a motion with my hand, "Not everything. Did she get your letter?"

He shook his head and said, "I don't know. I told you I was thinking *yes, no, maybe*, waiting for a letter, and it came in January. I thought she would write about the birth, but all she said was that the baby was gone. She never saw it."

"Never saw it?" I was shocked.

He said, "Never saw it, never saw it," and rocked Nuai back and forth. "She asked for medicine and slept and when she woke it was gone and she didn't know if it was a boy or a girl. She didn't give my name as the father. She never said, 'It was your baby,' or 'You are the father.' She only said that she didn't tell the government it was my baby."

I said, "Oh, Elliot, my friend." It was a terrible thing, what Anna did. If Anna had been in the garden with us I would have cut a ginger stalk and danced and threatened her with it, to show my anger.

Elliot said, "When I read that, I cried out 'Ah, ah,' even though I was in my house and could be heard. Then I spoke quietly. I said, 'I'm somebody's father.' I felt all the air go out of me. I collapsed onto my bench. 'I am nothing,' I thought, 'I am the father of nothing.' And I couldn't talk to anybody, not even you."

Sorrow made it hard for me to speak, but I said, "It's true. You can't have that kind of secret with me." I paused to think about what I'd just said. "But now you do."

He made a little gesture with his hands and sat quietly. Nuai stood up and started playing with his hair.

I said, "Anna?"

He said, "In the same letter she said she was going to a new town, but she didn't name it, and she said she wouldn't see me again. She said that at the birthing place she used someone else's name. But even if I find her, she knows nothing about the baby, my child, so I'll never see it. If it ever tries to find its mother or its father, it will fail."

Now I couldn't speak. There was more than I could understand. Running away? Baby gone, Elliot's the father but he'll never see it and never see Anna again?

I thought of him alone in his house holding these terrible things in his heart. It made me so sad that I started crying.

After a moment I said, "You have Nuai," and then he was crying again, but more freely, saying "I have Nuai," and Nuai was playing with his face, saying "El, El," and we were still sitting in the open, in the sun and again I thought *weareoneperson,* which helped me control my weeping. I got up and went to Elliot and took hold of his arm and pulled up a little.

"Come," I said, "there's too much sun for Nuai. We'll sit in the house and drink some water."

Elliot stood up and put Nuai on his hip. In the garden house we sat and cooled off. My hand hadn't stopped hurting. He said he'd go and quickly finish digging out, and we could go home.

He filled my basket and brought it to me. I slipped into the carrying straps but I couldn't adjust them with one hand, so he faced me, put his hands under the straps, and did it himself. He never had put his hands on my chest before. Indeed it was only the back of his hands, and he did it not to put his hands on me, but to help. Even so his closeness and touch went to my belly and stayed there.

I can tell you that that didn't make me want to go into the forest with him. I am telling you that it was impossible to sit with Elliot, and see him holding my child as if she were his own, weeping for a woman who ran away from him, for his child he never saw and never will see, feeling his pain and my pain from hearing this, and then have him touching me, and not understand that the feeling in my belly was what *weareoneperson* meant.

I knew it then and even now I know it.

When we came into the open at Tutueo and headed along the wide trail toward Osileni, Elliot didn't speak. We must have looked as we always had, except for my bandaged hand. Anybody seeing us would have thought, *There they are again, heading back from their garden.*

No one could know what we'd learned about each other there.

You can see that *weareoneperson* comforted me so long as no other woman claimed Elliot. But what of Anna, who surely had thought of Elliot as hers? Perhaps she still did, but I'd never know.

What Elliot and the child might mean to her was completely beyond me. I would never see Anna. There would never be a way for me to enter her thoughts. Thinking about her was like thinking of a stone that contained knowledge or understanding that would make everything clear, but that could not be cracked open.

I thought that for Elliot it was no different, for all that he knew Anna's ways, that he held her. That he knew her voice, her smell. They did what men and women do but when she threw aside her baby and ran away, she became as much a stone to Elliot as to me. He had letters and memories but although he could read and remember he would never learn anything new.

In this he and I were the same.

What Elliot and Anna did was only a small part of what men and women do, perhaps the smallest part. As for the rest—what was there?

Did they look after each other? No.

Did they make a life? No.

Do they have a child? No, I thought, and I almost spoke it there on the trail where my white man could hear me: *No they do not have a child.*

A little farther along the trail, holding my hand to my breasts so as to lessen the pain, it came to me that Elliot was also wounded, wounded as surely as I was, as surely as if he'd been in a knife fight, or speared. It wasn't important what wounded him. What was important was how I might bind his wound as he bound mine.

I am telling you I had no idea what to do.

Everything I might do if he were my husband, I couldn't do. I couldn't hold him. Putting my hand on his arm as I had when he bound my wound was as far as I could go, and I wouldn't have that chance again—not along the trail, not openly in the village, not in my cookhouse, not in his false one, not at the Wetu.

I couldn't go to him.

I couldn't say "Come into my arms and weep," as I might to a child or another woman.

All I could do was let him have as much of Nuai as he needed, and as if I'd spoken and they both heard, she wrapped her arms around his head and he reached over his shoulder and rubbed her back.

Coda

You're slashing Hawaiian vegetation with a "Crocodile" machete, the brand Solomon Islanders call *pukpuk*, and it's all coming back to you. You're in a patch of your dead mother's yard, a hundred feet by fifty, right at the end of the driveway. From your childhood you remember *Monstera*, *Cordyline*, *Cestrum nocturnum*, and an ornamental plant you can no longer name. It's all covered by creepers and a sullen dark-green vine you don't recognize. Everything's growing wildly in clumps and heaps, because nobody's cared for this patch since your father died.

At first your body didn't remember how to do this, but after an hour you've loosened up. You have to hack and slash and pull away the overgrowth before you can see the structure beneath. Then, maybe late in the afternoon, you can start the fine work.

A rooster crows next door, there aren't many cars on the road that runs beside your mother's house, and the Wailuku River is up because of the rain last night. You can hear it plainly.

Your arm goes over your head, you smell your sweat, and that opens the gate to other odors. You realize with pleasure, delight really, that the combination of slashing and heat, the saps and juices on you and the close quarters of the area you're cleaning have made you smell the way you used to in Nagovisi, on Bougainville Island, thousands of miles from here. The sounds were already with you, your motor memory has awakened, and now with the smells you can believe that you're working in a Solomons garden, perhaps your favorite, Wanawo-nami.

You start imagining that when you're done you'll walk back to the village laden with food, your friend Siuwako's little daughter on your shoulders, and after you go to the river and wash you can sit with somebody you like and chew a little betel and talk about things that might turn out to be interesting.

If you were in the village you could tell how you spotted a pukpuk in Garden Exchange, the store where in the nineteen-fifties your mother bought a wooden-handled castrating knife, which she used to cut and shape tree fern trunks for her orchids. When you lost your Boy Scout pocketknife she gave it to you. You carved your name in the handle and you still have it, the blade no longer gracefully curved, straight-tapered instead like a dagger from a half-century of the whetstone. The Nagovisi called it your *small knife.*

So here you are, slashing vegetation with your pukpuk and thinking about wars and killings, because it's just been reported that a Solomon Islands revolutionary named Harold Keke has killed six Anglican Brothers on the Weather Coast of Guadalcanal.

You've never heard of Harold Keke, because the wars and truces and flareups and uneasy peaces you've been following have been on Bougainville, four hundred miles to the north of Guadalcanal. On Bougainville the war's gone on for longer and there's been more carnage, and Bougainville's where your heart is.

You read about Harold Keke and the Anglican Brothers in the Honolulu newspaper that's flown to Hilo in the pre-dawn darkness, you've seen postings about it on the Internet, and in the very early morning you heard about it on shortwave radio, direct from the Solomon Islands Broadcasting Service, reported in South Solomons pidgin.

Nothing you know helps you understand why Harold Keke first killed one Anglican Brother, and then killed the six others who came to see if their brother was dead, and take away his body if he was. That's not like any of the Bougainville killings you've been told about.

During the crisis there, groups of fighters killed other fighters or Army soldiers or were killed by the Army or thrown from helicopters, and yes, there were murders and extra-judicial killings but so far as you know, never a group of peacemakers going to get one of their own and being slaughtered for their trouble.

You feel as though you're betraying your Bougainville friends by following Harold Keke's war, because it has nothing to do with you or your past or for that matter your present, except that you were in Keke's territory once, that wooden-handled castrating knife in your pocket, and Keke's killings are all over the news and Bougainville's aren't, because nobody's killing anybody on Bougainville just at the moment.

You're still chewing on the Anglican Brothers business because it makes no sense to you. The lunatic charismatic leaders in the Solomons *you* know about show great respect for religious people, and you've heard nothing about religious wars in the Solomons.

The last time you went to Bougainville and worried about encountering juiced-up young fighters who might be hostile to white strangers, you were advised to start out by saying *I greet you in the name of Our Lord Jesus Christ.* And you decided that if it came to a test between your beliefs and your life, you would betray your beliefs and declare that Jesus Christ was your personal savior.

Here in your dead mother's patch of vegetation, you're trying to hang on to the mystery of Harold Keke and the six Anglican Brothers. You want to keep it with you. You can't understand it so you're letting a phrase, a droning chant, run around in your mind:

harold-keke-killed...six-anglican-brothers...why-why-why
harold-keke-killed...six-anglican-brothers...why-why-why

It's a mystery, so it makes a good chant. It's English, but that's all right, and not from Bougainville, and that's all right too. It's a strand, sometimes braiding itself with your Bougainville strands, and sometimes splitting itself off in the same way you're slashing and slicing the jungle you're in, sometimes pulling apart vines, sometimes gathering them together the better for slashing.

You don't want an empty mind, even though you're in a zone, even though you're doing Zen cutting and have become one with your machete.

Thick growth everywhere; motor memory lets you pull handfuls of vines with your left hand as you slash with your right. Your fingers are an inch from where the sharp blade strikes but there's no danger because *you remember how to do this,* and by now you're doing it well. It's all coming together: chant, strands, memories, vines, sharp edge, action.

When you slow for a little slack time you hope that Harold Keke killed the Anglican brothers quickly, and didn't torture them. Thinking about executions makes you think about a tape recording you made thirty years ago, in which a Bougainville man named Mesiamo tells you in his high-pitched whispery voice how he killed starving Japanese soldiers.

He tells you how he approached them one by one as they searched for food they could steal from the native gardens, and offered to show them where it was. He would feign fatigue, a harmless fool bewildered by the fighting, and when the soldier relaxed and put aside his weapon Mesiamo would take out the hatchet he had concealed, and kill him with it.

He would take the soldier's weapon, and search his kit hoping for grenades, because in the little guerrilla army Mesiamo raised there was an excellent grenade thrower. Then he would drag the body into the bush and leave it.

He told you he always struck with the flat of the hatchet, so that when the body was found the other soldiers would think it was an accident.

That seemed unlikely to you, but you didn't press him on that point.

He was fast and strong, deadly, and he kept his people safe during the fighting.

You're remembering how he finally allowed you to record his voice, having for months refused to be taped, which you thought might be for spiritual reasons, but finally he said it was because he didn't like to think that after he died, people might hear his voice and cry.

You said nothing, but thought there were some whom his death would relieve, since he was still feared as a fighter and sorcerer who, with the war over and the Japanese gone, might find new enemies.

He never told you why he changed his mind about the taping, and you could not see how to ask him.

You eventually came to love him; there's no other word for it.

When you returned to that village thirty years later, in the dead of night as it happened, you shocked the young people who had come a hundred miles down the coast from Buka with you, they told you this later, by veering off the trail into the cemetery at Wapola where you knew he had been buried, by walking to where you knew his grave would have to be, and saying to him in his own tongue, "Mesiamo, I've returned."

And you sobbed a few sobs at the sound of your voice saying his name, speaking his language, but not so loudly that the young guys could hear over the shrill insects and the Wetu River. You knew they would be afraid to approach Mesiamo's grave at night.

Nobody ever asked you what you had done in the graveyard but you knew them well enough to know it would be much talked about.

In the tape, he's telling how he saw the Japanese execute two Nagovisi, and you can be heard interrupting him asking if they beheaded them, and he says, *No, they shot them.*

They shot them suddenly, and the leaders gathered as witnesses were so shocked when Japanese handguns were quickly put to the heads of their friends and the triggers pulled, blowing the men's brains out onto the trunk of the coconut palm they'd been tied to, that they screamed and fell down. Some fainted. The blood and brains splattered on the trunk were washed away by rain, but the two bullet holes stayed as warnings.

After the Japanese defeat, the palm was felled and burned. You knew Mesiamo betrayed one of the men so as to deflect suspicion from himself. He did not tell you what witnessing the execution of someone he had betrayed to his enemy felt like.

When Mesiamo was telling you the story, the famous image in which Colonel Loan blows out the brains of a Viet Cong suspect with his revolver during the Tet Offensive of 1968, yes, that same year you first went to the Solomons, flashed into your mind. The image seemed repulsive and yet compelling; when you saw it on television you immediately understood you would not forget it, just as you have never forgotten No, *they shot them.*

In the clearing you've made your feelings are as tangled as the aerial roots of the *Monstera deliciosa* you're grubbing out, although at least your tangles lie along a single path. Why do you feel differently about Harold Keke than you do about Mesiamo, who killed more men than Harold Keke has? Mesiamo's victims were not all Japanese soldiers.

You feel certain of the difference, you know it in your bones, your heart, but if closely questioned about it now, you would have a hard time explaining it, which is why it seems good to be attacking tangled roots.

You begin thinking about the trail, the overgrown pathway that leads from your old work to your new, from what you did with your old pukpuk to what you're doing with your new one. On Bougainville, your old one and its work were about food and shelter, serious matters, but here in Hawai'i the new pukpuk and the new work are only making up for neglect, improving the yard, keeping you busy. You aren't producing anything. Your new pukpuk is a landscaping tool.

You remember that once, in Nagovisi, you started to the other side of the island, carrying your pukpuk as everyone always did. You didn't notice that the other villagers weren't carrying theirs. They stopped you and told you to take it back to your house and leave it, because even though it was all right to carry it in Buin, a bushy town where some women walked with their breasts uncovered, you were going to the white town Arawa and the Panguna Copper Mine, where it wasn't.

In those places, they told you, whites sometimes got excited by the sight of men with no work to do walking around with pukpuks swinging from their hands, and they would get even more excited to see a white man they didn't know carrying one.

It was best not to excite the whites.

It was best to avoid explaining anything.

You did as they wanted you to, but complained *It's only a tool.* They told you, *To us but not to the whites. They think* pukpuks *are weapons.*

You could not have known, and neither could those men have known, that within two decades pukpuks would be used as weapons, that spearguns of the kind you had used in the Wetu River would be launched at people rather than fish, that waterpipes and scrap metal would be forged into crude shotguns to be discharged at soldiers who would return fire with automatic weapons, that captured grenades would be thrown, and that thousands of Bougainvilleans would die.

You couldn't have known that, but the Bougainvilleans in your old village believed you *had*, that you had the gift of prophecy, that you had seen what would happen and had warned them. When you returned you were told to your surprise and consternation that you had predicted the carnage, and that it had unfolded as you said it would.

You were stunned, and asked in what manner you had predicted it. A young fighter quoted you: *Once you understand what the copper mine has done to you, there will be trouble.*

You did remember saying that, but in your mind that was not the same as predicting a revolution, great destruction, and the deaths of eight or ten thousand people, some of whom were your friends.

And yet it *had* happened, and people believed *you* were the one who foretold it.

It was hard to know what to say.

Hard to know what to do, back in your village, almost an old man, uncomfortable being treated with restraint, even fear, as a seer.

Uncomfortable with the deference shown an elder.

Uncomfortable having young people come to you saying *Tell us about Mesiamo*, as if you were the only person who knew him.

Uncomfortable having a woman you didn't recognize greet you saying *Once, when I was little, I saw you.*

No one had ever treated you as an elder and prophet before, and you did not know how to behave appropriately.

So you did as you'd done years before: chewed betel and ate sweet potato and taro and bananas and attempted but failed, as always, to make the garden fire by friction.

And you worked in your old garden's dirt with your old garden partner Siuwako, which gave you great pleasure, but you couldn't work with Siro because he was dead, and you chewed betel, but not with Mesiamo, because he too was dead, and you sat and talked and talked with Lalaga about everything in the world, and you ate your meals in Siuwako's cookhouse and she wanted to know different things than the others did, and you told her, and you both wept.

One day you helped butcher a pig with the cheap Brazilian Tramontina machete you had been forced to buy because the store in Buka, where you landed in a jetliner rather than a roaring DC-3, had no pukpuks. The shopkeeper said he couldn't get them any more, and then he said he was surprised that a white man was looking for a pukpuk. When you told him you had lived in Nagovisi he spoke that language to you, and you responded in kind, which gave you both great pleasure.

Two years later in Hilo, part of your delight in finding the pukpuk was that it was hidden beneath a heap of Tramontinas on the shelf in Garden Exchange.

The pig would be eaten at a feast in your honor on the day you would formally announce the new school everybody already knew you were paying for. You had not been a rich American when you were there before, but you had money now, and you had brought five thousand American dollars to give them.

At the ceremony you got to listen, for the first time in your life, here you were nearly sixty years old, listening to people making speeches about *you*. The speech makers talked about your mother and how she raised you correctly and allowed you to come to them.

One speechmaker declared that although it was said you did not believe in God or Jesus Christ, this might not be true because you were behaving as a Christian ought to, but should it be true, then surely your goodness came from your mother.

The young fighters you encountered were thoughtful revolutionaries rather than juiced-up killers, so you returned safely.

Later, you flew back across the Pacific to see your mother. You showed her a videotape of the speeches, and although profoundly deaf she understood that the speakers were praising her son, because she could see you decorated and sitting among them and the speech makers turned to you often. And you shouted into her ear, *They're praising you too*.

In the videotape you're dressed nicely, heading a procession of villagers, preceded by a panpipe band, marshaled on one side by a man who was called the Chief, which was a surprise because in the old days of this matrilineal society there was no such thing as a male Chief, and on the other side by a small woman a few years older than you, who one day long ago in the big bush had tempted you, seemingly prepared to betray her husband, the excellent grenade thrower.

Before the procession she decorated you with the wealth of her clan, your clan, the fiber-strung red shell disks called *wiasi*, traded up the Solomons into Bougainville, decades, even centuries before. And when you bent over towards her so she could slide the thickly coiled strands, some silky and polished from generations of handling, some new and rough, slide them over your head and onto your neck you, the clanmate she had incestuously tried to seduce, you smelled her breath peppery, her lips red from betel, you looked into the one eye, merry as always, still inviting, and not into the black vacant socket of the other, lost in the fighting.

You saw her breasts now withered and lying flat against her chest, and you wished you had yielded to her.

When it was your turn to speak, you asked that the school be named for your mother, who had been a teacher as you were a teacher, and as the villagers had been teachers to you long ago when you were an unformed human being, too young to know very much.

And then because you had not been speaking their language for thirty years you stumbled and meaning to say *You taught me to become a man*, you said *You taught me how to make men.*

You tangled up the verbs *to become* and *to create*, and to your surprise nobody laughed or mentioned it afterwards. You first thought this might be a sign of respect, but decided instead it was evidence that during the long hot afternoon the villagers tuned out of the speeches, proving once again the psychic unity of humankind.

Your mother's yard guy comes to mow the lawn, backing down the driveway in a giant pickup truck as if he owns the place. He steps down from his truck and sees you emerge from the jungle with a long machete in your hand, and you can tell that he's startled.

You've never met; you've been paying him by mail, writing checks from your mother's checkbook, signing her name because you've been avoiding the hassle of telling the bank that she's dead.

You sense that to him, you don't belong here, so you don't wait for him to come to you. You go over to him, shake hands, talk a little, and then return to the jungle to cut bush with your machete. He gets on his riding mower and cuts the grass.

When he's gone, having promised to return and haul away your cuttings because on the island of Hawai'i in 2003 burning yard trash is forbidden, you return to your work, which has become less work than glorying in the power of motor memory.

Your arm has remembered and remastered that slight pull-back at the exact instant your wrist angles the blade when you're cutting a stem and it goes *ching,* which to your hungry ear is a beautiful sound, the sound of a small thing perfectly done.

Your wrist recovers the correct motion for cutting trees too small to axe, pukpuk angling down, then twisted straight in. On your backstrokes you never tangle the machete in the vines. Your breathing is regular and deep; your heartrate is up but steady, as if you were on a long run, completely in control of your effort. You have settled into a pace you can maintain for hours.

You're making nice moves on the small trees you're cutting, twenty or thirty of them, the trash tree your mother always called by its Latin name, *Cestrum nocturnum,* Queen of the Night, an exotic jasmine, an invasive species brought to Hawai'i from the Central American tropics many years ago.

As a boy you were allergic to their flowers. Keeping them cut back so their night vapors wouldn't constrict your throat was your job because in the day you could fell them without incident.

They have beautiful white berries, which are poisonous, and the flowers release an intoxicating scent that at night drifts into your mother's room, where you've been sleeping. Queen of the Night no longer disturbs you but even so you feel compelled to cut them down, perhaps because your father is dead and your mother is dead and this is now your own house and yard and trees, not just in a manner of speaking, but legally, and you can cut them down if you want to.

You're getting used to the idea that this house, the one you grew up in, the yard where your mother sometimes made your life miserable, making you work, that it's *your place* and nobody else has any claim to it and that clearing this little patch, Queen of the Night and all, has made it the only place in the world that is truly yours.

And you're getting used to the idea what you're doing is returning you to your childhood as well as to your young manhood. Merging the wheezing boy cutting *Cestrum nocturnum* with the young man cutting Bougainville bush and the old man again cutting Queen of the Night seems as though it should be easy, but it isn't and this bothers you.

After a few more trees you realize this isn't something that needs *making sense of.* It's something that *is.* Vines, tendrils, roots, trunk, leaves. Tangles. Blossoms.

And now as you near the end you're remembering the last time you cleaned this place, when you came back from the Solomons with your first pukpuk, the one that you could pack in your bag and carry through Customs because in 1974 an edged weapon in your bag troubled no one.

Your mother asked you to cut everything back, and you did. You didn't think about your life while you were slashing. All you felt was satisfaction in transplanting what you had learned on one tropical island to another.

The Nagovisi also taught you gardening firecraft so after you cut you built a banked fire which dried out and reduced to ashes a giant heap of cuttings, even though it rained and they were sopping with it and their own juices.

You kept the fire burning in the rain for two days and your mother and father were impressed, and praised you. But you shrugged off their praise, believing you had failed to reveal the heart of your pukpuk and fire work, sure that it seemed to them a delightful parlor trick rather than a sightline into another way of life. And fearing you might slip into lecturing them, you couldn't bring yourself to explain. So you let it drop.

Now there's no one left who can peer along that sightline from this end with you, and from the other end, only Lalaga and Siuwako peer back.

You look down at your shoes. You've ruined your marathon shoes, shoes you left in Hilo when your mother was dying and you knew you'd be making trip and trip again, and didn't want to pack them each time.

You left your shoes here and instead of running in them you've been wearing them without socks, in the mud and sap, trampling bleeding *Monstera*, painted by the Night Queen's drizzling white.

Your mother is dead, reduced to ashes, the friends of your heart on their distant funeral pyres the same, and you're still slashing, chopping, aiming always for the sweet sound of a clean stroke, perfectly executed.

Acknowledgments

No one has been more important to me during this project than Ruth Thompson. Her writing counsel and loving support have meant everything to me. I could not have succeeded without her.

Irving Feldman knows the debt of gratitude I owe him for many years of friendship, advice, support—and criticism.

I thank Ann Pancake for her insightful, patient reading and suggestions.

Carol Flynn, Stefan Kiesbye, Ginia Loo, Stacey McGirr, Michael Ritterbrown, Judy Slater, and David Tarbet read and commented on some or all of the stories.

The Nagovisi anthropologist Simon Kenema, PhD, not only read and commented on the manuscript, but helped with translations and clarified some ethnographic material for me.

The year 2019 marks the 50th anniversary of my walking into Pomalate Village, not knowing what to expect, but hopeful that the Nagovisi would allow me to live among them, and teach me. They did, and they still do.

My gratitude to the people of Pomalate, Biroi, Osileni and Wakoia villages and the Biroi, Bero, and Lavali clans is enormous, but perhaps greatest towards Nebura, Tevu (d. 2000), Nuai (d. 2016), Mesiamo (d. 1976), and Lalaga (d. 2010).

I'm especially grateful to Karinaba (d. 1990s), Papanuba (d. 1990s), my namesake Don Kanai, Takawai (d. 1980s) Taliau (d. 2009), Otoloi (d. 2009), Joe Musa and his wife Elizabeth, Big Nuai, Tang, Nicky Koiropa, Peter Kobua, Peter Siana, and Peter Chanel Lovio.

And I have to mention my dozens of interesting and engaged Nagovisi Facebook friends, who keep me not only up to date, but on my linguistic and cultural toes. Knowing that Nagovisi have read my book gives me enormous pleasure. I'm still getting used to being considered one of the *pagau* (elders), but I like it very much.

I'm also grateful to Shelley Aronoff, Sean Beaudoin, Lisa Brothwell, Rae and Jim Burchfiel, Becky Cooper, Martin Danahay, Veronica deGrieff, Anthony Doerr, Ronlyn Domingue, Bill Engelbrecht, Carol Clark Erwin, Gail Fischer, the late Toni Flores, Duke Haney, Gloria Harrison, the late Norma Kassirer, Pat and Laurel Leone, Piet Lincoln, Brad Listi, Ed McClanahan, my sister Gayle Mitchell Lambert, my late parents Neva and Glenn Mitchell, my late uncle Don Kilolani Mitchell, the late Margaret Dukore Mitchell, Zara Potts, Kate Reilly, Trudy Stern, Caitlin Sullivan, Edith Turner, Donna Wierzomeski, Karen Wiley, Michel Wing, Sarah Willis, Rolf Yngve and Irene Zion, for general advice and encouragement.

For inviting me to read portions of this material in public I thank John Ahjudah Barr (Portales, NM Arts Council), Carol Flynn (Tufts University), Stefan Kiesbye

(Eastern New Mexico University), Perry Nicholas and Jennifer Campbell (Just Buffalo/Center for Inquiry Literary Cafe), Deborah Reed-Danahay (University at Buffalo), ryki zuckerman (Earth's Daughters Gray Hair Series; Wordflight), Lori Hettler (The Next Best Book Club, Goodreads), Joyce Kessel (Villa Maria College, Buffalo), Talking Leaves (Buffalo), Peg Alford Purcell (Why There are Words, Sausalito CA), Michel Wing (Books on Stage, Cloverdale CA), Jennifer Douglas (The Brooklyn Cottage, NY), Zara Potts (Radio New Zealand), Pegasus Books (Berkeley CA), the Hilo Public Library, Basically Books Hilo, and the Society for Humanistic Anthropology.

I nod to the academic custom of acknowledging support for the research on which some of these stories are built by thanking Harvard University's Department of Anthropology, the National Institutes of Health, the Australian National University's Research School of Pacific Studies and its New Guinea Research Unit, and the ethnographers Jill Nash and the late Gene Ogan.

GLOSSARY

Aid Post: a government medical station, staffed by an Aid Post Orderly, known commonly in Melanesian pidgin as *dakta boi*. These men were trained about to the level of a practical nurse, and were skilled in many medical techniques. A single Aid Post might service from a few hundred to perhaps a thousand people.

Banoni: the Austronesian-speaking group on the coast to the west of Nagovisi.

Betel nut: the fruit of the betel palm *Areca catechu*. Chewed with betel pepper (the fruit of the vine *Piper areca*) and lime powder, it's a short-acting stimulant and appetite suppressor. Chewing produces copious red saliva. Chewing betel is an important social interaction.

Big Man: a classic Melanesian leader whose power and authority are earned by his demonstrated political, economic, judicial, and military prowess. It is not hereditary. In Nagovisi, they are called *momiako* and can be female, though they are overwhelmingly male.

Boi/boy: Melanesian pidgin/English for "native man." Can be used as *kanaka* (below) is but is potentially more insulting if spoken by a white. Use of pidgin *boi* isn't always insulting when talking pidgin, but is very insulting if used in an English sentence. It's also used for "workman," in which context it's less insulting. Nagovisi will use it, when speaking pidgin, in a casual or joking sense, as Americans might use "guy" or "dude." An example: *boi Siwai emi bin spak nogut tru na boi Nagovisi ibin paitim het bilongen* (the Siwai guy was really drunk and the Nagovisi dude punched him in the head).

Boku Patrol Post: the colonial administration outpost for the Nagovisi Census District, which is now called the BANA area. Boku in fact lay well outside Nagovisi, at the Siwai border, on the Puriaka River. There was a good-quality airstrip near Boku.

Bougainville: with Buka, the northernmost of the Solomon Islands chain. It lies between 5° and 6° South, and about 155° East. It is a mineral-rich volcanic island with a 2013 population of around 200,000. During the time of these stories, its population was about 100,000. See references in *Exploring Nagovisi* for more information.

Buin Town: the town at the southern tip of Bougainville; in the time of these stories, it was the only commercial center accessible by road. It was the Sub-District Headquarters, and had an airstrip and a surf port (Kangu).

Bush kanaka: see *Kanaka*

Clan: Nagovisi are divided into matrilineal clans, descent groups traced through women, said to be descended from a single woman or set of sisters. Clans are grouped into *marriage groups* or *moieties*, Hornbills and Eagles; you must marry someone in the other group. Nagovisi clans are further divided into *lineages*—named subgroups of a clan, descended from a known woman. *Example*: Siuwako belongs to the Hornbill moiety, the Biroi clan, and the Waina lineage. Her husband Siro belongs to the Eagle moiety, Bero clan, Tolesina lineage. Siuwako could have married a man of any Eagle clan—for example, an Eagle Lavali Pakawoi man.

Clan incest: members of the same clan (and especially the same lineage) must not engage sexually, regardless of "genetic" closeness. In other words, marriage or sexual relations between individuals a geneticist would not regard as closely-related is considered as incestuous as marriage between siblings. The greatest restraint is between opposite-sex siblings, who must not hear anything sexual about each other. This is why the curse Elliot delivers in "Dog Fights" is so reckless—in the old days it could have led to lethal physical violence.

Didiman: the name used for the colonial Australian Agricultural Officer.

Japan War (*tauto Siapan*): the commonly-used Nagovisi name for World War II.

Kanaka: Melanesian pidgin word for "man," or "person." As used on Bougainville it is generally pejorative or used in joking. When a white person uses it, it's often a term of derision. "Bush kanaka" translates roughly to "hick" or "rube."

Kiap: the name used for the Australian Patrol Officer, a colonial functionary with considerable power; the Kiap administered Nagovisi, from his seat of authority at the Patrol Post.

Lineage: see Clan

Master/*masta*: the Melanesian pidgin word for "white man." During the time of these stories, older Nagovisi treated it as merely a descriptive word, but the younger generation was perfectly aware of its derivation and either used it jokingly, or insultingly.

Matrilineal descent: tracing descent through the mother's line. You belong to your mother's clan and lineage, not to your father's. This has nothing to do with "matriarchy." It's the mirror image of "patrilineal descent," in which descent is traced through the father's line, not the mother's. Patrilineal descent similarly has nothing necessarily to do with "patriarchy." Matriarchy and patriarchy are all about power and control, not descent. It's important to keep these concepts separate. See the Oliver *Pacific Studies* article listed in *Exploring Nagovisi*.

Marriage group/moiety: see Clan

Missus: see Master/*masta*; this is the female version.

Nagovisi (Nagovis'): a linguistic and cultural group occupying south-western Central Bougainville. During the time of these stories, they numbered about 7,000. Currently their population is more than twice that number. Politically, their territory lay in the Buin Sub-district (during Colonial times); currently their region is called BANA (BAnoni-NAgovisi). They are bordered on the west by the Banoni, on the east by the Nasioi, on the south by the Baitsi and Siwai, and to the north by the Rotokas and some Nasioi. The area is tropical rainforest and where these stories are set, the altitude is about 600' (200 m) and the average rainfall is about .5" (12 mm) per day. It is heavily dissected by rivers. During the time of these stories, Nagovisi were primarily subsistence shifting-agriculture sweet-potato horticulturalists who were increasingly planting the cash crop cacao (cocoa). They raised pigs. They are matrilineal and uxorilocal; settlements comprise a core of related women whose husbands come from elsewhere.

Nasioi: the people on the other (east) side of the mountains from Nagovisi. Their language is closely-related to Nagovisi.

Patrol Officer: see *Kiap*

Pidgin/*tok pisin*: the Melanesian lingua franca (creole). Many people speak *tok pisin* in addition to their own language. Because on Bougainville alone there are at least 14 mutually-unintelligible languages, tok pisin is essential when traveling away from your own language group. Tok pisin is not very difficult for an English speaker to learn, although there are many false cognates. Nagovisi have an endless store of jokes and funny stories involving English and Chinese speakers and their tok pisin attempts, because few outsiders take tok pisin seriously and learn to speak it well. Interestingly, in the years that I've been speaking tok pisin, the language has changed considerably. On the one hand, there are more English words, and on the other, a number of words with clear English origins have been shortened. For example, *bilong* (a possessive) has become *blo.* As everywhere, mobile phones and texting have altered orthography: it's common to see "U" and "4" used exactly as a young person in North America would, even though the sentence may be in tok pisin or Nagovisi.

Rabaul: the major town on New Britain. Although it's on another island, Rabaul was the largest town Bougainvilleans could easily reach, typically by coastal steamer.

Rotokas: the people living inland from Wakunai and Numa Numa plantation. Their language belongs to the North Bougainville language group (Nagovisi belongs to the South Bougainville language group).

Sekentu: the snake in the title story, sometimes known as Paramorung. His mythological position is analogous to that of Homoromun in Siwai culture. The Bero clan possesses a smoothly-shaped stone said to be Sekentu's heart. See the Oliver *Pacific Studies* article listed in "Exploring Nagovisi."

Sibbe: the Nagovisi's name for their language, although it is commonly referred to simply as "Nagovisi."

Siwai: the large group to the south of Nagovisi and Baitsi.

Slit gong: a drum made by hollowing out a log, beaten by a heavy stick. The opening is a narrow slit parallel to the gong's long axis. Some are very large and can be heard for miles.

Sovele: the Catholic mission at Sovele, in Nagovisi. During the time period of these stories, it was staffed by Marist priests and nuns belonging to the Sisters of Mary. Sovele operated a primary school and a hospital.

Wiasi: ceremonial shell valuables, made from small shell disks, most often red, strung on fiber.

Exploring Nagovisi

Background information about Nagovisi can be found at

a-red-woman-was-crying.com/exploring-nagovisi

The folktales and myths formerly in the first edition may also be found there, in their entirety.

The book-length ethnographic works about the Nagovisi are:

Kenema, Simon. 2015. *Bougainville revisited: understanding the crisis and U-Vistract through an ethnography of everyday life in Nagovisi.* PhD thesis, University of St Andrews (Scotland).

Mitchell, Donald D. 1976. *Land and Agriculture in Nagovisi, Papua New Guinea.* Institute for Applied Social and Economic Research, Monograph 3. Port Moresby, Papua New Guinea.

Nash, Jill. 1974. *Matriliny and Modernization: the Nagovisi of South Bougainville.* New Guinea Research

Bulletin No. 55. Port Moresby and Canberra: Australian National University Press.

Other useful articles include:

Kenema, Simon. 2010. An Analysis of Post-Conflict Explanations of Indigenous Dissent Relating to the Bougainville Copper Mining Conflict, Papua New Guinea. *eJournal of the Australian Association for the Advancement of Pacific Studies* Issues 1.2 and 2.1, April 2010

Mitchell, Donald D. "Frozen Assets in Nagovisi," *Oceania*, v. 53 no. 1, 1982.

Oliver, Douglas L. 1993. "Rivers (W.H.R.) Revisited: Matriliny in Southern Bougainville. Part 1: Introduction, The Siwai, The Nagovisi." *Pacific Studies*, v 16, No. 3.

Some general book-length publications:

Oliver, Douglas. 1991. *Black Islanders: a personal perspective of Bougainville, 1937-1991*. Honolulu: University of Hawaii Press.

Regan, Anthony and Helga-Marie Griffin, Eds. 2005. *Bougainville Before the Conflict*. Canberra: Pandanus Books. (The Regan-Griffin volume is a useful resource that includes the work of many authors, including Bougainvilleans such as James Tanis, a Nagovisi, who was for a time the President of the Autonomous Region of Bougainville.)

Novels that include Mesiamo as a character:

Pinney, Peter. 1990. *The Glass Cannon*. Brisbane: University of Queensland Press

Hungerford, Thomas. 1952. *The Ridge and the River*. Sydney:Angus and Robertson.

In Pinney's novel, Mesiamo bears his own name. In Hungerford's, the character "Mummawa" is clearly Mesiamo.

Internet Resources

There are many, and considerable caution is advised. Bougainville's post-1988 history is contentious and highly-charged politically.

Many Nagovisi and Nagovisi groups have Facebook pages.

As for Nagovisi-related resources, beware the unwarranted characterization of the Nagovisi as "matriarchal." Simon Kenema, Jill Nash and I are the only professional ethnographers to have done field research in Nagovisi. We are in agreement that the Nagovisi are not a "matriarchy," unless the definition of a matriarchy is so diluted as to mean only "women are respected and control important resources."

Indeed woman are respected and powerful, and it's certainly true that women control land and many other assets, and it's certainly true that if there ever was a society in which men and women have approximately equal power, it would be the Nagovisi. But for all that, they're *not* a matriarchy.

Names, characters, places

There are living and dead Nagovisi with the same names as my characters; this would be true in any culture. There are, after all, a finite number of names. My use of a name does not imply that the character is based on an identically-named person from the area in which I worked. Even so, two narrators—Mesiamo and Lalaga—*are* meant to closely resemble the men whose names they bear. Both these men, now dead, were good friends and wonderful teachers, and I have chosen to honor them in this way.

Some names I've used for characters are not Nagovisi names at all; my Nagovisi readers will understand why and will, I hope, be amused by them.

The Nagovisi moiety, clan, and lineage names I use are not necessarily the kin group affiliations of particular characters.

Not all of the named locations I refer to are actual locations, although many are.

For geographic coordinates of many places named in the book, see the website. The coordinates can be used to view Nagovisi via Google Earth (or the equivalent).

About the Author

Don Mitchell is an ecological anthropologist, writer, book designer, and photographer. He grew up in Hilo, on the island of Hawai'i, and graduated from Hilo High School. He studied anthropology, evolutionary biology, and

creative writing at Stanford and earned a Ph.D. in anthropology from Harvard.

He lived among the Nagovisi people of Bougainville for several years in the 1960s and 1970s, and returned in 2001 after Bougainville's war of secession.

For many years he was a professor of anthropology at Buffalo State, a unit of the State University of New York.

In his non-academic life, he was a dedicated marathon and ultra-marathon runner and a professional road race timer (operating for 25 years as Runtime Services). He continues to tackle long distances on foot, though much more slowly.

He lived in Buffalo and later in Colden, New York, where he and the poet Ruth Thompson lived before they returned to his childhood home in Hilo. In mid-2020 they left Hilo for Ithaca, New York.

He published an academic book and articles about Nagovisi, but in the early 1990s returned to writing fiction and poetry. His stories have won praise from many quarters, including a Pushcart nomination and awards from the Society for Humanistic Anthropology, *New Millennium Writings* and other journals.

His photographs have won competitions and have hung in several Hawai'i galleries.

He designs books for several small publishers.

He has been an Artist in Residence for the City of Portales, New Mexico, and in 2019 shared (with Ruth Thompson) the Jack Williamson Visiting Professor of English Chair at Eastern New Mexico University.

In Hawai'i, he was actively involved in matters concerning Mauna Kea, Hawai'i's tallest and most contested mountain.